❉

The
Point of
Return

❉

AN IMPRINT OF

HARPERCOLLINS*PUBLISHERS*

The Point of Return

A NOVEL

SIDDHARTHA DEB

Published in Great Britain as *The Point of Return* by Picador,
an imprint of Pan Macmillan Ltd.

THE POINT OF RETURN. Copyright © 2002 by Siddhartha Deb. All
rights reserved. Printed in the United States of America. No part of
this book may be used or reproduced in any manner whatsoever without
written permission except in the case of brief quotations embodied in critical
articles and reviews. For information, address HarperCollins Publishers
Inc., 10 East 53rd Street, New York, NY 10022.

HarperCollins books may be purchased for educational, business, or sales promotional
use. For information, please write: Special Markets Department, HarperCollins
Publishers Inc., 10 East 53rd Street, New York, NY 10022.

First Ecco US edition published 2003

Designed by Claire Vaccaro

Printed on acid-free paper

Library of Congress Cataloging-in-Publication Data
Deb, Siddhartha, 1970–
The point of return / Siddhartha Deb.—1st ed.
p. cm.
ISBN 0-06-050151-0
1. Fathers and sons—Fiction. 2. Violence—Fiction. 3. India—Fiction. I. Title.
PR9499.3.D433 P65 2003
823'.92—dc21
2002035300

03 04 05 06 07 BVG/RRD 10 9 8 7 6 5 4 3 2 1

To my father
Ranjit Lal Deb
1926–1992

"You can go home again . . . so long as you understand
that home is a place where you have never been."

URSULA K. LE GUIN

"It is not down in any map; true places never are."

HERMAN MELVILLE

acknowledgments

I incurred many debts in the writing of this book, some of them invisible even to my conscious self, but I would like to thank the following people for the tangible nature of their help, encouragement, and friendship: Tahmima Anam, Katie Kilroy-Marac, Lauren Meeker, Pankaj Mishra, Syed Nauman Naqvi, Rob Nixon, and Nermeen Sheikh. To my agent, David Miller, and to Mary Mount, Rebecca Senior, and to Julia Serebrinsky at Ecco/HarperCollins, I owe the certain, dedicated labor that transforms a manuscript into a book. I am grateful to the editors of *Civil Lines,* especially Mukul Kesavan, for publishing an early version of the chapter "Night Journey."

Above all, to my mother, Manju Rani Deb, and to my wife, Amy Rosenberg, my gratitude, my love.

Contents

3. Terminal

4. Travelogue

prologue
1987

When Dr. Dam woke up, his eyes catching the stained white canvas stretching across the rafters of the house, his only thought was to go to the bathroom. In the cold December dawn, his feet touched the wooden floor with uncertainty, curling into worn, rubber slippers, trying to keep a precarious balance on the sloping, shifting world that had been his home for forty years. Hand on the rickety clothes rack on which shapeless winter garments lay huddled in preparation for the day's bus ride, he moved carefully toward the bathroom, anticipating that one little step down from the bedroom to the passageway. He did not want to wake the boy sleeping on the other side. Vague shapes gathered around him, faintly discernible through the mist, figures whose paths had intersected with his in the course of a tumultuous life, now ranged around him as spectators, helpers, and opponents, some of them urging him to hold himself up while the others anticipated his fall. Dr.

Dam put a foot forward, from the wooden floor to the small, threadbare carpet in the middle of the room. He took another step toward the passageway but he stumbled and the movement became a plunge away from the world he had always known. He fell softly onto the carpet.

He was lying there, hands braced to break the fall—or to accept it—when Babu found him half an hour later. "Ma," Babu called, lifting his father up to the bed, thinking about the bus that would leave for Gauhati in a few hours. "Ma, come here, he's not well. Something's wrong."

At that hour in a small town in the Northeast of India, neither doctors nor medicines were easy to obtain. If they still had the phone, they could have called someone, sent their hushed whispers scurrying across the wires strung out against the sky, mouthing their worries over a thick black tube on to the winding paths and narrow steps of the neighborhood of Rilbong, over and across the pine trees. But they had not had a phone since his retirement, so they waited, Babu's mother fanning her husband with a newspaper. The boy washed his face and came back to his father.

"What's wrong? Where does it hurt?"

There was no reply.

"Tell me what's wrong," he insisted, leaning into the fetid breath.

The answer came as a gasp. "Feeling . . . uneasy."

Babu stood up and looked at his mother. "Maybe I should get some medicines. Perhaps it's indigestion. The shops in Police Bazaar open in a little while." His mother nodded, looking as if she wanted to add something.

"And Ma?"

"Yes?"

"I think I should sell the tickets. We can take another bus if he feels better."

"Yes, Babu. We'll go later in the day. But put on some warm clothes."

Babu dug his socks out from under the mattress, where he put them at night ever since the rats had begun stealing them. He looked for his running shoes, the white sneakers with an uneven brown patina spreading across the canvas like a map still being drawn. He checked his wallet for the three tickets, then buttoned his coat methodically.

"Go carefully, Babu, it's still dark," his mother called out.

"Yes, yes, I'll be careful," he muttered, pulling the bolt down. The small glass panes set in the door were frosted over and his fingers left impressions on them as he pushed the door gently, out into the cold.

1.

Arrival

the pension office
1986

Through the small opening in the grimy pane that separated clerk and pensioner, an impasse had been reached over the responsibilities of the minister in charge of the veterinary department. There was no reason for the minister to be aware of this particular set of papers, the clerk repeated, or even of the person trying to push the papers through the opening, he suggested a little more sarcastically. Dr. Dam, however, insisted that everything was in order. The file that would validate his claim for full payment had been sent directly to the Treasury by the minister's personal assistant, he said.

"She told me so herself," he said. "She told me the minister had asked the Treasury to process my papers immediately."

The clerk shrugged. "Your order will come back," he scowled. "What do I care? Won't get a paisa," he muttered in a lower voice, dropping the red booklet onto the pile gathering in front of him. "Next," he called out, the word rising with authority over the shrunken heads in the dim corridor, arousing into sudden motion those who had not yet handed in their papers.

The clerk's voice sank back into a customary monotone while he quickly scanned the last of the pension orders, offered through the window by nervous, fragile fingers. When he looked up, he saw the obstinate, elderly man in the background, still watching him from a distance. He felt his irritation resurfacing. "Move back. Let the others get to the window," he cried out, sinking back into his seat and picking out one of the numbered metal tokens that were impaled on a long spike on his desk.

The widow to whom he handed the token, a small woman whose eyes barely came up to the counter, brought her fingers together and bobbed her head. "Thank you, *sahib,* thank you, you'll see to it that I get my money today, won't you?" she muttered and some of his ill temper was assuaged.

Babu was embarrassed to be standing in this prison of paper-crammed cubicles with his father, feeling trapped by the pensioners as they flapped around awkwardly, filling up the passageway with their birdlike bodies. Experiencing at first hand the humiliation of being old and at the mercy of the state, he felt a sudden empathy for his father, who suffered this every month. But, feeling the minutes wasting away, he wished he could be somewhere else. The narrow corridor was lit by electric lights even in the morning, while beyond the teller windows all he could see was an endless sequence of rooms, disturbingly similar, like a series of receding reflections in parallel mirrors. Outside, Babu knew, the streets were full of people, the town and its inhabitants alike released from the long hibernation of winter by the touch of spring.

The pension office was located in a hollow between the Additional Secretariat and the Governor's House, along the small road that ran from Police Bazaar toward the State Central Library situated inconspicuously at the heart of the government section that bordered the main commercial zone of the town. On his walk to the pension office, Dr. Dam, therefore, was forced to revisit those imposing structures of power he had been so much a part of until the year before.

The Additional Secretariat had been built some years after the Principal Secretariat, when the hill region broke away from the state of Assam to form an independent political entity in 1972. The new hill state found itself with an old capital town—after all, the town had been the capital of Assam from the time of the British—and although it welcomed possession of the old building, it felt the necessity of erecting fresh monuments to the vastly different political aspirations of the hill people. The time of its self-assertion had left its mark on the architectural style of the Additional Secretariat and you could read the seventies in it as surely as if the decade was etched onto its facade. It was a rather large administrative complex for a town of this size, a poseur of a big city office block whose white concrete and tall glass panes had been beaten into a template of dull stains by the monsoon weather.

Towering over the street, the view from its windows reduced

pedestrians passing below to mere specks. When Dr. Dam and Babu had passed the building earlier in the morning, their anonymity was not challenged by the slightest flicker of recognition from within. They had walked on and waited for the turbaned military policeman directing traffic to wave them through to the pension building, where they joined the flow of hopeful pensioners: bent old men with memories of office, widows who put thumb imprints on official documents, and disabled men of an uncertain age who lounged around with a faint aura of alcohol about them.

Work, that is the disbursement of money, did not begin until after lunch, although the pensioners had to hand in their Pension Payment Orders (PPOs) at counter three by eleven o'clock in the morning. The counter closed after the clerk had accepted the PPOs and given out numbered, round brass tokens. What happened between eleven and two when the numbers were finally called out was uncertain, but in some ways it was the most important procedure of the day. It usually ended with some of the supplicants being summarily rejected, while the lucky ones were given slips of paper that they exchanged for checks at counter five. A slightly different system was followed for those who received cash—these were people whose monthly pensions amounted to less than three hundred rupees—but barring the few who claimed to have a close relative among the clerks, the entire sequence was fraught with that strange mixture of tension and boredom that only a practiced bureaucracy is capable of producing.

Babu had not wanted to be part of this. The college was closed for student elections, leaving him totally free. He had planned to follow his usual holiday routine, leaving home right after breakfast to meet his friends at the tea stall near the bus stop. Last Stop, everyone called it, to mark the rather arbitrary point where the bus route from Burra Bazaar terminated, and here it was that his friends collected with cricket stumps and pads, hurling joyous insults at each other as the group swelled in number. They moved back and forth between the shops and the street, commented on the characters of the habitual late-comers, and after pasting a note on a tree or on the window of Dadu's chai stall for the final stragglers, they trekked to the playing ground available that day. Here they played, among other games, cricket, which included much bantering and ac-cusations of cheating, frank remarks on the inability of a par-ticular player, and brief words of glory for the fortunate one favored that day. Sometimes—mostly on Saturdays—their games were shorter and after they put away the cricket kit they set off on a long, looping walk. They wandered toward the movie the-aters and shops of Police Bazaar, carefully smoking Wills Filter cigarettes, cupping their hands every now and then when a fa-miliar adult figure appeared in the distance. On these ma-neuvers, Babu sometimes saw Dr. Dam on his lonely perambulations, but father and son usually passed each other without acknowledgment.

Dr. Dam had had difficulty walking since an accident some five or six years ago, but he still took on the steep slopes of the town every day. Shuffling slowly, a short, once broad figure now thinning with age, he moved in silence through people and neighborhoods, submerged within his own reticent world. If the gray eyes took in anything of the places he passed through, they restricted their attention to the nonhuman world: a sudden flower among the weeds, the damaged branches of a tree, a clogged drain that needed to be cleared.

The blows had fallen steadily, at regular intervals, on Dr. Dam's life. Nobody had ever heard him assign any cause to these events; neither wife nor son had come across references to bad luck, system, fate, or god. He fell, he picked himself up, and he went on, absorbing the effects of the disruptions into a ceaseless but unemotional routine. Ill health, legal cases, financial setbacks, they were all worked into a regular pattern of behavior, as Dr. Dam added one more set of medical checkups to his schedule or began a fresh stream of correspondence with a new group of government agencies.

There were three things that carried the burden of Dr. Dam's stoic rationality: his official letters, the carefully balanced accounts he kept on loose, numbered sheets of paper, and a series of matter-of-fact diaries that for over four decades had incorporated daily entries about the hour he had gone to work, the things discussed at official meetings, references to health problems, all in the compressed, telegraphic language that expressed his personality so well. The days he had not worked for the government were marked "HOLIDAY" in large capital letters spreading diagonally across the entire page, as if there was no further meaning that could be given to these interruptions of work. Even the entry for April 13, 1970, merely read "Babu born. Weight 9 pounds. Attended office later."

When I try to recapture the scene at the pension office, I see my father standing in the corridor, lines on his face, the shape of the bones pushing their way up through the thin coat, the network of blue veins on his hands that shake ever so slightly. Despite the clarity of the details, there is something forced about my memory of them—like in a studio portrait. Other contesting images come to mind immediately, for example, my father self-absorbed and very certain of himself. This was the way I saw him most of the time at home, always doing something, scribbling endlessly on small, yellowed sheets of paper, sometimes returning from mysterious appointments with a more somber look than usual, an act that was followed by the extraction of strange pills, syrups, and prescriptions from his bag, each object being examined carefully against the light.

Sometimes he asked me for help, but the moments of alliance did not last very long, like the time he wrote a letter to the minister in charge of pensions. He seemed unusually frustrated, angry, and resentful about the way people were treated in the pension office. "Like cattle," he said. Then he revised his comment, the animal comparison unsatisfactory to someone who had been a practicing veterinary surgeon for the first ten years of his career. "Worse than cattle. The clerks, the

officers, they're always rude and inconsiderate to the pensioners, and then they're inefficient on top of that. I am going to
complain to the minister." I had not understood his frustration with the pension office, but the fact that he was going to
do something about it made me happy.

But his form of protest was different from mine.

"You always sign 'Yours Humbly,'" I commented. "That's
so demeaning. The British taught you all this bowing and
scraping."

"We weren't sent to expensive schools. Besides, he's a minister."

"But you're not doing anything wrong. You're complaining about inefficiency in the pension office. The humiliation
a lot of people go through. You have a right to complain.
Maybe the minister will do something."

It ended with my father looking at my changes, rejecting
most of them, and sending the letter off anonymously. This
decision not to sign his name seemed to strip the whole project of its purpose. In my eyes it made him as meek as those who
never protested, but there was no arguing with him. "If someone gets hold of my name, they could harass me even more,"
he said and turned away.

It was not unusual, this feeling of inadequacy that each of
us often felt in the other, a feeling that was somewhat stronger
on my side. My father seemed to have calculated all the possible courses of action and behavior, and there was no room in
that system for varying opinions about the situation. I suspect
that he felt equally dissatisfied with me; if I found him bound

by rules—a little like one of the fraying files in his trunk, wrapped in endless loops of ribbon—he considered me over-confident and stubborn, unaware of the world as it really was. We used different languages even when we were both communicating in English, my father always circumspect and cautious in his choice of words: "Yours humbly, I beg to inform you . . ."

It was a small household but the spaces in it were vast. We sat on opposite sides of the room, waited politely for the other to finish with the newspaper, and went to our meals silently. If we ever found ourselves agreeing, it was only when my mother talked to us. She knew no English—her schooling had been brief and perfunctory—but she had the ability to see our opposing points of view. We lapsed into Bengali in her presence, in deference to her, and sometimes came to a temporary understanding. That morning, when my father asked me to come to the pension office with him, I was surprised. It sounded too much like an appeal to be ignored, but a day with him at a government office was not an attractive idea. My mother intervened. "Your father never asks anyone for help. Do you really want to let him go alone? I would go, but it is your company that he wants." I couldn't say no after that.

Having finished talking to an acquaintance he had just met, my father joined me on a wooden bench in the passageway. We sat with our backs to the window, looking at the notice boards on which government fliers had been pasted in layers over each other, shifting our feet to let the peons with their bulging files pass. Behind us, a sunny vista of roads radiated outward from the cluster of lawns and shrubbery and guardhouses that encircled the governor's residence. Our wait opened up space for a small, rare conversation.

"How are your classes? Are the teachers any good?"

"Some of them are okay," I replied. They were so dull that I had skipped more classes than I had attended.

"And are you going to take any of the entrance exams? For the IIT engineering college?"

"I don't think there's any point. Hardly anybody from here makes it. Almost everyone who gets in happens to be from the cities, or living near the cities, where they have these coaching centers. I don't want to waste money and apply for a course pack just because the other boys are doing it."

My father nodded, approving of my parsimony.

"Still, if you want to try, I'll pay for a course packet. How much is it?"

"It depends. Usually a thousand bucks."

"Bucks? What's bucks?"

I became a little flustered. "Rupees. Money."

He looked thoughtful. "Slang. They taught you slang at school?"

"Everybody speaks it. There's nothing wrong with it."

"I suppose it makes you confident. When you can speak like that, you're not so nervous at interviews. You don't spend time choosing your words carefully. Most of the Bengali boys I interviewed for jobs couldn't speak. Tongue-tied. They knew their medicine but couldn't explain anything."

"How long do you think this will take?" I asked, anxious to change the subject.

"Who knows? They say the papers are not in order. How can they not be in order? The minister's personal assistant told me she sent the order to the Treasury."

"Do you know the minister?"

"In an official capacity. He was the minister of my department."

But he still *is* the minister, I thought, and it no longer is *your* department. The slip was unusual, this assertion of power, because at home he seemed to have let go of the entire structure that had held him up through the years. He had always been different from the fathers of my friends, but that difference was never more visible than after his retirement. The days were heavy with his presence now, the morning light revealing his figure squatting on the floor between two open metal trunks, an old, somewhat infirm magician at the center of a circle of papers and files that represented the four decades of striving.

That was bad enough, but it was even more embarrassing when his attention turned to our surroundings at home. Friends taking a short cut through the Dutta house sometimes saw him in the unkempt backyard of our bungalow, hoeing the soil with his striped pajamas rolled up to the knees, back bent with effort so that his fair, mottled skin showed through the holes in his undershirt. On Sundays, he would turn his attention to the front, to the drain running along the street below the steps leading up to the house. Using one of those spades with the blade at right angles to the wooden stock, he would meticulously dredge the soil and dirt that had collected in the unpaved drain, fully absorbed in the task that others left to their servants. It was as if, with retirement, the layers of life as a veterinary doctor, as an officer, had fallen away to reveal the peasant who had always lived beneath the suits and ties. He had returned to his rightful place in the world, regardless of how awkward it was for others. I ignored him if I was at home, but our neighbors usually gathered on the road when he cleared the drain, reluctant to join him but uncomfortable that an elderly man was doing this work on his own.

My father's request for an extension of his position as the director of the veterinary department had been turned down, though he had not known his exact fate until the last working day in January, the day he turned sixty. I think he went to work with a certain degree of hope, his rationale being that he would have been informed earlier if they were letting him go. Around three in the afternoon his colleagues had assembled in the minister's chambers to make farewell speeches. There had been tea (one cup for him without sugar), samosas, and small pastries from the tea stall behind the office building. Everything had been quiet, very sedate. Then they had given him a plastic VIP briefcase and sent him home as if encouraging him to sally out the next morning, new briefcase in hand, like a young man stepping into the job market for the first time.

"Is he the same minister who used to get drunk and call at night?" I asked him, anxious to fill the gap that was threatening to overwhelm our conversation.

"No, this one's from the new party. He's shrewd, but at least he's polite."

"You think you'll get a full payment today?"

"Maybe." He stood up. "Let's go out and have some tea."

Outside the pension office, a fresh afternoon had seeped through the town. People around the tea stalls jockeyed for a spot in the sun, away from the cold shadows of the government buildings. Unlike in the plains, there was no suspicion or wariness here about the sun. Spring had released the warmth that had burrowed underground during the long months of winter, and in the wake of that warmth emerged the life of the town. Groups of young men and women walked past the pension office and the Governor's House, heading for Police Bazaar with its fashionable shops and movie theaters, or toward Wards Lake with its carefully tended flowers. The eyes of father and son followed the strolling groups to the lake. Across the lake, its grounds patterned with flower beds and stone-chipped pathways, was the town's most expensive hotel, the Ashoka Pinewood, where Dr. Dam had once gone to meet the two Danish specialists.

Dr. Dam shook his head. After all these years, he still had no idea what exactly they had wanted. Tall, white men emanating what he thought of as typically Western confidence, they had been full of questions, many of which had not been technical and had had little to do with the Indo-Danish Dairy Project. Did his wife work or did she stay at home? Had he taken a dowry from his wife's family? Did she wear a veil? He had snorted indignantly at this last question and the bald one with the glasses had switched subjects. So his son went to a school where the subjects were taught in English? Indians spoke English well, unlike Africans, who talked as if they had hot potatoes in their mouths. Had he been to Africa? Did his government believe in sending people abroad so that they could learn from other places and cultures? They had been like children, and almost as tiresome, insisting on getting out of the car to look at anything that interested them: an orchid among the branches, a vendor's woven fruit basket, the military helicopter fluttering down over the air force base.

A white Ambassador car with an official red light on its roof headed toward the governor's bungalow, slowing down before the guardhouse. The soldier saluted and let it in. The trail of gray, diesel-flavored smoke wafted in the gentle breeze, like the tail of a cat going after an injured sparrow trapped in the shrubs. The smoke drifted and then disappeared as a fresh gust of wind came up from the lake. Springtime in this town was a short season between the long months of winter and monsoon, and underneath the pleasant air of relaxation there was a sense of urgency. College students were displaying their T-shirts for these few weeks until the rains forced them under dark umbrellas and raincoats, while the black marketeers outside Kelvin movie theater raised their prices swiftly, responding to the crowd swelling through the lobby, anxious in its quest for entertainment.

These tremors of pleasure and excitement reached Babu as he stood outside the pension office with his father and his mind took off in pursuit of his friends up the steep steps of Jacob's Ladder, moving toward Don Bosco Square with its missionary schools and colleges—Loreto's, St. Anthony's, St. Mary's, St. Edmund's, Sacred Heart. In contrast to this silent sipping of tea, his friends would be involved in a raucous session of passing around samosas and tea cups at Appayan. If they had a little more money, they would go to one of the Chinese restaurants around Don Bosco Square, smearing hot red sauce onto steamed *momos*. Then they would head down Jacob's Ladder on their way to Police Bazaar, passing the pension office without so much as a glance. "Thieves," someone muttered, as Babu and Dr. Dam sat on the little bench in front of the tea stall, absorbed in their separate thoughts. It was a man on crutches, breathing heavily. They made room for him to pass as he leaned toward the tribal woman in her gingham dress behind the tea counter, his fingers fluttering, snatching at the glass jar containing biscuits the color and texture of cracked earth.

The two of them sat behind the pension office, sipping tea and nibbling at their biscuits, not looking at the lame man, who had placed himself on the bench next to them, head sunk upon his broad chest. The cup in Dr. Dam's hand clinked against the plate and the man looked up at them fiercely, the piercing eyes set in a sunburnt, wrinkled face that had once been light in color. A tribal man. Many of them were light-skinned, especially those who were said to have some English blood in them. The man scrutinized the pair closely, squinting in the sun. "Bengalis," he growled, arriving at a decision. "No use for Bengalis, always coming over the border." They said nothing, looking away at the Indian flag fluttering in front of the guard-house. The plaque in front of the gate announced, in golden letters, the name of the current governor of the state. "I've no use for politicians either, the thieves," the man went on. He had not eaten his biscuit yet. The shirt he wore lay open at the chest, revealing a shiny chain with a cross. The rough wooden crutches with rubber tips were leaning on the bench. His hand curled around a crutch, raising it in the air, a salute to the sun or the flag in front of the Governor's House.

"Riding in white cars with red lights these days. Whatever you choose to call them, ministers, politicians, legislators. Thieves with promises before the elections and orders after they win their seats. They gave me a stall once. Then they took it away. They promised that things would get better if we had a separate state. Then they said it would be better once the out-siders were thrown out. Promises, promises. Now going to the North Indian who lives in that house. You know his name?"

"The governor? Raghunath Reddy. He's not North In-dian," Dr. Dam said.

"A South Indian, then. North Indians, South Indians, East Bengalis crossing the border, what does it matter? East Ben-galis crossing the border, back and forth, up and down. Why *do* they cross the border, hey?"

No one answered the question. The man went on, continuing his investigation into the ethnic origins of the pair. "Back and forth, up and down. In '47 they came across because the country was being divided. In '71 because there was a war. After that, they were coming because there were no jobs, no homes, no land, too many mouths, too much water. Always coming across the border, with hordes of squealing children, coming across like locusts, like rain." Dr. Dam and Babu now looked at him, the references much too barbed for them to ignore him any longer. The red eyes stared belligerently at Babu, then at Dr. Dam, and then became suddenly milder. "Grown-up grandson you have with you. Probably doesn't remember the ancestral land," he commented to Dr. Dam, making the mistake most strangers did when they saw the teenage boy with the old, retired man.

"No, he doesn't."

"Tell him about it. Tell him about the past. How can you forget about your land?" he said, very agitated. "I'll tell him about it. Listen, boy, I saw your land, during the war. Do you have any idea when the Bangladesh War was?"

"The Bangladesh War? 1971," Babu replied, a little tersely, offended by the manner of his speech.

"I was there. With the Army. We went down the hills, across the river near Dauki, with a Bihari officer in charge, traveling in bullock carts because there were no roads. But these days, I can't remember why the war happened in the first place."

He waited for an answer and Dr. Dam felt obliged to respond. "West Pakistan was unhappy with the election results. Mujib and his party, mostly Bengali-speaking Muslims from

East Pakistan, had won the elections. So the military imposed martial law and the killings began."

The lame man nodded vigorously. "Oh, yes, it was all about stealing an election, wasn't it? I can understand that."

The white Ambassador appeared again, emerging from the gates of the Governor's House, and the three of them turned in unison to look at it. There was a jeep standing at the intersection in front of the guardhouse, black flags on its hood, sending out waves of loud music. The military policeman was waving the Ambassador through, his other hand raised at the jeep in a stop sign, when the jeep lurched forward, disregarding the signal. The driver of the Ambassador braked and the policeman turned, the even demeanor of his face breaking up as he raised his voice in a shout. The jeep accelerated and swept past with shouts of laughter and jeers and they saw that it was packed with young tribal men. As the jeep moved away, the music was cut off by a hoarse, blaring voice on a mike, beginning to break into an even chant. The Ambassador, forced to a standstill by the antics of the jeep, picked up speed and raced off toward the Additional Secretariat.

The lame man recovered his train of thought. "Look at that, now. There's a little stand-off for you now, some maneuvering with the elections. The one in the car is running around getting support, telling the South Indian that the chief minister has lost the confidence of the assembly. Thinking, even as he talks to the governor, that he's going to be chief minister now. For the next thirty days, maybe. And the boys in the jeep, they don't care so much about elections or parties, do they? They want to bash in a few heads instead, huh?"

There was nothing to be said in response to this and Dr. Dam and Babu went on drinking their tea, both of them suddenly anxious to be done with the pension office and get back home. The crowd had begun trickling back with the end of lunch hour, clutching their little bags and shawls, their umbrellas, knitting needles, and balls of wool, shuffling across the corridors to take their seats near the counter where the numbers would be called out. Dr. Dam stood up, putting his cup down on the little wooden bench with one shorter leg balanced on two stones. "You're not coming in? They'll call out numbers any minute now," he asked the lame man, who had slumped down again.

"You go," the man said, with a wave, not looking up. "Get your money and go through the border again." He hunched down in sleep, the cross glinting as his chest began to heave in a steady rhythm. Babu, who had already started for the office, stopped and turned around, looking for his father. The man stirred violently and woke up, looking at Dr. Dam. "You will go back, don't worry," he said. "You will be able to return," he said, waving again, as Dr. Dam nodded uncertainly but politely and walked on to join Babu.

After lunch, if the day was not too warm or too cold, the clerks usually managed a brisk, businesslike air. On these days the counter window went up as soon as the break was over and the numbers were called out so fast that some people missed the call and had to wait for their turn all over again. That this was not going to be one of these days became clear when at fifteen minutes past two there was still no sign of activity. Babu waited near the window as the crowd slowly clotted around it in varying degrees of expectation, waiting for the numbers to be announced. It was a little bit like a lottery, Babu thought, and no doubt some of the men who received checks would head for the newspaper stands in Police Bazaar, choosing from different stacks of brightly colored slips with rows of zeroes on them. The clerks could be seen in the central room, hanging around desks overflowing with piles of paper with crumpled markers sticking out. They crossed their legs, rested hands on hips, fingered the long metal spikes on the desks, gesticulating and talking as the afternoon edition of a local newspaper changed hands. Some of the pensioners, the men, walked up the corridor and turned back again, coughing self-consciously as they passed the open doors. This had no effect on those inside. An officer appeared and asked questions of the head clerk, who pointed out the newspaper. The officer took the sheet and read carefully while the head clerk slumped back in his chair, his hands behind his head. It was no use, nothing was possible in this state. He was going home early today, he thought. In a final gesture of disgust and resignation, he picked up the newspaper the officer had left behind on his desk and impaled it savagely on the spike.

At two-thirty the clerk in charge of counter four appeared

with a weary look and a shake of his head, reading out the numbers with a detached air. Dr. Dam had pushed his way to the front, but it was Babu who was closer to the counter, so he waved his hand at his father from time to time to indicate that he had not heard the number. At last it appeared, the magic sequence, and the thinning crowd parted to let Dr. Dam in to receive his slip of paper. Dr. Dam and Babu waited at the next counter for about half an hour for the check, a crisp, pink rectangle with scrawled signatures and figures and the all-important stamp of the Treasury on it. Babu wanted to leave immediately now that the ordeal was over. With the whole day gone, he might just be able to catch some of his friends in the neighborhood tea stall where they usually spent the last couple of hours. But Dr. Dam was poring over the check, peering through his bifocals and speaking to himself. He looked up and turned back to the clerk who was handing out the last bunch of checks with much greater speed than he had managed so far. Dr. Dam weaved his way through and began to argue in a low but insistent voice, displaying the check across the opening. The clerk shrugged, reached for the register, and slapped it emphatically across the window, his finger marking out one little row toward the bottom of a vast grid of red and black.

Babu saw his father emerge with his face flushed from the effort, still holding the check in his hands. "What's wrong? They didn't pay the full amount?"

"Must be some mistake somewhere," Dr. Dam replied. "We'll sort it out. Need to speak to an officer." Babu followed his father, who had maintained, in spite of his anxiety and urgency, an air of routine calm. "I would like to point out a mistake in my check," he said to the officer who motioned them into his room. The officer examined it, went through another register with a similar grid, and looked up. "There's no mistake. That's the amount on the Treasury order."

"But if you look at my PPO"—at this point Dr. Dam produced his papers, the booklet turned to the correct page for the convenience of the officer—"my dearness allowance of two hundred and forty-seven rupees, twenty-two paise, has not been added on to the amount on the check."

The officer leafed back to the opening pages. "But this is a recent pension order. Two months, that's all. The dearness allowance takes time to be added on, you should know that."

"But sir"—Babu flinched to hear his father calling this man "sir"—"the minister's assistant assured me that it had been sent, at his personal orders, to the Treasury for clearance."

"The minister of your department?" the officer said with a look of interest.

"Yes, the minister of my department, who took some personal care in the matter."

"Which department is this? I mean, who's the minister we're talking about? There are so many of them, you know. Sit down, sit down," the officer said, indicating the chair in front of him. "When we had a new state, there were six ministers. Now there are more than twenty. As many ministers as there are legislators willing to pitch in with the government."

Dr. Dam told him the name of the minister. The officer looked at him with a grave but sympathetic air.

"Perhaps you don't know. The government's fallen. A no-confidence motion was passed in the assembly today. The governor accepted the change in the situation and invited the opposition to form the government. Your minister is a key figure, along with Mr. Leapingstone, leader of the Opposition. Your minister resigned to show that he supported the Opposition and not the current, corrupt government—which is not very current at the moment." He laughed at his own wordplay and looked quite willing to discuss the matter in some detail. "He's switched sides. So maybe he was busy and had other things to do. But I would be hopeful if I were you. Maybe he will be the next chief minister. Then things could get done really fast. He can do so much for you then if he cares. A second gas cylinder, maybe, a telephone connection if you don't have one, admission for the grandson to an engineering college, and even the pension order. Anything's possible when you have a powerful politician on your side."

We left the main branch of the State Bank of India at three, having managed to deposit the check just before the bank closed. "Hungry?" my father asked and I shook my head, wanting to get back home. "Maybe we can get something here, we're close to Police Bazaar. *Puri-sabzi?* From Delhi Mistanna Bhandar."

"But they'll get cold by the time we get home," I protested, even though he had already set off past the newspaper stands toward the restaurant. I caught up with him and began to repeat my argument but stopped midway. It had been a long time since I had been anywhere with him. When I was small and very keen on the Independence Day Parade, and we lived at the Veterinary Compound at Garikhana, we always returned this way from the parade ground, stopping for *puri-sabzi* and *jalebis.* It had been a ritual for some years, the walk to Garrison Ground with dozens of white Ambassador cars in the official parking spots, everyone standing up as a politician in a Congress cap shook the tricolor loose and the band played *"Jana Gana Mana."* On the way back, just before the food was bought, I claimed the one present my father gave me every year, a bottle of orange squash with a sticky, sweet aftertaste that was my birthright as the citizen of a free country, for not being born a slave, he said.

"What are you?" I once asked my father on the way back.

"Eh?" He had been confused.

"What do you do? What should I tell the boys and teachers in school when they ask me what my father does?"

"I'm a government servant."

"But you're not a servant. Servants clean dishes and sweep floors."

"I serve the government."

"Why do you say you're a servant? Aren't you an officer? You have a telephone and a jeep with a driver. Servants don't have these things," I had finished triumphantly.

"But that is the truth. One shouldn't have problems with the truth. Those things belong to the government. They're not mine. When I finish serving the government, somebody else will use them."

He stood on the road, preferring to avoid the steep steps

that led up to Delhi Mistanna Bhandar, while I waited at the window opening onto the kitchen where the *puris* were bubbling in a large black pan.

The *puri-sabzi* broke through in oval stains of oil across the brown paper bag, a small center of warmth amid the chill of the evening falling swiftly around us. As we crossed the main street of Police Bazaar a sudden flow filled out the marketplace, people clustering at bus stops and huddling around shops, the clerks on their way home from the accountant-general's office picking up the Calcutta editions that had arrived in the afternoon. The young men who had satiated themselves on the sights and sounds of Police Bazaar stood around the newsstands, sharing a last cigarette before breaking up into smaller groups to make their way home. It was like Independence Day, I thought, the holiday mood, the weather. The traffic policeman who had been placed there for the evening crowds put his hands out to let an Ambassador pass, a white Ambassador with a red light on its roof. The wind had picked up and people drew their light summer clothes closer around them, and as we passed Regal Restaurant we could see the waiters in shabby white uniforms crowding around the kitchen, all of them trying to get their orders in first.

"You were right," my father said. "Let's walk fast. The *puris* will get cold."

highway journey
1984

The quietness of a Sunday afternoon drifted through the house with the triangular rooms, the two heads inside it bent over their work. Mrs. Dam was visiting friends in the neighborhood, and Babu and Dr. Dam were immersed in their discrete projects. Dr. Dam's fierce, unyielding posture indicated that he had found something worthwhile in the files he was examining, only the sudden rustle of paper or a series of rapid scribbles punctuating his intense scrutiny. Babu was aware of the hum of life outside, of the slow unraveling of the sun across the corrugated tin rooftops of Rilbong, the passing sound of a car, and the shouts from a group of children at play somewhere, but he made an effort not to be distracted. Then he caught the sound of footsteps outside, the hint of an alien presence near the front door that promised a break in his routine. He waited for a sound, a sign that would allow him to go and greet the visitor.

The man delivering the express telegram was in the habit of doing his job quickly. Going up the steps, he jammed the doorbell button hard into its socket, following this up with a loud cry announcing the name of the recipient, introducing a sense of urgency not unpleasant to Babu. It was Dr. Dam who went to open the door, in response to the name being called out. Handing over the envelope with one hand, the pen with the other, the postman waited silently for Dr. Dam's signature. Having received this he left swiftly, without a backward glance at the elderly man opening the thin envelope with the plastic window, his short, thick fingers unfolding the creased, recycled paper with the smudged blue type.

Babu saw his father enter the room with the telegram. Minutes passed, and he returned to his homework again, now filling sheets of paper with little charts that served as mnemonic devices, while his father sat hunched at the table on which stood the black telephone, cradling his head in his hands. When Babu looked up, he saw that his father was rubbing his eyes. "Your grandfather is dead," Dr. Dam said. "And I wasn't even there."

This was the only time in his life that Babu had seen his father come close to tears. He didn't know what to do. The word *grandfather* fell in endless spirals through the recesses of his mind before he managed, through some act of will, to bring up the image of a dark, lined face trapped between bony knees, periodically bending to a cheap wooden hookah like a toy bird. It was followed by other scenes of the old family house in Silchar, shimmering over the page and interfering with the geometric precision of his diagrams. Weed-choked pond and unkempt garden, the hobbling figure of his grandmother, his uncle Biren's irritable commands, a swimming lesson that had gone wrong, these images poured out of some hidden cylinder in his head, vaguely familiar but ultimately unknown, like the fact of death. He rose to go and find his mother.

It seems strange to think that people can die just like that, in the condensed phrases of a telegram, and that the only apparent signs of my grandfather's death were the restrictions on what we ate at home and the sight of my father's shaved head when he came back from Silchar. The cremation was over before my father reached Silchar, and my grandfather had had to set off on his journey to the next world without the guiding hand of his eldest son. Not that he could be considered unlucky because of this. He had fathered enough sons to leave himself with the high probability of at least one of them being around at any given point in time. Biren, who lived with my grandparents, was the one on whom the necessary duties had fallen. It was he who sent the telegram, arranged for the death certificate, and carried out the cremation.

For a peasant who had undergone the greatest disaster that can fall upon this social class—the loss of ancestral farming land—my grandfather had not done too badly in the final assessment. The burden of the Partition, of finding a new way of life in the country that had been fashioned so bloodily in 1947, he had left to his eldest son, my father. My grandfather's references to the home left behind as East Pakistan, decades after East Pakistan had seceded from Pakistan to become the independent nation state of Bangladesh, revealed something more than a limited grasp of geopolitical shifts. It showed that the landscape of his past would forever be permanent and unchanging, not something that was historical and therefore open to perpetual revision but a place beyond the vagaries of time.

When word reached the family sometime in the autumn of 1947 that they must leave for India, it was said that he rose, grasped his stick, and set off without a word or a glance back, leaving it to his wife and children to gather what belongings they could. When my father rented one room for the seven refugees in the slums of Thikarbasti, my grandfather lived there without comment for years, never once leaving the neighborhood to see the town of Silchar except when my father moved them to the land he had bought near Aizawl Road. There, my grandfather watched the trees grow and the fishes multiply with equanimity for the next thirty years, until the day he was carried out through Lane 13 on a modest bier, emerging from the property that was registered in his name at the Land Records Office, helped along this last journey by a touch of fire from the resident son's hand. The other sons came at varying speeds to be tonsured and to wear their white, unstitched garments. After the funeral feast, the Brahmins burped to indicate their satisfaction that things had been done quite properly. They said they had no reason to doubt that the departed soul would indeed reach its final resting place.

My father returned from the funeral seemingly unchanged, except for the shaven head on which a coarse white stubble grew back tentatively. Though the customary period of asceticism was not over, he had worn his usual clothes on the ten-hour bus ride from Silchar. Nor had he insisted on special observances at home, although my mother switched over to vegetarian food of her own accord. These were the outward signs, however. For all I know, below that placid surface he was struggling with a strange mix of sensations and images, buffeted by the residual chant of the *sraddha* ceremonies centered around the bed made empty by my grandfather's death, the sounds fading again and leaving only the image of that dark little house and the open stretch of land next to it. It was unlikely that he would have willed these thoughts, but they may have overrun his mind swiftly, mercilessly, arriving in waves of consciousness as he sat by himself late into the night. Above him, the rats would have scurried in little bursts of activity, while my mother and I slept on. He would have thought about the vacant land in Silchar next to the old house, thought about his mother bent double, and of his brother Biren. At that moment, the land in Silchar and its promise of an extended family may have seemed more real to him than the rented house we lived in, with its odd, triangular rooms at two ends, a shadowy structure looming over Zigzag Road.

I don't know that this is the way any of it happened, but we did see where his thoughts had led him when he began his calculations. My mother and I found the evidence on the table, the expense list for bricks and cement and work hours and permits, the amount of money he had in a fixed-deposit account and in his provident fund, a tug of opposing forces out of which would emerge the thing he was trying to create. My mother confronted him about these secretive plans one evening, and he furrowed his brow, pushing together the steel-gray clumps of his thick eyebrows, seemingly annoyed at the interruption. He hit a button on the massive calculator he was using, looked in my direction to see if I was listening, then announced calmly that he was going to build a house on the vacant land in Silchar. That was where we would live after he had retired, he said firmly; no more government quarters, no more rented houses with strangely shaped rooms, but finally a house of our own.

The generations that grow up in the stability of a family home know nothing of the uncertain process that went into creating that home. Human memory is frail, and the children who leave the front door and a firm, unchanged mailbox on their way to school usually care to know nothing of how this point of stability, this steady center, was found. When they grow up and move on, it is usually a simple principle of expansion, of adding the extra wing or buying the big city apartment. For those who go through the vagaries of creating a house and a home, however, there is a fragile magic in the set of operations that leads from the blueprint to the actual structure.

Dr. Dam had only known temporary places of various kinds, ever since he had left the village and the mud hut he had

been born in, turning his back on the unpredictable, tempera-
mental river around which the settlement of Baniachang had
grown through the centuries. At the age of fifteen, his quest for
a place in the modern world had taken him to MacPherson
Hostel in Calcutta, across the street from the Bengal Veterinary
College in Beliaghata. The hostel rooms had green windows
and doors, their thick layer of paint broken up by the acute
angle of wooden slats through which one afternoon, on Direct
Action Day, had come the cries of murder and riot. With grad-
uation and a job as a junior doctor with the Assam Veterinary
Department, he had accompanied his metal trunk to different
towns and outposts of the vast northeastern state of Assam,
sprawling wildly across a distant corner of the Indian subcontinent. He had unpacked his same meager belongings over and
over again in lonely bungalows with their wooden frames
painted in fresh black tar, thinking mostly of the money order
to be sent to the Thikarbasti slums in Silchar where he had settled his family.

There had been attempts to redress this flux, to put down
roots. First, as always, something had to be done for his parents and the three brothers, for the widowed sister and her
small child. Dr. Dam found a piece of land in Silchar in the
fifties, directly across from the Aizawl Highway, being sold off
cheaply by a Muslim peasant who had decided to migrate to
East Pakistan in a mirror image of the movement of the Dams.
Over the years, as brothers and nephew stepped into the adult
world, the mud-and-thatch structure in Silchar hardened into
plaster and tin. A bamboo fence cordoned it off from other

houses and the first thin cord strangling a naked bulb brought the light of a different world into the gloomy interiors inhabited by his half-blinded parents. Then, in the sixties, as a measure of independence following his marriage, he had acquired a plot in the suburbs of Gauhati, not far from the Narangi oil refineries.

All this occurred against the background of larger changes sweeping the region in the years following Partition. The state of Assam to which he owed allegiance became smaller as new tribal states were formed, their fresh cartographic boundaries indicating more than anything a growing uncertainty about the relationship between the hills and the plains. His life took on a familiar pattern; he would be sent to distant hill areas with phrases from the Five-Year Plan ringing in his ears, armed with new vaccines for inoculating the animal populations of different tribal groups, driven by targets and directives, enthralled by ideas of development and self-reliance. Then would come the signs of dissent among the hill people, the armed insurrections and kidnappings, negotiations between ministers and bureaucrats from Delhi and tribal leaders that recognized the need of the hills for autonomy and freedom. Recalled by the Assam Government from the outpost that had abruptly become part of a new hill state, his jeep would crawl past long army columns on their way to these new capitals, the soldiers rushing in to fill the breach left by doctors and agricultural officers. The highways, the small roadside stalls, the faces of nomads who waited gravely and silently for him to look at their animals, the Caesarean operation at night on a skinny cow with its owner holding a rapidly dying flashlight, these were what remained constant factors even as the administrative divisions of the Northeast were shuffled around desperately in an attempt to defeat the specter of secession.

Until the seventies, Dr. Dam had chosen to remain with his original employers. He liked the Assamese, he was comfortable with them. The land he had bought in Gauhati was an expression of this belief, even if he had not been able to stay there for more than a few years. In 1969, he was transferred to the state capital, a town in the neighboring hills. He went dutifully, with the consoling thought that it was no more than four hours by road from Gauhati. On alternate weekends he visited the Narangi plot, an empty stretch of land with a ragged wire fence on the edge where it met the uneven road. Gauhati was hot and humid in summer, the air reeking of chemicals from the refinery, but as he sat on a tin chair and watched the laborers go about their task of building his house, he was filled with a sense of quiet achievement. The one room that had been put up hurriedly at the beginning metamorphosed from mud to cement over the years, adding on the limbs of bathroom and kitchen.

Entranced by the prospect of the house coming up in Gauhati, he had ignored the advice of his associates in the hill town, many of them Bengali immigrants like him. They pointed out the good fortune that had brought them to the one place in the region that was not fractured by ethnic divisions and insurgency. There were no guerrilla groups here, longtime resident Dr. Chatterji told him, no masked men who could march into your office one day and take you away into the jungle. Land was cheap and the air crisp and clean, these men told him as elders of the immigrant Bengali community, their eyes cast proprietorially over the hillsides aflame with orange and peach trees. The schools were the best in the region, the hospitals clean, there was amity between the tribal leaders and the immigrant settlers.

Dr. Dam agreed with them about the town, but he saw no need to let go of the house that was being built in Narangi. If he succumbed to the persuasive tones of his friends, and to the lure of the place, it was only in agreeing to serve the new veterinary department that was formed when the town became the capital of a new hill state in 1972. His visits to Narangi became less frequent through these years, the effort of creating and shaping a new department demanding his complete attention. The house remained, he reassured his wife, for them to return to when he retired. He could not ask for more than to live in Gauhati, a day's journey from the rest of the family in Silchar, and with the hills always present for a break from the clammy summers of the plains.

This pattern could have continued indefinitely, perhaps up to the day of his retirement, if the wire fence around the house in Narangi had matched a government surveyor's plans for the area. But the boundaries of human expectations rarely match those set by higher powers. He had spent six years with the new department, even risen to the rank of deputy director, when he visited his Narangi house for the last time.

His wife and son were visiting his in-laws in Bihar, setting off on a train journey that would take them over two days. He had accompanied them to Gauhati by bus and seen them off at the small platform, crowded and smoky under the clear winter sky. He decided to visit the Narangi house before taking the bus back to three months of solitary existence. On his way, he stopped at a small shop in Pan Bazaar to buy a broom, remembering that when he had last been there, nearly six months ago, the broom in the house had been falling apart. It was something of a ritual, this act of visiting the empty house in Narangi for half an hour, opening the lock and inspecting the walls and ceilings, sweeping the floors if he had time. There were few houses and shops near his plot, but he thought the city would expand over the years to meet the refinery.

He noticed nothing untoward when he got off the bus near the gates of the oil refinery. He walked with a sense of purpose toward his house, broom in one hand, and it was only when he approached his land that he saw the government bulldozers standing on what supposedly belonged to him, surrounded by vats of black pitch bubbling and trickling onto the road being expanded, creating a smooth, flat surface over the rubble of his desires. A supervisor in a blue helmet had tried to chase him away as he stood there with the broom in his hand. He had stood there aghast, not even knowing where to begin, so total had been the demolition, not even protesting when one of the workers walked up to him and asked to borrow the broom.

Nothing had survived of his Narangi house except the papers testifying to legal possession of the land, the correspondence with various claims offices and tribunals, all the papers bundled into a fat file that was added to the collection occupying his battered metal trunks. By the time he realized that he would never get his property back, it was much too late to buy land or a house in the hill town, even if he had had the money for it. The town had changed too, and under the aegis of the new state the laws prohibiting outsiders from acquiring land were already in place. He went about his work and his life without faltering, moving from the official quarters in Garikhana to two rooms in Jail Road when it became much too unsafe to live on the fringes of the town. Then he found the house with the triangular rooms in Rilbong, from where he would gamely emerge on Sundays, walking past the others sitting on the lawns of their houses. Kar, Mukherjee, Dutta, they all waved at him respectfully with their newspapers, asking him to stop in for a cup of tea on his way back from the Bishnupur market. But Dr. Dam knew that unlike his neighbors, who had laid a claim to the town—or at least to this section of the town—through the solid foundations of their houses, he had not shaken off the stigma of the refugee. He was still uncertainly poised, growing old, depositing the monthly rental checks, carrying out repairs on the plumbing, and writing to the owner that the holes in the ceiling needed to be fixed before the monsoons.

The house he would build in Silchar was a last-ditch attempt to find a resting place, to face the reality of retirement and not move from rented house to rented house on an ever-tightening spiral, so that he could ultimately set forth on his final journey from the same emotional space at which he had arrived fifty-six years earlier, the space some of us call home.

❀   ❀   ❀

The new house was to be built on a rectangular strip of land. A green, weed-filled pond took up a third of the plot, skirted by a wild mix of trees and plants that Dr. Dam's father had tried to shape into a garden. On the other edge of the land was the house where the entire Dam family had lived through the fifties and sixties, waiting for the money orders to come in from the eldest son's latest outpost. Now most of the family was dispersed. Two of the brothers had settled in Calcutta, while the sister had followed her son to Gauhati. Only Biren and his wife had stayed on, using the room adjacent to the one used by his parents. It was a quiet house that did not adapt well to change, and Dr. Dam did not think it desirable to add on rooms to the existing structure. He decided to build another house between the old one and the pond, a modest building that would slip into the existing order of things. This, he thought, would allow for intimacy without his encroaching upon those who had lived there from the time he bought the land.

The work began cautiously, Dr. Dam arming himself with a very plain and austere blueprint that Chakraborty, the super-intendent of constructions in the veterinary department, had drawn up for him. A building permit was acquired, the foundation laid. Chakraborty had insisted to Dr. Dam that the foundation should be deep enough to take the weight of three floors. It was too expensive, Dr. Dam had protested, and be-sides it was much too grand for him. Chakraborty's will prevailed. It was a typical middle-class ploy, this building upward, but he had to emphasize to Dr. Dam that it was only sensible to keep the option of expanding vertically, given that Silchar was ravaged by floods every year.

Those in Silchar showed little interest in Dr. Dam's project. His mother, Mayarani, grumbled about her gout on hearing that he was planning to live next to her after he retired. If Biren was surprised by the sudden announcement of building plans and the construction that followed, he did not show it. He displayed no unusual interest when the bags of cement and sand were carried in on cycle-carts through Lane 13. Only when he was sure that he was quite alone would he emerge from the house to inspect the raw material lying on what had once been vacant land, scratching his armpits, testing a stray wooden beam with his toe. He had quietly agreed to distribute the builders' weekly payments on behalf of his elder brother.

Then the figures began to take over, assuming a life of their own. The permits had cost a great deal of money, Biren informed Dr. Dam in his letters, since the clerks and their supervising officers had demanded very high bribes. There was a building boom in Silchar, he wrote next, and work on the foundation had extended well beyond the initial calculation. The room for visitors was dropped from the plan, erased before it came into existence, the sizes of the rooms reduced, the stairway to the roof left out. But it still did not add up.

It was the most commonplace of situations, to which men react in the most commonplace of ways: by consulting astrologers, buying lottery tickets, increasing the frequency of elaborate *pujas,* cajoling or bullying wives into pawning their jewelry, appealing for loans from friends and relatives. Dr. Dam's response was in keeping with his character. The answer lay in rationality, in an approach that assessed possibilities and weighed outcomes, in an application of that strain of thought that the first impressive schoolmaster, in standard eight, had reiterated constantly in the village school, that ability unknown to the East and that had been the blessing and weapon of the West. Rationality told him to look at everything again, and over the days he thought it over dispassionately, reducing what could have easily become a lament in someone else to a matter of figures and numbers, materials and manpower. Nothing could be done about the manpower, he decided swiftly, since he was dependent on local labor. As for the raw materials, there was little possibility that he could cut costs by transporting them from somewhere else.

For the fact was that Silchar produced nothing: not cement, bricks, or electrical components, not vegetables, grains, or fruit, not even poultry or mutton, as could be verified by going to the markets during Bakr Id. In this it was not especially unlike the region it was part of. All of the Northeast, largely severed from mainland India by the Partition, depended on an overburdened artery of rail and road to bring it the things that could not be produced on its hilly, waterlogged soil or in its small, primitive factories. Every mile beyond Calcutta was painstakingly gained, up through North Bengal and the narrow strip of land between Bhutan and Bangladesh into Assam. The trucks toiled up from Gauhati along National

Highway 36, lumbering into the hill state that lay between the two ends of Assam, some of them ending their run in the hill town while others soldiered on toward Silchar, descending along NH 44 to the plains of lower Assam before heading for Aizawl. Silchar produced nothing, nor did the town he lived in, Dr. Dam told himself as he considered the possibilities. Silchar was a muddy and waterlogged little place, a transit point between state capitals and a trading center for the tea plantations around it. But even this town, with its parks and pastures and cottages, with the postcards proudly proclaiming it as "Scotland of the East," was no different. There was nothing that was produced in this land of monsoon clouds.

"Not true, not true," Chakraborty told him, having pestered him for a while about work on the house. They had bumped into each other at Police Bazaar, and since Chakraborty had insisted on finding out how the construction was going, they had decided to talk over a cup of tea. They were in Delhi Mistanna Bhandar, both men enjoying the luxury of greasy *puri-sabzi* and sweet *jalebis*. "There isn't much that is available here, that is true, but there is something that could bring down costs," Chakraborty said. He was in his late forties, an immigrant from East Bengal like Dr. Dam, his origins written plainly on the contours of his body. Short and paunchy, with a receding hairline for which he tried to compensate by wearing his hair long on the sides, Chakraborty was skilled in the matter of breaking deadlocks, having dealt with striking laborers, impetuous officers, and canny contractors in his early days as an overseer of construction gangs. There were some who called him a "fixer," but Chakraborty denied this vehemently. His work as an overseer had left its mark upon him, he told everyone, the sunhat that he had been forced to wear for long hours having destroyed his hair.

He dabbed his head with a handkerchief and turned his attention to the matter of Dr. Dam's house. "I have suggested the same thing before as well, sir, to others who were building houses. Cement—that we have here, in plenty. At the Cherra Factory. And I think I can get it. I know the man in charge there. I did him a favor once."

The Cherra Factory, Dr. Dam mused, the cement factory in Cherrapunjee. A forty-five-minute drive took one to the important geographical spot of Cherrapunjee, a motley collection of huts, cottages, fruit stalls selling sour pineapples and overripe jackfruit, with a signboard that claimed this out-of-the-way hamlet to be the recipient of the highest annual rainfall in the world. During the happy years tourists had gone there in droves, vomiting into plastic bags as their plainsmen's stomachs reacted violently to the blind curves, then stepping out to stare at the clouds wandering below. And here, on the mountain range that braced itself every year against the southwest monsoons, was the cement factory belching smoke into the clouds, processing the limestone quarried from nearby to churn out sacks of Cherra Cement.

Dr. Dam checked the estimates Chakraborty had scribbled out on a scrap of paper and found the calculations accurate. If one could buy the cement from the factory, the difference in price was substantial enough to allow work on the house to proceed, if only a method of transportation could be worked out. What he needed was a truck to carry the cement sacks across the 400-kilometer stretch that led to Silchar. "I can take care of the truck too," Chakraborty said. "One of the department contractors could be persuaded, sir."

"No, no, that is an abuse of one's position. I will try the transport companies."

"Well then, I will arrange for the cement, sir."

"It's not illegal?"

Chakraborty looked shocked at the suggestion. "There's a quota for all class-one officers, sir, as long as it's for personal use. Sometimes one must take advantage of the privileges one is entitled to," he said. They had finished their snack and were about to go their separate ways.

"It leads too often to the abuse of one's position," Dr. Dam repeated, as they went down the cavernous steps leading out from the restaurant and joined the evening crowd. They hesitated at the bottom and Chakraborty once again asked Dr. Dam to let him know if the truck proved to be a problem.

There was sufficient distance in age and rank to allow the men to part immediately. Dr. Dam, in any case, was immune to the pleasures of tobacco or *paan*. Chakraborty stopped at a *paan* stall below the restaurant and waited for his leaf to be rolled up, watching the figure of Dr. Dam weaving its way through the crowd. Those scuffed shoes, the threadbare coat, they were the signs of a government official who lived only on his salary, without the commissions and percentages and favors that swelled the bank balances of many others. Chakraborty may have been a fixer, but there was a part of him that admired the principles that men like Dr. Dam upheld, and it was this part of him that had responded to the task at hand, although there was nothing in it for him. He chewed his *paan* thoughtfully and began walking back home, aware that he would do well to be off the streets before dark. As he walked, he mused over how Dr. Dam would go about finding a truck.

That Saturday Dr. Dam went to the transportation companies in Burra Bazaar, housed in little offices huddled between auto workshops that could be reached only by squeezing through parked vehicles and jumping over deep ruts of slush with tire treads cut into them. It was one of the ugliest sections of the town, a little segment that lay to one side of G.S. Road, full of the belching smoke of trucks and the thud of sacks, with long tunnel-like warehouses crammed with spices and grain. Night never stopped work here. Trucks roared in from their enforced daylight layovers outside the town, burly Sikh and Punjabi drivers handing their consignment papers to cadaverous Marwaris. Mornings began early with the grunting shuffle of Nepali laborers as they walked the wet ramps of the trucks, bent double under loads of 100 kilos or more. Policeman, teashop boys, short and wily Bengali *babus* hoping to find a cheap deal, tribal women bringing in vegetables, fruit, and dried betel nuts, all converged around Burra Bazaar for money and work. It was totally out of character with the rest of the town, though, and few people went there for pleasure. Anjali movie theater marked the dividing line between the rest of the town and Burra Bazaar, and after the movie theater everything fell into a neat, regular pattern again, beginning with the straight lines of the military establishments around Garrison Ground.

Dr. Dam's venture to Burra Bazaar was brief, consisting of a visit to one office containing a particularly large picture of the goddess Shakti. A fat, smooth-skinned man sat behind the counter, taking his time to acknowledge the visitor. Dr. Dam had toyed with the idea of going in his official car but had then decided against it, thinking that appearing to be poor might fetch him a lower and more realistic price. "Ah, getting trans-ferred, moving household belongings," the man said when Dr. Dam told him that he was hoping to hire a truck for a one-way journey to Silchar. "Only one-way? Means an empty truck on the way back, but same cost of labor, same cost of fuel."

Dr. Dam explained that he wasn't moving household goods, though if this trip worked out he might be some day. "Not household goods. What, then? You running a business?" The man's look indicated how unlikely he thought this to be. Dr. Dam replied that he was taking some bags of cement to build a house in Silchar. "Floods in Silchar all the time. Your house become sinking houseboat if you don't build two stories. Better, build three stories and rent out bottom floor. I'm looking for an office. Your house have a big road in front for trucks to get in?" Dr. Dam said no, and the man immediately lost all interest in the subtleties of the situation and became very businesslike.

"Okay, give you a price," he said, scribbling rapidly, pausing only to take fistfuls of fennel seeds out of a plastic box, chewing on them noisily. "Driver's charge, handyman's labor, fuel costs, bridge toll, road tax, insurance, toll charged by state being exited, toll charged by state being entered, money to town police allowing truck to exit, money for town police allowing truck to enter, sundries, truck rental for two ways." He stopped.

Dr. Dam protested, "What are all these tolls? That's too many. It's only a ten-hour journey."

The man crunched on his fennel seeds and looked at him thoughtfully. "State to state is interstate, two hours or twenty hours is no difference. And is commercial load."

"I'm not selling the bags, they're for my own use," Dr. Dam said. The man opened a drawer noisily and took out a grimy pamphlet. "Cement bags. Commercial goods under department of transportation and highway-traffic regulations. You want to tell me I don't know? You want to explain to the police and customs fellows? State to state is interstate."

"So how much is it?" Dr. Dam asked. Now that his eyes had become used to the strange lighting inside the office, he could see a partly drawn curtain behind the man, a figure muffled in a shawl sitting on a chair midway through the receding darkness. The paper was pushed across to him, swiveled around to reveal the zeroes. He swallowed. It came, roughly, to the price difference he had worked out with Chakraborty. "You let me draw up the papers, half upfront, twenty-five percent day of journey, twenty-five percent day of delivery to agent in Silchar, all cash."

Dr. Dam got up from the chair with some effort. "Let me think about it. I need to compare prices."

"Wait, wait." The man raised his voice. "Some concession if you sign now." Dr. Dam was already leaving, picking his way out hurriedly, wanting to avoid the absurd quotes and the claustrophobia of the office, aware that the shawled figure in the back—no doubt the actual proprietor—had stepped out and was now bending over the fat man at the counter, muttering a low string of words that followed him as he stepped hurriedly under the dark, sodden skies of Burra Bazaar.

I had stood in front of the house, leaning over the railing to look at the truck loaded with the cement bags being taken to Silchar, while inside, my father drank tea with Talukdar, a policeman hitching a ride in the truck. I had a camera in my hand, a small Halina automatic I had borrowed from a friend at school, and when I peered through the viewfinder I could see streaks of grease and engine oil smeared on the truck's hood. The canvas lashed around the back of the truck was taut and bulging, powdered with gray cement dust that rose in little clouds when the driver slapped the canvas. There were twenty-four color exposures in the camera, a brand-new film I had bought just for this trip, film that was useless because I had found out the night before that I could not accompany my father. The policeman had taken my place; he had come with the truck provided by Khitin Das, the department's feed supplier.

I had heard my parents arguing over the truck, my father unhappy about the way Chakraborty had arranged the truck with Das without letting him know. "It looks bad," he had grumbled to my mother, as they sat in the kitchen, "when officers start accepting favors from businessmen."

"You're paying for the fuel," my mother said. "There are some people who wouldn't do even that."

"Had to insist on it," he replied tersely. "Had to insist on paying for the fuel, for the driver and his handyman."

"Chakraborty and Das did it because they like you."

"Like? What has 'like' to do with it? What about service rules?"

My mother sensed a small lecture in the offing and continued hurriedly. "Chakraborty and Das came to see me, you know. They are very concerned about the house and want you to be able to finish it. But they said you would not want to accept their help because your principles got in the way."

"So they should. Otherwise, what good are principles? Anyway," he said, a little annoyed because the topic had been diverted. "This is not about principles. It's about rules."

"Yes, yes, but who says you can't accept the help of people? He's just lending you a truck. He has many trucks, he's not going to ask for any favors in return."

"Oh, Das doesn't need any favors. He would get the department contract anyway. His feed is the best in the business. No adulteration at all."

"Exactly. So there's nothing to worry about."

"Das also wants me to give a ride to some policeman. Thinks it might help."

"What about Babu? Aren't you taking him with you?"

"I wanted to, but there's no room. Anyway, the policeman might be useful in getting through the customs posts. Otherwise, they might ask me for bribes, or even seize the truck on some pretext or the other."

That was how I found out that the policeman had taken my place, well before my mother told me about it. I tried to let go of the images I had held in my mind, of the things I had hoped to see along the highway, the scenes that had stayed in my brain from a trip made years ago. I remembered the road to Silchar as remote and mysterious, the sudden change in landscape as you crossed the border into Assam across a long bridge spanning a fast-flowing river. The bridge appeared after Sonarpur with its little shacks serving rice and fish curry, with rickety wooden balconies at the back where people washed their hands, the water falling from the aluminum jug to their fingers before slipping down to the river more than a hundred feet below. When you crossed the bridge, you came to the worst stretch of the highway, the road twisting around forests and gorges, dipping, doubling back furiously on itself while the gears and engines of cars and buses and trucks and jeeps were hurled against the road mercilessly, reverberating across the land day and night. The vehicles slowed down when they came to a little shrine after the bridge, coins tumbling out like slow sparks in a Diwali night, but I had never been able to make out what this particular deity looked like, whether there was an idol at all or if it was just a slab of stone.

I wanted to photograph the bridge and the shrine, the lime trees that appear in thick bunches on the hillside, the plains of Bangladesh that seem faraway and mysterious from the road. But that was not possible now, and the camera felt like a toy in my hands.

My father and Talukdar appeared from the house and, in a small gesture of revenge, I squeezed the shutter as the fat, uniformed policeman came down the stairs, stepping slowly and awkwardly like a crab. "Damsahib, Damsahib," he cried, "your son is taking pictures of us. We should pose properly so that we look good." My father looked surprised. That surprise is still visible in the picture I took of him, standing stiffly next to Talukdar, who has puffed out his chest, arms akimbo, fists on his Sam Browne belt. I took some more pictures of them: standing near the truck, inspecting the back, my father climbing into the cabin, and a last snapshot of the truck itself, partially obscured by its thick plume of diesel smoke and cement dust as it takes the curve near the IB bungalow.

They had set out early in the morning, hoping to clear the town limits in the two-hour window allowed during the day. They fell in with a very small convoy of Ashok Leyland and Tata trucks monotonously circling the slopes on the outskirts of the town, the houses becoming farther apart from each other and smaller, the bus stops more and more crowded with tribal villagers waiting for a ride. Most of the traffic they came across consisted of the battered Bentley buses common in this region, their exhaust pipes mounted in front and pointing up, a few old cars and Willys jeeps with canvas or plastic hoods, all of them crammed with people traveling toward the town from the outlying clusters. Commercial truckers preferred to sleep through the day and pull out at night in large groups, headlights blinking and swaying against the dark slopes rising toward an equally dark sky, lit up on winter nights with the pinpoints of celestial travelers.

The driver and his handyman sat in the front of the cab. Talukdar and Dr. Dam rode behind them, the policeman trying to begin a conversation but not doing very well because Dr. Dam was taciturn, working with figures in his head. They made it through the boundaries of the town and began to run into the checkpoints set up by the state police, customs, and forest departments, and Dr. Dam acknowledged ruefully that the Burra Bazaar businessman had been right about the police.

The checkpoints were not very impressive in appearance, looking as if they had been placed on the road almost as an afterthought. A large tin signboard carried the rules and regulations about octroi and excise, weight of vehicle and kinds of goods, placed next to a swiveling bamboo trunk operated by a rope from the little out-house in which a couple of policemen usually sat, waiting for their prey. There were not many trucks at this time of the day and, almost inevitably, the barrier remained in place when the truck approached a checkpoint. Dr. Dam tried to negotiate his way through the first one with the help of his papers, having equipped himself with every single permit or piece of paper that might be required by law.

The whole business of bribing petty officials was distasteful to him. Whatever he spent came out of his paltry salary and he saw no reason why others should not adopt the same mode of living. At the same time, he was anxious to avoid a confrontation, unlike Babu, who always argued that such people should be threatened and exposed to higher officials. Dr. Dam had little faith in higher officials, being one himself. He knew that justice did not follow swiftly even when an honest officer was willing to take action. He always attempted to circumvent the procedure of bribery by making sure his papers were in perfect order, and it was in this symbolism of papers and rubber stamps, in the weight of the Ashoka Chakra and the pillar with three lions that appeared on every official document, that he could be said to have some residual faith.

These symbols of the Indian state, however, had little effect on the guardians of the first checkpoint. Shirts hanging over their trousers, their feet clad in slippers, *bidis* stuck into the inevitable stubble on their faces, the policemen took remarkably little time to inspect the papers. Talukdar watched knowingly from inside the truck as they sized up Dr. Dam and named a price, waving away the papers he offered them again and again.

"Open the door," Talukdar snarled at the driver, who came around and held the door as he climbed out and stood next to the truck, waiting for the constables to approach him. Shirt-tails were tucked in surreptitiously as the men approached Talukdar, saluting him. "Dr. Dam, I think you should stay in the truck from now on," Talukdar said as they climbed back into the truck. Not a word had been spoken by him, but the constables had hurried back to their post, the green bamboo trunk already up against the blue sky, waiting for the truck to pass.

Talukdar was intrigued by Dr. Dam's behavior, having heard something about him from Khitin Das. Most officers would have done this business of carrying cement differently, he reflected, but he had met a number of eccentric people in his line of work, characters who refused to behave according to the norm. He saw that Dr. Dam was grateful for his interven-tion and a little more at ease, so he began talking about the nephew he had been visiting, a boarder at St. Edmund's, the school Dr. Dam's son went to. They had left the little settle-ments of Jowai and Garampani behind and the truck gathered speed as it hit the highway proper and began the process of de-scending toward the plains of lower Assam. The two men chat-ted away comfortably in Assamese now, Talukdar pleased at Dr. Dam's fluency in the language and at the prospect of passing the time quickly on such a long journey.

A junior official in the Assam police, Talukdar would go on to Karimganj from Silchar, where much of his work involved dealing with the fluid local population, he explained to Dr. Dam. The local population, unfortunately, was neither law-abiding nor very patriotic and spent a great deal of its time in smuggling things between India and Bangladesh, which lay just beyond the Sonai River. Then there were soldiers from the Border Security Force, who alternated between making peremptory arrests and taking bribes from the offenders. "Everybody blames the police, sir," he said, "even though they are only part of the system. The politicians want to make money quickly and please their voters before the elections. The Border Security Force guys want to have it easy and get their cut without fuss. The people don't care about laws and are only earning a living as far as they're concerned. So what should we do?"

Dr. Dam nodded in assent, even though he didn't completely agree with this sort of ethical compromise. "Then there's the border, which can do funny things to people. You've been to Karimganj, haven't you, *Dada*? Well, you know it's the district headquarters. But I'm sure you didn't know that it made a national record in the amount of money deposited in small-scale saving schemes. That's how much money is made there."

Dr. Dam remembered Karimganj as a small town with dirt roads and a perpetual shortage of electricity, more a large village than a town, so he was surprised at this account of wealth. But he did not interrupt Talukdar. "Even with the money there's not that much to do. They're basically old-fashioned people, no good schools, nothing, so it's not like the town you live in. They depend on family ties, religious festivals, weddings, and the day-to-day business. Running the trucks close to the banks and then carrying the goods in cycle-carts up to the river, loading the stuff onto boats and moving them to the other side. Small-scale stuff, sir. No guns or heroin, that's in Nagaland or Manipur. It's mostly biscuits—no, not gold biscuits, just the regular stuff—Phensedyl cough syrup, rice, mill-made cloth. Electronic goods from the other side, Funai VCRs, two-in-ones. Anyway, when I was first posted here the biggest guy in the business was one Rajab Ali. Strong fellow who didn't just sit in his shop or warehouse but went along to the boats. He carried a piece, they said, and it wasn't just any Chinese stuff. Real American gun.

"Rajab had a big family. Wife, three or four kids, and one brother, much younger than him. He was very fond of the brother, treated him almost like a son. College-going type. Studious, went to Cotton College in Gauhati. Came home during the holidays and stayed by himself. Not into any of the business. Anyway, the BSF had a new commandant posted here around the time of Bihu, who was creating a problem. Trouble was that he was really greedy. He had been transferred from Punjab, a Sikh, and told everybody as soon as he took charge that if he could handle the Punjab terrorists, he could handle fish-eating Bengalis—so what if some of them were Muslims? Most of the fellows resisted at first, but he was tough, had good information, and began seizing a lot of consignments. They gave in but they were unhappy about it. It's not as if the profits are that good, if you consider that the business really suffers during the monsoons. Now Rajab Ali decided that he wasn't going to increase the cut for the BSF. The others, they thought they would give in and wait for this guy to get transferred, and some of them even began making noises about him to the press and the politicians. But Rajab was big man around here, you see, he wasn't going to give in.

"But he wasn't just a tough guy. He was smart and he wanted to avoid a confrontation if he could help it. He decided to set up a meeting with the Sikh, invite him for dinner, show him that he was different and not like the rest, the small-timers. The Sikh agreed and came over with a couple of his cronies, bringing some army-issue bottles of booze with them because they knew that Rajab wasn't that religious. So here they were, eating and drinking in Rajab's house, and Rajab slowly but carefully showing off his status. His push-button phone and fancy television and VCR with remote, his big house and car, slowly giving the Sikh some idea of his connections even at the state capital. 'I got my brother a seat in the best college in Gauhati. He's going to be an engineer, or maybe an Indian Administrative Service officer. Wait, I'll introduce him to you.' The Sikh's actually quite impressed, though he doesn't show it. He knows that if Rajab Ali has a brother who goes to Cotton College, he probably really does have good connections, maybe even with the defense people. So he's contemplating maintaining good relations with Rajab, maybe asking for a few extra favors but not a blanket raise in his case as with the others. Outside the drawing room, Rajab meets his brother, who's come down with the servant sent to call him. Rajab explains that he wants his brother to meet the Border Security Force guys and chat for a while.

" 'Talk smart, talk English. They'll be impressed. It's important.'

" 'I don't want to go there. I want nothing to do with these people. They're drinking alcohol.'

" 'Drinking alcohol is a problem?' Rajab nearly hits the ceiling. 'You a Jamaati or what? I thought they were all modern in the college I send you to. So why're you talking like a mullah?'

"The brother doesn't answer the question. 'Anyway, the entire business is illegal. What you do. What those men do. I want nothing to do with this.'

"Rajab starts shouting, he's that mad, thinking of his bringing the boy up, giving him the best of everything and then being stabbed in the back. Problem is, he's so loud that the Border Security Force fellows have heard him and the Sikh has come out and is standing there laughing, his big body shaking. 'So, Rajab, since you seem to be having family problems, maybe we should leave you alone. Illegal business, hah? That's not good, is it? When your brother becomes engineer or Indian Administrative Service he'll either have to disown you or send you to jail.'

"Before leaving, one of the Sikh's men tells Rajab that they don't expect to be seeing him again but they'll be waiting for their cut to start flowing in at the same rate as everybody else, no nonsense, or they'll make him illegal nice and proper.

"Rajab doesn't say anything. He doesn't do anything for the next few days. Doesn't speak to his brother but doesn't throw him out either. The brother leaves at the end of the holidays. Rajab doesn't see him but has his wife give the boy the usual amount of money for his room and board and college expenses.

Now around this time, Rajab has a big load coming in to be delivered to his contact on the other side. His people are used to the same old routine, so they begin early in the morning and the stuff has been transferred from the trucks to the carts, which are used for the last leg because there are no paved roads next to the riverbank. But they have proper roads right on the other side in Bangladesh. Can you believe that, *Dada*, that little underdeveloped country has paved roads when we don't? Our politicians! Anyway, it's barely light when they have everything ready to be loaded onto two boats and they're waiting for Rajab because he likes to be in charge when this is happening. He comes on foot. 'Nothing's going across today. Leave,' he says. He pays the cart owners out of his own pocket, tells everyone to go. He's there with the sacks and boxes and cartons piled up on the ground, the two rowing boats with no one in them bobbing on the river because he's sent off the *majhis* as well. And what does he do? He begins throwing the stuff into the river. Sack by sack, he lifts and swings and throws them into the river—rice, saris tied together, biscuit tins, packs of Frooti—all falling into the river somewhere between India and Bangladesh.

"Some of his cronies are still hanging around, watching him from a distance, but they don't dare approach him. He's not acting crazy, he looks controlled and careful, methodical. Only the end result is crazy because if those things don't get anywhere, what's going to happen to everyone, the buyers and sellers and the people in the middle? The river can't use that stuff, it's not like throwing a coin for luck in the river or something. After about half an hour, the Sikh arrives with about eight men, all of them armed. They walk straight into Rajab's cronies, slap a couple of them around because the Sikh's in a tough mood and wants everyone to know that he's the big boss around here. He walks up to Rajab and says, 'Where's my cut? You think you can do business out here without listening to me first?' Rajab doesn't say anything, just goes on with what he's doing. The Sikh starts to get mad and yells, 'You think you'd rather put the stuff in the river than pay me my share? Where did you get so much stupid pride from? You think I'll weep for you and go away?' He gets no reply and now gets really mad. 'Okay, that's the way you want it, that's where the stuff goes,' he says and takes off his shirt and picks up a sack. That's what they do for the next hour, the two of them. One of the Border Security Force guys tries to talk to the Sikh but gets abused loudly and decides to stay out of it. The soldiers stand there and watch the two madmen working away at putting those things where nobody can ever use them. What waste! No one can take that stuff, just lying there in no man's land and going to rot at the bottom of the river.

"Rajab's business folds after that. No one will work with him, especially as his counterpart in Bangladesh was really mad when he found out what happened. As for the Sikh, he got transferred out real quick. That's the end of the story," Talukdar said, seeing the plains falling away in front of them through the window of the cab. "What do you think, sir? That's Bangladesh out there, isn't it? Your village was somewhere there, no?" Dr. Dam shook his head. "Hey, driver, stop here for a second, will you?" Talukdar called out.

They stepped out to look at Bangladesh.

There was nothing particular about the place where they had stopped. It was like almost any other spot on the road traveled so far, the thinning, cracked tar running into the soft earth and a tattered sheet of dry grass and twigs before the ground fell away toward a thicker underbrush burrowing toward densely intertwined trees and stagnant pools of black water. Across and over the treetops, they could spot the valleys and ridges yielding place to each other with the practiced ease of runners in a relay race until there was an openness, the air plunging toward distant flatlands, green and blue, waters and fields shimmering in the distance.

"Bangladesh," Dr. Dam breathed, while the driver and his assistant stretched themselves on the grass, scratching idly. Nothing save the topography distinguished it, no flags, guns, signposts, nothing that was visible at this distance, not even the thick dash-dot-dash of the political semaphore of atlases. No sound of *azaan* or temple bells, not even the splash of fish interfered with the still landscape, the flattened-out blank spaces with their soft colors running into each other, waiting for a black grid to impose meaning on the land that seemed for the time being to belong to no man at all.

There were questions in my mind about the exact nature of the house my father was building, now that there was "enough cement for two houses," as my father said in a moment of uncharacteristic exuberance when he got back home from Silchar.

The idea of a house of our own was exciting, but both my mother and I were uncertain about how it would look. My mother wanted nothing so much as shelves built into the walls, and when she asked him if there would be shelves, he replied cryptically, "There will be bunks."

"Bunks? What do you mean by bunks?" I asked. The images I had of bunks were not comforting. "Bunks as in trains, things that you pull down to sleep on?"

"Bunks near the ceilings, running across a whole wall," my father said. "They will be useful to store things in, especially if there are floods."

"How high are these bunks?" my mother asked, a little suspicious.

"Oh, a foot from the ceilings, which are—let me see—twelve feet."

"Eleven feet from the floor?" my mother said, beginning to lose her cool a little. The average height in the family was five feet.

My father dismissed the question with a grand gesture of his hand, so I decided to take up another issue. "What about the toilet? Is it going to be Indian-style or will you have a Western commode?"

Now he lost his temper. "Your forefathers went to the fields for their morning chores. In the cities, people use train tracks. Who do you think you are, with your ideas about reading magazines in the toilet?"

"What about when you and Ma get old? What happens then, when you find it difficult to squat?"

"Your grandmother still squats, doesn't she? Listen, we're not Englishmen, no matter what you might think because of your school."

So the conversations went, amid the letters arriving sporadically from Biren in Silchar, thin, yellow postcards that the postman slid between the door panels. My father scanned them hurriedly, but when I read the postcards I felt an undertone of complaint in the brief, scattered pieces of information. "Respected elder brother, the work is taking time, although the front rooms have frames for the doors. Ali and his men are not very good workers and I will have to give them a little extra money the coming month. Mother is not doing very well. Yours in all respect, Biren."

My father seemed immersed in his work, pushing around more files than ever, trying to adjust himself to the demands of a new officer from the central government. Since he had become the director of the veterinary department, he was attending meetings and conferences most of the time, but he had not let go of the old habit of attending to every small detail. I heard him on the phone talking to managers of farms in distant places, placing "person-to-person" calls on lines that were unpredictable and frail, going over precautions against possible epidemics. He always worried about diseases and epidemics just before the monsoons, and the frequency of his weekend inspection tours increased as he tried to visit each dairy and poultry farm to satisfy himself that things were in order. For all I knew he checked every single cow and bird for the state of its health and I think he felt personally betrayed when any of them died.

The monsoons arrived with their usual theatrical gesture, building up over the town for a few days like alien spaceships before letting loose. At first they were a diversion, but as our days settled into a steady patter of rain, the monsoons became a tedious, gloomy time. With the roads coming apart under landslides, my father was confined to the town, and the telephone lines worked so sporadically that he spent more time talking to the operators than to the managers at the farms. It seemed to release in him a certain detachment from the affairs of the department, and he sometimes talked about the two years he had remaining as director, that it was time for him to forget about the department and think of life after retirement.

I had to spend more time at home too, the rains putting an end to outdoor games, and we wiled away the evenings reading, drying our socks and shoes on the gas oven, and eating large amounts of *khichri*—our standard fare during this season. The trees and plants and weeds grew furiously outside, their tendrils tapping on the windows through the windy, rainy nights, and sometimes the power got cut off as poles came down somewhere. In the light of candles and kerosene lamps, with moths hovering around the flames, my father talked about having a real garden in Silchar, with rows of beets and turnip, of putting up a small chicken farm at the back of the new house. My father informed me that I would have a room of my own, with the best possible view. "You'll get to see a lot of birds, and if you're lucky you'll see a kingfisher because they come to the pond looking for fish." There had been no news from Biren for a while, however, and my father was worried about the bags of cement. It was almost time for Silchar's annual flood, for the water overflowing from rivers up in Manipur to sail into the town. I had never seen the floods, but I remembered the lampposts and telegraph poles on the streets with red lines painted on them, almost near my shoulder, with the letters H.F.L.—Highest Flood Level—and the numbers indicating the year of the flood.

When news finally came from Silchar, it was not a special telegram of any sort, just a blue inland letter that the postman handed to my father when he opened the door. With the coming of the rains, the postman had stopped jamming the mail into the door, and he waited for us to take it from him. I saw my father enter the room with the letter, the paper wet and pliant. My first thought was that my grandmother had died too and that Biren had decided to economize, but the look on my father's face was not that of grief. There was an expression of disbelief, even incomprehension, on his face as he read through the letter and finally handed it to me.

We sat there together, looking out at the pouring rain that ruled outside, emptying the town of the detritus of human life. Biren's letter had informed my father that it had not been possible to move the remaining bags of cement out of the front yard to a sheltered place before the floods. He had been busy, the workers had not been around, and there were too many bags to be moved by one man. The water had subsided now, his message said, and although I had no idea what it looked like when the flood waters retreated, I could visualize the scene very clearly, the sacks of Cherra cement that had returned almost to their natural state, uneven lumps of stone stuck inside gunny bags, strewn around with other debris on the site of the house being built.

the minister's chambers
1983

It was a good thing, everyone agreed, that the program for the tenth anniversary of statehood had been conducted indoors. The creation of India's twentieth state, the carving out of a separate ethnic entity from the unwieldy mass of plains and hills that the British had administered as Assam, was undoubtedly a cause for celebration, but nobody wanted to get soaked in the process. Not being on the same scale as Independence Day—with its grand demonstration of emancipation from colonial bondage—the smaller celebration could do without marching bands, unfurled flags, distribution of free food, and unrestricted admission to movie theaters for the day. Just as well or it would have been a washout.

The evening had consisted of the usual speeches, one from the chief minister on behalf of the tribal people and their steady arrival as a notionally equal partner to the socialist, secular, democratic republic of India, another from the governor who represented the larger entity. This had been followed by a routine of song and dance: a performance of Bihu to show that there were no hard feelings toward the Assamese, who had originally objected to the shrinking of their state, then a couple of local dances, some choral singing, and finally the national anthem—with much shuffling of feet and scraping of chairs as the audience stood up as a mark of respect—followed by refreshments for invited guests.

The invited guests were the usual mix of bureaucrats, politicians, and the heterogeneous assortment of individuals who usually go by the collective designation of "local dignitaries" in all government affairs. Almost everyone was impatient, waiting for the final business of milling around to be finished quickly, clutching their glasses of juice or cups of tea with a faintly desperate air. Dr. Dam, the new director of the veterinary and dairy department, was relieved that the celebration was a "dry" affair. He did not drink alcohol, and he disliked the subterfuge of having his glass filled with whisky and then surreptitiously pouring the liquor into a potted plant. There was a party later on at the residence of the veterinary minister, which certainly would not be dry, but he had not been invited. He watched the figures circulating around the large room, the motion of bodies toward the long table stacked with plates full of samosas and vegetable chops, and then the rapid dispersal as some of the people realized that the entire affair was vegetarian as well as alcohol-free.

Dr. Dam wandered around, a little absent-minded, feeling the waft of wet, cold air as the hall doors opened and closed, plucking at a button on his coat. He was well aware of the different hierarchies operating in the room. There were rules of rank and privilege that separated the politicians from the bureaucrats, the Indian Administrative Service officers from those working for the state government, while within the state government there was the subtle distinction between tribal officers and those who, like him, were immigrants. There had been a time when the ethnic differences had been unimportant, and when he thought about it, even now most of his tribal colleagues were remarkably unprejudiced. If anything, it was his fellow Bengalis and the other nontribal groups who were insular, with a vague sense of superiority over the tribal officers.

That was back in the Additional Secretariat, however, in contrast to this staid congregation where the presence of the politicians had caused everybody to gravitate to their own groups. He had himself been unconsciously heading toward the nontribal officials without realizing it, so that he found himself face to face with Bora, the Assamese director of the agriculture department. There was a natural affinity of temperament between the two men, and the sense of kinship was heightened by the fact that they both headed low-budget departments that did not possess the glamor and weight of industries or tourism. "Been thinking of your new scheme. Very impressive," Bora remarked, without much of a preamble, and for a while both of them forgot the dreariness of the surroundings and their own insignificance.

"How's the quality been so far?" Dr. Dam asked anxiously.

"Pretty good. And they seem to be much more on time."

"Well, they used to be late before because they would go to Burra Bazaar to sell off part of the milk."

The revamped town milk-supply scheme was a week old, but it was the result of careful planning on the part of Dr. Dam and his colleagues. Booths had sprung up everywhere in the past month, small structures of tin and wood painted a pale yellow, with the words "Town Milk Supply Scheme" emblazoned in bright blue on three sides. The booths had gone up near bus stops, post offices, and marketplaces, arousing the curiosity of people until they found out that the old practice of delivering bottles of milk to their doorstep was being discontinued. There had been mixed reactions to this change, and some of Dr. Dam's neighbors had grumbled that collecting milk from the booths would take up their time. "It's not that inconvenient," he had replied. "They are not more than ten minutes away, and the poorer people used to collect milk from the vans anyway." The booths opened in the early hours of the morning to the sound of trucks depositing the day's load, a signal to the people to come and collect their milk instead of having it delivered to their houses.

Not only did this lead to economy in terms of labor and fuel costs, Dr. Dam asserted to Bora, but the polythene packets replacing glass bottles were far cheaper. Then, of course, there was the old practice of watering down the milk, which had now been stopped. Once the packets had been sealed at the plant in the presence of a supervisor, he explained earnestly, it was impossible to open them without breaking the seal.

"Did you have trouble getting your superiors to approve the scheme?"

"Well, it was pushed through some months before. I don't know how the new minister will react to it," Dr. Dam said, lowering his voice slightly.

Bora whispered back conspiratorially, and they looked like two schoolboys, warily looking out for Dr. Dam's minister. "Quite a character, isn't he?"

The minister was in fact not too far away, a tall, well-built figure nattily dressed in a formal white suit whose lines were a little spoiled by the bulge under his left armpit. That bulge was prone to speculation among the officers and staff at the Additional Secretariat and both Bora and Dr. Dam found their gazes drawn to it. They hastily turned the conversation back from the minister, and Bora tried to lighten the mood. "There's an old joke about Indian milk—you know it, Dr. Dam?"

"The British joke about Indians and their habit of watering milk? Yes," he said sourly.

Bora was not to be dissuaded from reciting it.

"One part milk and three parts pani
Is what is called doodh *in Hindusthani."*

Dr. Dam was not amused. Bora saw him frowning, the lines on his large, light-skinned face emphasizing the jowls, making him look, oddly enough, like a caricature of an Englishman, a real John Bull, he thought. The same speculation that had crossed the minds of most of Dr. Dam's colleagues and neighbors occurred to Bora as well, and he wondered how an East Bengali had such white skin and gray eyes. Dr. Dam was still looking impatient, however, and Bora quickly began talking about the aspect of the milk booths that interested him.

"Do you have other plans for the booths?"

"You mean?"

"Well, you're having them manned from nine to one. Is that cost-effective in terms of labor?"

"Ah, there's no hiding things from you. We were considering selling dairy and poultry products. Butter, cream, broiler chicken, eggs. Much better things than what is available on the market, at lower prices."

"Excellent. What about agriculture-department products? Potatoes, which could be sold at less than the market rate, that are now rotting because we have so few outlets. Fruit products, like jam and juice. What do you think about combining forces?"

"It's a wonderful idea," Dr. Dam exclaimed. "We should do it. You need to draw out a formal proposal. We could share the manpower and the trucks."

Perhaps there were other similar projects being floated in the room at the moment. But people had grown tired of the bad food and the weak tea, the austerity measures floated by Indira Gandhi's government in Delhi not conducive to the lavish feasts that had once been the norm. The bureaucrats and politicians and dignitaries had come from different directions, in Ambassadors with red lights and jeeps with white plastic canopies, and now they were preparing to go home. The veterinary minister strode through the diminishing crowd and stopped in front of the two officials. His tone was peremptory.

"Dam, you send them to my house?"

"Yes, sir, I asked them to be delivered this afternoon, fifty table birds. They're about a kilo each."

"Okay, you come see me tomorrow." The minister dismissed him and walked out of the hall. Dr. Dam and Bora looked at each other, Bora's eyebrows raised in a silent but eloquent comment on the minister's manners. The two of them promised to talk about the booths later that week, and then they were separated by the crowd pouring out of the hall toward the cars and jeeps.

Dr. Dam reached home around seven, having walked to Rilbong from the library, passing through empty, wet streets that merged into the darkness of the trees and the sky, in a thick silence ruptured occasionally by the hissing of car tires behind him and the muffled, fragmented sounds of the All-India Radio news from the houses along the way. He changed out of his wet clothes and sat down with a contented sigh, glancing at Babu, who was lying on the bed, circled by a cordon of books and pens. Dr. Dam pulled out the newspapers he had been carrying in his bag all day and began studying the front page of *The Statesman* methodically, its thick newsprint soggy under his hands. The rain had let up slightly and through the

dark came the sound of dripping trees and trickling drain-
pipes. There were more austerity measures being announced
by the Prime Minister as a way of restoring the Indian economy, partly because the World Bank had gone back on its
promise to lend 72 million dollars to the Indian government.
The money would not have come anywhere near the Northeast,
Dr. Dam noted automatically, since it had been earmarked for
improving the water supply and sewerage system in Gujarat. He
moved on to reports of the bitter antagonism between the
Congress government and the Opposition parties over presidential candidates, especially over the alleged comment by Mrs.
Gandhi's nominee, Zail Singh, that on becoming President
"he would even sweep the floor if Mrs. Gandhi wanted."

Sycophants, he thought in a sudden spell of bitterness,
bereft of dignity or belief, lowering the image of the country,
and of the Congress party itself. He put the newspaper down
on the table and studied the front page as a whole, the headlines in their bold type ringing the front-page picture of the
Prime Minister with her palms together, though what really
dominated the photograph was the giant cut-out of her son
Sanjay Gandhi, looking as if he was being hanged by the massive garland on his neck, his feet dangling above the men who
stood around the Prime Minister. The nation created by the
Gandhi family was starkly signposted by the headlines: the Opposition presidential candidate was lamenting the "decline in
political values," an eighteen-year-old woman in Haryana,
having given birth to a stillborn child, had been gang-raped by
medical students at the very hospital to which she had been

admitted, while the Defense Minister was boasting about the new fighter aircraft India would buy to match the American F-16s Pakistan had acquired. The austerity measures clearly did not apply to purchasing expensive fighter planes, he thought, and as he fidgeted with the button on his shirt he recalled the number of times he had heard the phrase "austerity measures." The previous Janata government, for instance, had reduced the whole business of governance to farce, their austerity measures consisting of substituting molasses for sugar on all Indian Airlines flights and ordering slices of papaya to be served as snacks. And on top of that, the last prime minister had gone around advocating a form of nature therapy that involved drinking one's own urine every morning.

Outside, the rain started again, continuing its demonstration of excess with zeal, shaking the trees and the tin roof of the house with such force that the rats above the ceiling scurried for a drier place. The telephone rang, dribbling its mechanical sound over and above the patter of rain. It was 8:30. What could be important enough to merit a call at this time, on a night like this?

The minister had been drinking something other than his own urine. With a difficulty in speaking that owed as much to his aborted schooling as to the bottle of Johnny Walker whisky he had finished off in the past hour, he tried to ascertain that the person he wanted was on the phone.

"Okay, Dam, listen now. Feefty, you hear, feefty birds to my house. In one hour."

Dr. Dam was mystified. "They didn't deliver the birds?"

"No, no. You listen. Want another feefty. More people. Very big party."

"But, sir, it's late now. The farms are closed. I can't take another fifty table birds without disrupting the market supply. It's not allowed, sir, by government regulations."

"You listen, Dam. I am gofment. Get me chickens. People hungry. Get other birds, is okay."

"The other birds are all laying birds, sir. Can't kill them. There'll be no eggs for weeks."

"Damn you!"

"Yes sir?" Dr. Dam thought he was being called.

"You get birds now. Get birds from market. Pay for it. I give you money tomorrow. Is a matter of prestige."

"Sorry, sir. It can't be done." He put down the phone.

Having caught one side of the conversation, Babu glanced at his father, peering over his book. Dr. Dam scrutinized the room dispassionately, taking in the signs of wear and tear that even his wife's inventive arrangements could no longer hide. The boy's head, crowned with dark, thick hair, returned to the book and Dr. Dam's eyes wandered over his curved back—too curved, he thought, he'll stoop when he gets taller if he's not careful, just like my father—to the end of the room. Over the clothes rack was a little scene representing an imaginative version of the Battle of Britain. Babu had cut out little paper planes, painted them with different insignias and camouflage colors, and hung them from the wooden frame of the ceiling. Spitfires, Messerschmitts, Focke-Wulf 190s, Hurricanes, Zeros, and B-17 Flying Fortresses bumped noses against each other when a draft came in from the direction of the kitchen, the eyes painted on them following the inmates of the house aggressively. Mrs. Dam appeared in the doorway, rubbing her face, wrapped in the smell of burning coal and spices, calling them to dinner. He stepped toward the kitchen, avoiding the paper aircraft swaying in the wind. He would not think of the morning to come. He had done what was right.

Through the break in the clouds perched threateningly above the town, a bird's-eye view would have captured only wet, deserted streets. Children were at school, adults at work, some of the women behind domestic walls. Those in-between individuals who populated the streets on a normal day during working hours—beggars, drunks, truant schoolchildren, gangs of young men—even they had taken shelter from the unbearable wetness that seeped through the town. The crows preened themselves, their tousled heads sticking out from dripping branches, belligerently proprietorial about the dry spots they had found. Only the immobile seemed to suffer stoically, the stone obelisks near IGP, the police headquarters, smooth and uncaring, the battle tank outside the library feeling a fresh patch of rust creeping up on its ancient war paint, the waters of Wards Lake restlessly receiving offerings from the new streams and rivulets that had opened up along its banks.

The human beings inside the various offices filled the air with the static and hum of their voices and signals, telephone calls and wireless messages bouncing around, from the police headquarters to the Assembly House, from the Principal Secretariat to the Additional Secretariat building, across houses and shops and schools and hospitals. The principal of St. Edmund's School, Brother Noronha, told the class teachers that the boys should be allowed to take off their wet socks so that they could dry their feet. Then he went to check that the school gates were closed, even though he didn't think there would be trouble on a day like this.

The veterinary minister was talking to his uncle, Leapingstone. Assaulted by a headache and nursing a cup of tea, he was trying to understand what his uncle was saying and although the words seemed to escape him, he did not miss the fact that Leapingstone was unusually agitated. The minister had a few things to say himself. He wanted to complain about what had happened last night but he found it difficult to think while Leapingstone went on talking at a furious pace.

Virtually illiterate, catapulted to this position of power by his uncle's skills, the minister was in awe of Leapingstone, the suave and shrewd veteran of political affairs in the state. He remembered that he had been insulted last night. The *dkhar* officer, a mere officer, had hung up on him. Uncle would know what to do about it. But Leapingstone, instead of listening, had dragged him out to the wet, cold lawn, slippery with the debris of fallen leaves.

"There's going to be another election soon, you understand? Another election." The minister nodded unhappily, beginning to sulk a little. He did not belong to any of the parties that had contested the previous elections to the state assembly. A local tough who had been elected on an independent ticket from the outlying constituency of Mawkhar, his victory had been largely engineered by Leapingstone. He had suddenly found himself with a cabinet berth, uncertain and confused during the oath-taking ceremony, hissed at by Leapingstone while stumbling to follow the words read out by the governor in his strange accent. Admittedly, the seat had not been as important as that of forests or industries, but veterinary-and-dairy was not bad for a newcomer providing support to the ruling coalition.

He was grateful to his uncle for propelling him to power, but sometimes he got tired of the obedience expected of him. Trying to find a dry spot and signaling to a servant inside for more tea, the minister watched as Leapingstone poked around in the shrubbery. He emerged with a small leaf in his hand. "Watch." Leapingstone held up his hand and opened his palm. A gust of wind swooped down on the leaf and snatched it up, twirling it a few steps in the air before letting it drop. The dry leaf, selected carefully by Leapingstone, tumbled to the ground and greedily drank in the moisture. "You understand, do you? You have to know which way the wind blows to survive in this game."

After half an hour of similar histrionics from Leapingstone, the minister could say he understood. Even he could figure out that the precarious government, shored up by defectors and hired guns like him in exchange for cash and cabinet berths, was about to topple. The governor had flown to Delhi in the morning and the prime minister was going to ask him to call for fresh elections in the state instead of swearing in another shaky government. And they—Leapingstone clapped his nephew on the back—would have to act fast. Things would not be easy, because the rules of the game had changed. They would have to do something but he shouldn't worry. "Uncle knows what to do." The minister, having recovered from the hangover significantly, shook his head grimly as he dressed. He too knew what to do with the officer who had snubbed him.

The Additional Secretariat was abuzz with two different topics of discussion. By far the more engaging was the business of austerity measures being proclaimed from Delhi by the prime minister, with bits of news and gossip traveling up through the sixteen levels from the main floor and circling around the corridors and typing pools. Rain was always good for talk, the wet trails following each newcomer into the building providing an excuse for slowness at work. The peons who were clustered at the corner of each corridor, ostensibly waiting for the bells inside the offices to sound, argued with each other with greater fervor than usual, knowing that only the most heartless of officers would insist on errands outside. The officers themselves, in any case, were busy on the phones or in person-to-person encounters. Was it true that they would have to walk to work or use public transportation? Considering that the most frequent users of official cars consisted of wives and children, this could lead to domestic strife, Chakraborty argued, adding that the divorce rate in India would definitely catch up with that of Western societies if these measures were pushed through. The governor had gone to Delhi and it looked like the state government wouldn't last long this time around as well. Along with these rumors there were also frequent references to the vigilance commission that had been empowered to investigate every official, no matter how senior, and many of the officers imagined sudden calls at night or late knocks that announced a raid on the house.

Below the main floor, however, on the three mezzanine levels, the day was tinged with slightly different expectations. The corridors here were a little muddier, the water sneaking in through the labyrinthine system of steps bringing in worries of a more local nature. Dr. Dam's response to the minister the night before had already become public through some mysterious media, and among the groups of peons and clerks and typists and officers and guards there was an uneasy tension. The consensus was that Dr. Dam had been stupid, especially since he knew as well as anybody else what happened when you got on the wrong side of politicians and their demands. By one o'clock, however, the minister had not yet come in, so the air of expectation began to give way and the staff here began to emulate their comrades above in talking about the new measures announced in Delhi, wondering if these had any resemblance to the declaration of the Emergency in the mid-seventies.

Inside his office, Dr. Dam had recovered his poise in the absence of the minister, and felt well disposed toward his colleagues and seniors. He had been clearing files, laying them in neat rows to his left, and his Nepali assistant, Murari, was kept busy in taking them to different cubicles, where the officers instantly broke from their worries about the nation to ask him if his boss looked tense. Oblivious to the speculation, Dr. Dam noted that repairs and maintenance had sent up a fresh set of bills for the vehicle LG 1456, and that the repair costs were beginning to total up to the price of a new jeep. He made a note for the possible phasing out of this vehicle, never quite the same after his old driver, Sam, had driven it into a rock face in 1980. Outside, the clouds kept up their bombardment of the town with precision, spraying the streets and buildings and trees evenly. The rain swept in crinkled, transparent sheets down the driveway just across from his windows, while far below in the gorge out of which the building rose the rainwater took on the color of mud as it collected in little pools among garbage heaps. The matter of New Delhi and its directives had come up in phone conversations with colleagues, but Dr. Dam had cut them short and stuck to business.

For the time being, the most important thing was strengthening the new milk supply scheme. There were many things to be adjusted and improved. Already, he had heard, there were complaints. One of the booths in Laitumukrah had been closed in the morning. Then there were the new ideas, Bora's proposal, for instance. The booths would have to be manned for longer hours, of course, but the agriculture people could provide the manpower for that. Perhaps there was a small employment opportunity here for neighborhood youths.

Anything was possible, he felt, if one had initiative. One must always have initiative.

There was a map of the state on the wall to his left and he walked across the room to look at it, seeing the existing farms and plants being supplemented by a network of booths, the red lines of supply snaking out to every single corner of the state, providing hygienic food—dairy, meat, vegetables—all of uniform quality and price.

Who said they were not capable of developing here, out in the Northeast? It took time and effort, but the possibility existed. He had colleagues who worked hard, who gave large portions of their lives to those segments of the five-year plans they were concerned with. It was not just darkness, corruption, rot, by no means. He knew of young men who lived miles from the nearest town, tending to the animals of villagers even as the health clinics next to them remained empty, bereft of doctors. He did not believe in these distinctions between people: tribals, nontribals. He knew dozens of names, voices that reached him on the phone from distant provincial towns, earnest and full of effort—Hussein, Marbaniang, Kharkhongor, Dhar—trying their best to immunize and administer. This was the real battlefield where the fight for a modern India was taking place.

Some of the papers on his desk rustled, as if they agreed with him. But then his eyes fell on the figures and charts, the memos and leave applications, the repair bills for the perpetually crippled LG 1456, and he felt his confidence draining out. They would not approve the scheme on a statewide scale, even though the farms could produce enough with the proper infrastructure. Could they? Was there not too much waste, si-phoning off, embezzlement? He would not think of such things, no, he could not think of these things after what had happened once. He had to remember the advice of well-wishers not to get too deeply involved in the activities of other people. He remembered the tense wait during those nights of blackout in 1979, the incident in Police Bazaar a year later. The booth at Laitumukrah had been closed; perhaps some-thing could be done about that.

The minister sent a peon to call Dr. Dam soon after he en-tered the building. The eyes of the staff evaded Dr. Dam's as he walked up the carpeted stretch of corridor, but they watched him from behind, following him all the way until he was swal-lowed up by the door. The lights in the room had been dimmed for the minister, who reclined in his foam chair, his black, zipped-up, ankle-length boots positioned carefully on the wonderfully bare table. Leapingstone sat perched on the edge of the desk, flicking an imaginary thread from his white suit as the official entered.

His hands damp against the files he was clutching to his side, Dam stood silently. Leapingstone turned his small head, nodding in a measured greeting. The official replied that he was very well as their gazes sought him out, the minister's glow-ering and belligerent, Leapingstone's shrewd and assessing.

No one said anything for a while, and the rain dripping outside the windows of the ministerial chambers was a heavy, potent presence. In that moment, whoever spoke first could have taken the conversation in a direction very different from that directed by government protocol or political needs. They could have shared their fears and desires, their distance from the decrees being issued from Delhi, their feeling that even at their most philanthropic people in the capital did not include the Northeast in any of their plans. Or they could have turned to themselves, each shown the other his real face. Leapingstone could have spoken of the throbbing of his heart, every year without exception, to the pealing of the church bells ringing in the new year, his one moment of peace. He could have spoken of his discomfort on those occasions when he was forced to visit Calcutta and Delhi, the cities and their people flowing past his eyes, indifferent and hostile. His only point of contact with those alien beings was the unpleasant taste of their failures and frauds permeating the streets, the clamminess of the city air and the viscosity of his sweat as he peeled his shirt from the seat of the car he was being chauffeured around in.

Even the minister could have spoken, if only haltingly, of his first careful foray into the streets of this town from his small village on the border with Bangladesh, the tension in his groin as the eyes of the smart town girls flicked past him, even though he was one of their own, of his feeling of bewilderment until his uncle had taken him under his wing and shown him a way to get to the top.

As for the official sinking into his shoes, he could have perhaps explained that he was not as different from them as he ap-

peared to be. He could have given an account of the history that
had brought him here along with countless others, to their
hometown, of the fateful time of the nation's birth in 1947
when decisions were as much about preserving lives as about
homes. Or if that was much too large a subject to be broached
by him, he could have told them a story about how he came to
love and fear this town at the same time.

He could have spoken about his father and himself walking
across the flatlands of East Bengal and climbing the Pandua
hills, coming ever closer to the clouds hanging over the rising
slopes of green. They had looked at the town silently from the
fork where the dirt track met a paved road, guided there by a
tribal shepherd they had met along the way and who had understood what they were looking for, although they communi-
cated only in broken phrases and hesitant gestures. He and his
father had entered the town fearfully, dirty, weary peasants
suddenly aware of their primitive status. That had been long
ago, when he had still been a student in his village school, the
country a part of the British Empire, the town mainly a sanitarium for white men. They had come to see his mother's
brother, who was an Indian Civil Service officer. He and his
father had come as supplicants; it had been the old man's idea
to ask his brother-in-law for help in paying for his eldest son's
schooling. They had sat outside the bungalow where the Indian
Civil Service man had his office. There were no buildings of
concrete and stone then, the trees far thicker and the houses
long distances from each other. They had waited on the

verandah, the old man with his almost African face, the boy with his white skin and gray eyes, an incongruous pair waiting for recognition from within. The Indian Civil Service uncle had not received them. The police constable had come back and, after a hard stare, he had handed back the note the boy had carefully written out in English, hoping to impress the uncle he had never seen. The constable had also given him three coins as a gift from the official and told them to clear off. They left immediately, waiting till they reached a tribal village some distance from the town before they bought food. For years to come, the boy had retained images of the town he had seen that day, though it had always been tinged by a sense of inadequacy.

None of this happened, of course. If such thoughts and images of their own histories passed through the minds of the three men, they did not express them fully even to themselves. They had government business to conduct, decorum to maintain. After some initial businesslike queries that circled around the matter at hand, the official suddenly found that the tone of the conversation had changed, that the questions had become pointed and antagonistic, and that he was defending his beloved new scheme.

"And the paint job? Did that cost anything?"

He replied that it had not cost much and that painting the cheap structures had been necessary to protect the wood. Gathering a little courage, he reiterated that very little money had been spent on putting up the booths. No unnecessary expenditures had been made; it would be extremely cost-effective in the long run, including the phasing out of glass bottles by poly-thene packets.

"The polythene packets cost nothing," Leapingstone said. "What happened to the bottles? What was wrong with the bottles?"

"The bottles," repeated the minister, thinking of the party the night before.

"That was part of an earlier plan, sir, because of the pilfer-age problem. The phasing-out of the bottles was approved last year."

"Pilferage?" Leapingstone looked at him.

"We've been having pilferage problems for years, sir. It's not possible for anyone to remove a portion of the milk and replace it with water because these packets are sealed. There was also the question of frequent breakage of the glass bottles, sir."

"So people steal, that's the problem. Does everyone steal?"
"Sir?"

"Except for you. Everyone else is a thief. And you want to save the government's money, the people's property, from the thieves, who are also the people. What do you protect, and from whom?"

"Sir?" he repeated, not understanding entirely.

"Schemes to make things better. To supply quality milk." Leapingstone's voice grew soft, thoughtful. "While the town is ready to burn, to go up in smoke. There are people, young people, who care nothing for your milk or the petty jobs the scheme will throw their way. They," he said, "are drunk on something other than milk." He slid off the desk spryly, feet coming together neatly on the carpet. "The new supply scheme will be scrapped. Do it the way it has been done all along."

He could say nothing right then. The pause in the room brought in the sound of running water, which seemed to come not from dripping pipes and eaves but from the recesses of the forests where the hill streams overflowed in abundance, sallying over rocks that had lain dry and cold through the winter, gathering patches of moss like bruises on an old man's head.

"Draw up a report totaling the money saved by scrapping this ostentatious scheme. We need it by tomorrow. The report has to be sent to Delhi."

He would go to the secretary of the department, he thought. No, to the chief secretary. Then he remembered that the chief secretary was away. Even if they listened to him, what would happen? He felt the room blurring before his eyes and he tried to keep a firm grip on the files that threatened to slip off and spill his figures and comments and notations and proposals onto the floor. The sun, which had peeped out a little while ago, sent a finger through the window, kindling the map on the wall into a slow fire. The minister was speaking. The minister was speaking of last night. The minister was standing up, he had put his right hand inside his coat, he had taken his hand out and was pointing at him.

Having reasserted his control over his nephew and the situation, Leapingstone continued as though nothing had happened. "Forget this, okay? Just concentrate on the report. And one more thing. Where are the booths located?"

Somebody else seemed to speak through his body. "In different neighborhoods, sir. Malki, Mawprem, Kench's Trace."

"I know, I know. That's not what I mean. But where? In somebody's house? In their gardens, backyards?"

"Along the main roads, sir. Usually near the bus stops for easy access. It's government land, sir."

"Not in this state. There are special laws here. Did you get permission from the elders?"

"Sir, the *gaonburans* were happy about the proposals."

"I don't think so. The booths are built on the people's property. They have to be returned to the people. How many booths did you say there were?"

"Thirty, sir, in the town and the outskirts. We were planning to build more."

"Okay, draw up the report and have it sent over. Also, a list of booth locations."

He began to turn toward the door, feeling strangely detached from his own body.

"Wait, I want to tell you something."

"Sir?"

"You must let me show you how one can steal milk even from plastic packets," Leapingstone laughed. "When we have the time, I will show you. All one needs is a syringe to make a small puncture in the packet and a flame to seal the hole."

Dr. Dam opened the door and let himself out. Leaping-stone raised his voice, "Go home, Dam, you need some rest. Go home, take a break."

When the official was no longer to be seen, Leapingstone turned to his nephew. "One more stunt like that and you're on your own. Go join the student union boys. They'll like your style. Direct action."

The minister sat there sullenly, saying nothing. He had only wanted to assert his position, to have some respect from junior functionaries who hung up on him. "An outsider. A foreigner. Should have some respect."

"Yes, but that's not the way to get respect. Come on, come on, move your lazy bottom." Leapingstone slapped him on the back affectionately, light-hearted after the departure of the hangdog official. "We're just beginning to find the answers. We have so many gifts to give. We have to find the right people. People who will remember when the elections come that we gave them free stalls."

"We could sell them. Why give them away free?" the minister said.

"Because we're after higher things. Power. Because this is a solid start in terms of public support. We're robbing the rich government and giving to the poor people. We'll be popular. We'll have support. Turn the people in our direction. Come on, we have a new party to float."

The clouds, which had been listening to these plans, observing the drama being played out below, opened up their hatches again. A light drizzle began, the apostrophe marks of rain lit up by the lamps driven like anchors around police headquarters. The force that had marked the earlier bombardment was missing and the drops drifting downward moved cautiously, tentatively, toward the town.

wedding season
1982

In a way it was I who was responsible for the changes that took place that winter in the family house on Lane 13, for the wedding that marked more clearly than any other event a boundary between what had gone before and what was to come. The story can safely be told now, if it is a story, for there is little left that could be affected. Most of the characters are gone; some of them I have let go willingly, while the others I lost without wanting to.

My grandfather died peacefully a few years after the wedding, in the lines of a telegram delivered one afternoon, while his wife, Mayarani, rotted away in the general ward of a Calcutta hospital almost a decade after his death. She did not go easily, attempting to subject her sons and their wives to a final bit of ignominy by ending up in a morgue, a battered and ugly corpse to be cut and shredded before the final ride to the crematorium, but it was a pyrrhic victory. Tossed from son to son, her authority had disappeared in those last years of her life, which is why it is so strange to think of her at the house in Silchar, during that wedding when the entire Dam family came together one last time.

The prelude to the wedding was the autumn of 1981, when my mother and aunts began to seriously consider the bachelor status of Naren, the youngest of my uncles. We had all come to Silchar for the holidays, my eldest uncle, Ranen, and his family from Calcutta, my parents and I from the hills. The house my father had built for the family when they migrated from East Bengal was small and crowded even without visitors, its three rooms occupied by my grandparents, Biren and his wife, and Naren. I am not sure how all of us slept there, but during the day people flitted in and out of those rooms. My mother and aunts spent much of their time in and around the kitchen, while my father and Ranen usually found something that would take them into town.

My grandmother, Mayarani, normally took a nap in the afternoon, but that day she was awake and full of uncharacteristic energy. It was hot, so hot that even the crows and mongrel dogs that squabbled over the scraps of food near the tubewell had fallen silent, but Mayarani was in the room where my mother and my aunts had gotten together, sitting directly under the ceiling fan and snarling at everyone.

Lunch had been finished a while ago, an uneasy ritual during these holiday months when the extended family sat on a row of low wooden seats laid out on the verandah, trying valiantly to survive an intimacy the rest of the year did not demand of them. Only Mayarani would eat alone, sitting down to her strange, messy lunch at eleven. Though she did not wear a watch or know how to tell the time, she had an unerring sense of her meal hours and a fine awareness of the needs of her body. By the time the others sat down for lunch, she was fast asleep in her dark little room, uncaring and unheeding of those who had collected here like so many migratory birds.

It may have been some measure of the crisis she felt brewing under her nose that she chose to forego her afternoon nap and be present in the room. "Why are the lot of you so keen to have him married off? As if the three of you haven't blistered my bones enough ever since you stepped over the threshold of this house." The third daughter-in-law, Biren's wife, was not present just then, and my mother and Ranen's wife, Uma, took the brunt of her anger. Meanwhile, Naren had assumed a world-weary air at all this feminine foolishness. Now he put on his slippers.

"How can you run away?" Uma intervened. "Here we're being scolded for wanting to get you married. And you won't say a word."

Mayarani broke into a toothless, triumphant grin. "He's not like the rest of them. Loyal, blood of my own, he is."

I was in the room, following the conversation keenly. Believing foolishly that Naren's wedding would take place within the span of these holidays if only the question could be settled, I unknowingly swung the balance. "Hey, will you listen to what's being said?" Naren stopped. "Do you want to get married or not?" Silence. Naren shuffled out, head down, intensely concerned with his shirt buttons. I ran up and grabbed his arm, but he didn't look at me. "Fine, since you won't say anything. If you come back home by eight, we'll understand you don't want to get married and all that. If you come later, the answer's yes." Naren didn't look at me as he left, not even when I yelled out, "And don't, for god's sake, forget the fishing hooks today."

And that was how it was settled. Naren, who was always home by six, came back at midnight, a little drunk for good measure. After that not even Mayarani could dispute his need to get married.

By the time the event actually came around, I don't think I remembered how the wedding was initiated, or the role I played in eliciting an answer from Naren. More than a year had gone by and it was winter when we returned to the old house in Silchar. It seemed to be a different house now, having emerged from its habitual trance into a more communal world, as the noise of living that had been kept out for so long flooded its way in with a vengeance. The decrepit gate that had served to keep out cattle— few neighbors ventured here—was flung open now and people I had never seen before streamed into the house confidently.

The actual wedding ceremony took place in Calcutta, where the bride's family lived, and the preparations here were part of the reception my father and his brothers had decided to hold for Naren and his wife. I am not sure what prompted this uncharacteristic extravaganza and this sudden consciousness of social proprieties; perhaps it was the fact that Naren was twenty years younger than my father, who remembered going back to the village from the veterinary college in Calcutta and finding himself with a brother young enough to be his son. In any case, my father remembered dandling Naren in his arms, as did the other brothers, and this may have resulted in a certain relaxation in their attitude. Who knows? There are other explanations, but since there is no one around to speak of that time, I can only recall the unusual sense of effort and excitement in the days leading up to the reception.

The voices of querulous workers competed with those of uncles, aunts, and distant cousins who had come from their small towns and suburbs, a gathering of the clan dispersed through the decades after Partition. Weathered-gold bamboo poles and large, black-bottomed pans were dropped with a resounding clatter in the courtyard and the first static-filled burst from the speaker of a tape recorder that had been hired for the occasion slowly resolved itself into a *ghazal*:

To weep along with the walls
How wonderful it feels,
And even I will go mad now
Or that's how it feels.

In the glass palace each face is my own
Or that's how it feels,
And even I will go mad now,
Or that's how it feels.

My father was standing in the sun, ostensibly lending his authority to the operations, but I think he was just enjoying the chaos. I watched him across the string of wires the electrician was putting up, from house to tent, from the courtyard to the front gate, a web of lines with little nodes of light that were separate but connected. I was standing between him and my grandfather, who was near the pond watching the planting of tent poles with great interest. My mother and the aunts were busy in the kitchen, from which they emerged periodically with cups of tea that were delivered according to strict hierarchy: first to my grandfather—who drank it down noisily in one motion—then to my father, one cup without sugar, and then to the brothers and cousins and people working on different aspects of the reception.

An indignant cackle broke out from the direction of my grandmother's room. It was a delayed reaction to a raid on the Amul tin under the bedstead where she zealously hoarded her money. She had been doing this for so many decades that the copper pieces and quarter-paise coins—some of them with Victoria's face imprinted on them, no less—had long gone out of circulation. Of course, it was precisely this that sparked off my cousin Rana's interest. He had little regard for the exchange value of her trove and it was the older pieces he fancied. The electrician, a young man with long, well-oiled hair, had been humming along with the *ghazal* being played on the tape recorder. Now he was startled out of his romantic reverie by the loud laments coming from my grandmother's room, and he seemed suddenly aware of the strange reputation the Dam family had. He left saying he had six other places to visit, since it was the wedding season after all.

Uma emerged with a slightly desperate smile on her face as her son hooted and disappeared into the garden, followed after a considerable time lag by the bent, calcium-deficient figure of Mayarani. The old woman hobbled on, clutching her back, peering into the vast, fuzzy distance in search of the thief. Seeing my father standing there with an amused look on his face, she began complaining to him that the noise was driving her mad and that it was a conspiracy to rob her of the only son who had loved her. "You began all this," she moaned. "Why did you have to get married? Were we not family enough for you? Did we need these little demons to darken our lives? And now my youngest one has betrayed me as well."

My father smiled benevolently at her, indicating that he wanted no part of this, but his silent pleasure in the proceedings had been disturbed. He looked pointedly at his watch and disappeared into the house in search of his shoes. He was going out, that much was clear. My mother came out of the kitchen and whispered to me, "You'd better go into the garden too. She's really upset, don't hang around here. And it's not just her fault, either. Why do you children never talk to your grandparents?"

I proceeded dutifully toward the green pond, a place of mysterious fishy ripples beyond which lay the garden, with its strange stock of sugar cane, coconut, and banana trees. I found these trees with their big leaves and large fruits vaguely interesting but alien, far removed from the conifers I was used to in my hometown. The trees were a little like my grandparents, incredibly distant from me in spite of the claims of blood.

It was difficult even to conceive of a conversation with my grandparents, their speech slushed over with the earthy village dialect that clung to them forty years after Partition. I didn't mind my grandfather because he was so deaf as to make all languages and dialects redundant, his head usually sunk over a bubbling hookah held between cracked knees, his interests restricted to pipe and garden. When I wanted a cane stalk to suck on I would shout into his ears and he would clank his bones into motion to fetch his machete, showing in his stride a residual habit of open spaces as he hacked at the tall, leafy stalks and their will broke against his desire. My grandmother left me much colder. I knew she didn't like my mother very much, and she was not fond of children. I could see in her face the ties that connected my father to her, the same light skin and gray eyes, but in her these features had become the token of something disconcerting.

No one had ever told me how or why she looked like that, but what little I knew of her past suggested something very different from the peasant background my grandfather embodied. Her father had apparently been a wealthy landowner in East Bengal, and her brothers had all done well, one of them even joining the Indian Civil Service under the British government. Why and how she had been married to my grandfather, why her father's family never visited her after her marriage, these were things lost in time, like the past itself. What remained was her bent, ravaged body and wrinkled face, and the mind that ticked inside to a rhythm nobody else knew.

Dr. Dam left the house and walked down Lane 13, his professional interests appearing like a beacon in the distance, away from the wedding preparations and family conflicts. The Silchar office of the Assam Veterinary Department was not too far from the house and he thought he would walk rather than take a rickshaw. He found himself pausing on the main road, looking away from the town, following the highway as it tunneled through the last settlements of Silchar before heading for the hills of Mizoram. When he had bought the land on Lane 13, this stretch of the highway had been completely deserted, with only a few automobile workshops and tea stalls. Now there were houses and schools and shops along the road, which had shrunk even as the town expanded, and during rush hour the traffic was backed up all the way to Rangirkhadi.

It was dry and windy, and as he walked the wind blew clouds of dust at him, forcing him to cover his mouth with his handkerchief, filling him with a sudden longing to be back in the hills. The town was not a pretty sight, he thought, with its strange mix of decay and development: the crush of bicycles and rickshaws and small vans on its flat, narrow roads, the shabbily dressed office workers loitering at the marketplace during their lunch break, the thick layer of dust that lay on the signboards of the shops, the overflowing garbage bins with

thin, diseased cows rummaging through rotten fruit and vegetables. He had to check the impulse to examine the animals as
he passed them.

Silchar was a small Bengali island in the state of Assam,
heavily settled by immigrants from the villages of East Bengal
who had brought with them a sense of identity that allowed for
neither growth nor change. They were defined not by what they
were—that was uncertain—but by what they were not. They were
Indians because they were not Bangladeshis, Hindus because
they were not Muslims, Bengalis because they were not Assamese. They clung to their language fiercely, and yet they were
not really Bengali, because they spoke a dialect that aroused
only amusement and derision in the real center of Bengali culture and identity, in Calcutta.

Perhaps this was the reason that they had not been able to
create anything beautiful, Dr. Dam thought as he walked toward Premtolla, looking at the shops. Many of the shops were
hardware stores, revealing the immigrant's passion for construction, while others dealt in automobile parts, targeting the
tribal middle-class in neighboring Mizoram. The few book-
shops in the town were called "libraries," though they did not
lend books, and everything else, from a garment shop to a gro-
cery store, went by the generic title of "factory."

The sight depressed him so much that his mind involun-
tarily turned back toward what he had been trying to escape, the
family house on Lane 13 with its cracks and fault lines, with its
growing distance between generations and the yawning gap between the brothers. He had changed, as had Ranen and Biren,

each of them more concerned with his immediate family than with the ties they had in common, the memories of life in the hut in the village, a poor but happy life. Their wives were all uncomfortable with Mayarani, who had become increasingly querulous and self-centered. The only signs of affection he had seen across these barriers were between Babu and his grandfather. When Babu had been smaller, he would ask his grandfather for sugar cane, and the old man would be happy because he could give something that was from the earth, grown at home, not bought from a shop. But there was no sugar cane this year, he remembered as he entered the veterinary compound. The garden around the pond was only a bare, jagged piece of land waiting for the seasons to turn once again, tapped dry by the ending of another year.

With a day left before Naren and his bride came from Calcutta, the preparations for the wedding reception had reached their peak. The tent had been put up and trestle tables and folding chairs stacked in the corners. The chief cook and his assistants were setting up a huge earthen oven outside the tent, the smoke from the oven billowing all over the house as they stoked it with charcoal and wood. My mother was taking care of the initial ceremonies with my aunts, while my grandmother slept on in her room. It seems she had asked my grandfather to stay away from the ceremonies, so he watched the ritual around the tulsi plant from a safe distance, squatting on the veranda,

adding even more smoke to the proceedings as he pulled vigorously at his hookah.

My father had left early in the morning, saying something
about seeing pigs, and I was standing near the pond, watching
my eldest uncle, Ranen, oiling his tiny frame. I was surprised
by his preparations. I had never seen the pond being used as
anything other than a source of drinking water, and for fishing
on a few rare occasions. Compared to the house and the garden, it was huge, a green and opaque surface that was a concession to the past, to memories of the gardens and ponds that
had defined all but the very lowest castes in the village life left
behind. But in spite of my enthusiasm for the pond and the
fish in it, I was forbidden to approach it on my own. It was re-
puted to be very deep and its slippery mud banks were shored
up with crisscrossed bamboo poles at the end from which water
had been drawn, before my father had had a tube-well put up
some years ago.

I was impressed by Ranen's confidence as he finished oiling
himself and did some rapid squats. "Do you know how to
swim?" I asked.

"Of course I know how to swim," he replied, his mouth a
little open as he stared at me. "Everyone can swim, your father,
all your uncles, even my sister." I said nothing, digesting all
this information. "Do *you* know how to swim?" Ranen asked.

"No," I replied. "There's only one swimming pool back
home, part of a club. They had another one at school, but they
closed it a few years ago when a boy drowned."

"Swimming pool?" Ranen asked. "Why on earth would you need a swimming pool to learn to swim?" He thought for a while and shook his head. "I can't believe things have come to such a pass that a Dam boy cannot swim." Then he cheered up. "Time to learn, then, don't you think?"

"Me?"

"Yes, you. But we must ask your father first."

"He's not at home. Gone to see some pigs."

Ranen thought for a while. "Go change into a half-pant," he said. He meant shorts. "Your father won't mind. Nobody could possibly mind. It's a family skill."

Galvanized by the promise of activity, Ranen had fetched a machete and rope while I changed. The stem of a young banana plant was hacked down to serve as a float. I would have to cling to it while kicking out in the water according to Ranen's directions.

The event soon rivaled the impending festivities as people came up to the bank to watch. My grandfather, in spite of his deafness, had found out what was happening and he quickly appeared in the crowd, muttering approvingly. The women finished off their ceremonies in a final burst of activity and stood together on one edge of the pond, my mother watching me silently. I was aware of my aunts shrieking from time to time, while Rana hopped around on the bank, asking his father to take me deeper, to the center of the pond for just a little while. Even the men helping with the chores had taken a break and were clustered near the pool, laughing as they lit their bidis.

I struggled on valiantly, somehow conscious of everything

happening on land. I had swallowed a lot of water, the pond I was kicking out against feeling more and more rubbery with every passing instant, and if I felt buoyant for a fleeting moment I immediately began to sink again, but I was still aware of the people around the pond. Perhaps, like Bhim in the *Mahabharata*, who saw not only the target pigeon on the tree but also the branches, the tree, and the clouds in the sky, I wasn't concentrating very hard. I noticed that my grandmother was absent.

She appeared slowly, hobbling her way through the crowd. At first no one took any notice of Mayarani but when her presence became evident the younger women fell silent, the end of their shrieks bringing a déjà-vu quality to the scene at the pond as I kept my head above water, looking at the fronds of the coconut trees waving against the bright winter sky, feeling as if I had been like this for a very long time. Rana was still hovering around, his shrill voice becoming ever more urgent as he begged his father to release me for a few minutes, not too long, but he was sure I had learned to swim by now and wouldn't drown. Ranen and I had been in the water for about half an hour now, its coolness overridden by a sense of fatigue, when Mayarani called out, "Ranneney!"

Ranen snorted, as startled as everybody else at the unexpected involvement of his mother, "What?"

She pointed at Rana. "Look at your own son. What about him? Or is it only on your nephew that you can try your bravado?" Rana and his mother cried out in unison but it was no use. She had pricked some sense of fairness in Ranen that demanded that his son be put through the same process,

though it was quite clear that, unlike me, Rana was a very unwilling trainee.

"Take a break," Ranen said, and he began to guide me
toward the bank, my arms still around the banana stem as if my
life depended on it—which, at that moment, it probably did.
He put me on the bank and it took Rana a little while to figure
out what was in store for him. He was yelling at his father to
take me back into the water when he saw Ranen advancing
toward him. Rana screamed and started running but there were
too many people in the way. There was a loud splash, a blur of
arms and legs, muffled cries of "He's killing me, Ma," and then
all we could see was the banana plant bobbing furiously and the
sight of two heads, one bald, the other with full slick black hair,
surfacing periodically in the water.

Out of breath, I sat on the bank, feeling incredible pleasure at the sight of my cousin getting what he deserved. Ranen
was wrestling with Rana in the water, a clenched frown showing
his determination, heedless of his wife shouting at him to stop.
Uma suddenly turned to my mother. "You're the one who
started all this. Why couldn't you have said no at the very beginning?" My mother was startled at the accusation and began
to edge away uncomfortably, gesturing at me to follow her, but
there was no change in the situation in the pond. "I'm going
back to my father's house for good, d'you hear, if you don't
bring him back immediately," Uma shouted at her husband
again. It seemed unlikely that Ranen would give in, caught between mother and wife, and it was quite possible he would have
stayed in the water forever. His wife tottered toward the edge of

the water, wailing that she would drown herself rather than watch a heartless man playing with his son's life.

She paused as a collective cry went up, but no one made a move toward her. Ranen's will broke. He paddled back slowly and landed his son on the bank like a prize catch, looking around helplessly. Rana was hysterical, weeping and yelling at his mother as she sought to comfort him. Then he suddenly broke out of his mother's grasp and ran toward the house. Mayarani was standing there, nodding her head with an undeniable look of satisfaction, when Rana returned at full pace, his arms full with the slippers and shoes that had been left near the veranda by the many guests and workers. There were cries from all quarters now as Rana began tossing his collection into the pond. Men's shoes, *kolhapuri chappals,* women's high-heeled slippers, they all sank in the mucky water instantly, while a stray assortment of Bata rubber sandals floated upside-down. Rana broke down as his mother rushed to comfort him again.

It was not quite over. Some of the people were scrambling around with branches and sticks to rescue the blue-and-white Bata sandals, *lungis* and trousers rolled up high, while others hurried back to check their footwear, when Biren strode onto the scene. He did not shout at his elder brother but there was an icy formality in his voice as he stared at Ranen and spoke to him. "You've stirred up all the mud from the bottom. Could you tell me where I am supposed to get drinking water for all the workers and relatives who will eat today?"

An unseasonal rain arrived at night, turning Lane 13 and the courtyard where the guests would eat into a marsh, the winds accompanying the rain buffeting the tent until one of the supporting poles gave way. In the cloudy morning, repair work proceeded in desultory fashion while a small group, including me, proceeded to the railway station to greet the couple. The train reached Silchar late in the evening and Naren and his bride were quickly bundled into a rickety Ambassador hired for the occasion, and we headed back home through the crowded streets filled with people and animals and rickshaws as if the rain had driven them out into the streets instead of away from them.

At the head of Lane 13, which was far too narrow for the car, there stood a motley crowd, mostly neighbors. Since Mayarani had refused to come out to welcome the bride, citing the wet weather and her aches and pains as an excuse, the task had fallen on my mother. She stood at the head of the lane, holding a plate with leaves and flowers, stalks of paddy and *sindoor* arranged on it, ready to bless the couple with happiness and fertility. The bridegroom dodged past her furiously, speedily making his way through the crowd. His wife hung back, a dainty foot dangling from the car. Fresh from Calcutta, all she could see was the horrifying slush ahead. "Jump," some of the neighborhood boys encouraged her, while the more chivalrous among them scrambled back with planks and poles, which were placed over the especially tricky stretches.

My father was at the house to welcome and bless the bride. He had missed the entire affair of the pond the previous day.

He came back late at night, mildly curious about the incident but much more interested in the pigs he had been shown by Dr. Deka. He had visited a tribal settlement with Dr. Deka, some fifty kilometers from Silchar, to investigate these indigenous wonders that were far more resistant to tropical diseases than the animals imported or carefully crossbred by his department. He looked as if he was still thinking of pigs as he blessed the bride, and my mother had to guide him through the ceremony.

The hired tape recorder had been switched on and it blared out a baleful *shehnai* tune that drifted its way through puddles and wet chairs until the reception received a sudden lease of life in the inner room where the bride now sat, the last new member in this generation of the family. Someone had worked a miracle in the bridal chamber with flowers, colored paper, threads shimmering in gold and silver, lighting up the bride and the bed where she sat by herself. The guests were trickling in slowly, mostly people known to Biren, who was the long-standing local resident. My father stood in the covered space with the chairs, just in front of the tent, talking to the guests as they emerged from the feast, asking them the customary forgiveness for any omissions and errors in his hospitality.

The groups arriving now were much larger, many of them marching straight into the tent where the food was being served, and it began to feel more like an invasion than a reception. It had not been under way for long before Ranen approached my father, Uma and Rana standing outside the gate. "The boy wants some ice cream, so I'll take him out, if I may.

Biren seems to have the situation well in hand," he said. My father gave the assent required of him and then asked me if I wanted to go with them. They had already disappeared down the lane and I shook my head and went to look for my mother.

She was busy with the bride but when I peeped in she came out. "So how do you like a family wedding?"

I wanted to be nice about it but my feelings got the better of me. "Strange kind of wedding, isn't it, where everybody does their own thing? Strange kind of family," I said a little bitterly. "Anyway, why is that other room so dark?"

My mother held out a finger wearily. "See for yourself." I looked inside. The kerosene lantern that my grandparents used as a night lamp flickered in a corner of their room, its faint smoky flame unable to penetrate the shadows cast by the mosquito net they had set up before going to bed.

The evening wore on steadily to the sound of munching guests, to the cries of the servers and their manager, Biren, while I gravitated back and forth between my father at the reception area and the tent, a twelve-year-old with nothing to do. Rana and his parents did not come back until the feast was well over. Later I would be told that they had had dinner outside. Around eight, I wandered into the tent, much too hungry to resist the smell of food. Biren immediately pressed me into service and I was happy enough to carry the fried vegetables and the slices of lime, trying to keep out of the way of the men thundering down with the big, steaming pots with fish and mutton curry. But the pace grew more hectic as I stayed on, the guests loud and vocal with their demands, those at the table waiting for third or fourth helpings while others crowded around the entrance, impatient about having to wait.

Biren appeared from the kitchen with a flushed look on his face. "You, why are you still wandering around with that stuff? It's time for the sweets. Take one of the pots with the sweets."

I don't know why, perhaps it was his attitude or the boorishness of the people at the tables, but I refused. "I don't think so, the juice will get on my clothes," I said.

"What? You think knowing English makes you too good to listen to your elders? You're the one who started all the trouble yesterday. What are you doing here if you think you belong somewhere else?" He had brought his face close to me as he shouted, and I could see the graying hair around his temples, the veins on his forehead standing out, and his jagged, *paan*-stained teeth.

I went on serving the sweets mechanically, playing my part in the proceedings until the groups at the tables became smaller. Biren wasn't around and I went into the makeshift kitchen with the nearly empty earthen pot of sweets, a few dead ants floating in the juice swirling around. I put it down and slipped away, passing my father near the gate, one of his hands playing with a shirt button.

I stood in the lane, almost unseen by the groups that emerged from the reception on their way home. The music had been turned off a while ago and the lights strung up by the electrician were blinking weakly, some of them dying out altogether. Through the slats in the bamboo fence, I could see my father looking at the tent that stood between the house and the pond, as if he was looking for something specific. There was a sound from the direction of the house and I saw my grandfather appearing from the darkness, walking slowly past the tent. He was going to the bathroom, a cubicle near the pond surrounded by stones slippery with moss. My father went toward him. Taking out a flashlight and holding my grandfather's gnarled arm, he led him carefully toward the pond.

foreign visitors
1981

Dr. Ahmed blinks, standing next to the blue sign in front of the farm, awaiting the visit from the town. It is Saturday, but for the manager of a farm and a veterinary surgeon there isn't really such a thing as a free day. The official visits have a habit of falling at the most awkward times, the impulses and whims of government mandarins always running counter to the rhythm of animals and workers and machinery—a minister demanding one hundred liters of milk on the very day the cows are at their most unproductive, or when the plant equipment is malfunctioning and the technician who understands the machinery is away on leave. Everything seems in working order today, at least on the farm, although at home his son is suffering from diarrhea. Fate, Dr. Ahmed thinks. Manager of the best farm in the entire state and a son whose digestive system is strongly antilactose. The car honks, rounding the hill, breaking into his reverie. He steps forward to meet the guests, suddenly a little shy in the presence of the strapping white men emerging from the car.

They have strange names, the two visitors. Nielsen and Knudsen, Dr. Dam repeats to himself, looking at the page in his diary where he has laboriously spelled their names out from the official letter announcing their visit from Denmark. Professors at the Royal Veterinary and Agricultural University in Copenhagen, they are observers on behalf of the Danish government. They have come to see how their money, their equipment, their carefully packed bottles of serum, and the precisely bred animals dispatched from Denmark have been used in this far, underdeveloped corner of the world. They will go back and furnish serious reports in their own language to the Konsistorium, disseminate their experience to eager students, and work on papers that can be presented at conferences, then published in learned journals. They are nice people, tremendously interested in models of underdevelopment, concerned that they understand and be understood, so that people everywhere may benefit from new technologies and European knowledge.

In thirty years, maybe, people here too will be tall and strong like them. It is a small beginning, trying to raise the standard of dairy farming in this place, but it is all part of a great, long chain. The benefits of the vaccines and vitamins and steroids will pass on, from the cows to the human beings who drink the milk, forming bone and muscle, fleshing the people into shape. Both men are over fifty, but they spring from their chairs on the lawn in front of the Ashoka Pinewood Hotel with alacrity, backs straight, forearms hewn out of oak. The green car, built like a small battle tank, stops short of the lawn and their host for the day steps out to greet them.

Nielsen and Knudsen are very happy to be here, after their long, exhausting tour to hot zones everywhere. Their Scandinavian skins have been battered and bruised by the unrelenting sunlight and dust and pollution, the diesel fumes in Addis Ababa and Colombo and Delhi burrowing into their pores and settling there like foreign bodies determined to extend their parasitic presence all the way up to Denmark. Brave men with inquisitive and appreciative minds, Nielsen and Knudsen have accepted everything, the ceaseless churning of their bellies, the constriction in their bowels, but now they are glad to be here. Springtime in this town, with its surrounding hills and forests, does not make the place quite like home, but it is cool and fresh throughout the day, the early eastern light laying itself over a thick carpet of iridescent flowers around which butterflies and grasshoppers flit endlessly.

The two of them had walked around the town the previous day, gazing at the neat little shops that were a mixture of the modern and the quaintly traditional. Their large feet tripping around Wards Lake, they admired the views flung carelessly around the road past the Governor's House, where they were saluted by the military policeman. Then they returned to Police Bazaar, to the three government shops selling local handicrafts near the bus station, where they looked carefully at the friendly hill women with fair complexions and broad, muscular calves, shaking their checked shawls and spreading them on the ground before sitting down behind baskets of ripe fruit: pineapples, bananas, and dense, purple berries, and the last oranges of the year.

The town has prepared them, therefore, for the difference from the battered, dusty plains that are sprawling and endless and flat, but this government official with the thankfully short name has light skin and gray eyes. Nielsen and Knudsen look at each other quizzically, reserving their surprise. They don't quite understand how people can look so different from each other in the same country, dark and light, brown and red and white intermingling into a large map of shifting colors and shapes that goes by the name of India. Nielsen is the more expressive of the two, putting questions to Dr. Dam in the car to get at the heart of this mystery while Knudsen's ceaseless, brooding soul notes everything down and swallows it all into his invisible, impenetrable depths. They are very comfortable at the hotel, yes, they love the wooden planks of its floors, the feel of their wicker-backed cane chairs on the lawn, everything. They are very happy to be here.

The car heads out of the town, across a blackened, tar-coated wooden bridge to the upper reaches around the peaks where the Indo-Danish Project, a small complex combining cattle farm and dairy plant and semen bank, lies between different establishments of the army and air force and the weather observatory.

"No houses there? Only government institutions?" asks Nielsen.

"Yes," Dr. Dam says.

"And how old is the farm itself?"

"Very old. The dairy plant and semen bank were added later. The farm itself goes back to the time of the British, I think. It used to be run by the Army Veterinary Corps. They had as many horses as cows in those days."

"Any horses now?"

"None at all. There were a few left until six or seven years ago. But we didn't replace them when they died of old age."

"Why? Such great climate. The grass, so good," Nielsen gestured at the meadows rolling past thick courts of green broken up by potato patches.

"Too expensive, sir. No one plays polo out here anymore. There are no more competitions or riding clubs, either. A country like ours needs to concentrate on livestock. Much more useful."

Knudsen nods. He is thinking of the thin, rickety children clotting around him at the airport in Delhi, calling out for dollars before running away at the sight of an approaching policeman, pot-bellied and aggressive. He agrees that food should be the prime concern of people here. Anything else would be a disgraceful luxury. The car slows down near a little concrete bus stop where a smattering of tribal villagers wait for a ride to town. Knudsen clears his throat. "Local fruits?"

The vendor's basket contains ripening jackfruit, their sweet, sickly smell permeating the clear air as the car stops. "Mind?" Knudsen queries, always polite.

"No, no, go ahead. People are very friendly here, they

won't object." The two Danes have their cameras out, Japanese SLRs with swiveling, pirouetting lenses that hum and sigh as the objects are brought into focus. The woman with the basket waits for the shots to be completed, then digs in and brings out a fruit that has been cracked open. Parting the prickly, thick skin she reveals the white, fleshy interior, ripe and juicy. The foreigners peer inside. Moon, the driver, is poking the other jackfruit with concentration. The people at the bus stop are watching the big white men, nudging each other and commenting on their clothes and cameras. The Danes, unconscious of the scrutiny, buzz away with their cameras, capturing the fruits and the seller, the bus stop and the people, the forests and ridges with the radar station and the weather observatory looming in the background.

"Maybe we should leave now," Dr. Dam suggests. "Dr. Ahmed will be waiting for us." With a last glance at the jackfruit, they climb back into the car, the gangling legs of the white men folded uncomfortably inside the suede interior of the green Ambassador.

Dr. Ahmed is indeed waiting for them, and he turns toward Dr. Dam for some reassurance as everybody piles out in front of his farm, bringing an air of invasion to his life with their purposeful strides. They begin walking toward the office building that sits in the front, most of the farmhands suddenly visible in the veranda even though they have been explicitly told not to deviate from their daily routine. Dr. Ahmed has already launched into his speech, covering budget, acreage, tonnage of feed, total number of animals, number of calves and calving mothers, average daily yield of milk, method of pasteurization. The foreigners stop in front of the sign, peering at the letters spelling out the collaboration between the two nations, inaugurated by the Honorable Prime Minister Shrimati Indira Gandhi. The cameras are buzzing again, trying to capture the faces in front of the sign, now Nielsen, now Dr. Ahmed, now Dr. Dam, all of them except the photographer captured in a group shot, the paternal, proprietorial looks on the faces of Drs. Ahmed and Dam, the grin of the Nepali farmhand who is asked to pose by Nielsen.

They finally begin the tour, both the Indian officials slightly impatient because there are other pressing matters on their minds and because they are a little tense about this visit. The more time spent showing the visitors around, the greater the chances that something will go wrong. Spring casts a glow over the farm, the path to the animal stalls cut deep and framed by golden-green meadows on both sides. A Friesian cow appears silhouetted against the clear blue sky, its cartoon black-and-white patches adding a different color scheme to the scene. The stalls are largely empty, except for a solitary pair munching on feed. "These are sick animals," Dr. Ahmed says, clearing his throat, "so they are not grazing. Still recovering. If you look at the front right leg . . ."

Nielsen and Knudsen are very professional now, stooping to examine the animals, Knudsen noting with approval the round metal tags on the collar of each animal and the clean, narrow gutters running in front of the stalls. Farmhands are cleaning out some of the empty stalls and bringing in fresh feed. "So what are the major concerns for you?" asks Knudsen, looking down the hallway that opens at the other end in a framed patch of sky and grass.

"Foot-and-mouth," Dr. Dam says soberly, accompanied by the emphatic nods of Dr. Ahmed.

"Any recent outbreaks?"

"Well, two years ago, but not here. A farm in Kirdamkulai. Wiped out most of the cattle population there. But we went in for large-scale vaccination after that."

"Still, you can't always vaccinate animals owned by other people, I suppose. That's where the trouble comes from, I suppose, if your animals come into contact with these other ones."

"Not here," Dr. Dam says firmly. "This place is well isolated. And we don't have too many people owning cattle in this state."

"The local tribals," Dr. Ahmed explains, "don't go in much for dairy farming. It's mostly the Nepalis, people from Nepal who have settled here, who keep cows. The Nepalis usually cooperate because they don't want to alienate the state government." Knudsen and Nielsen look at each other, considering the relation between dairy farming and ethnic origins. "Besides," Dr. Ahmed goes on, "we have been trying to regulate hygiene and milking procedures among them, providing aid and medical attention, and pooling our resources to create a unified network. We don't see them as outsiders or competitors and we don't let them see us that way, either. It was Dr. Dam's idea."

"Very impressive," Nielsen says. They are in the open air now, both the Danes already sure that their reports will strongly recommend maintaining and even expanding the level of aid given to this project.

"Dr. Dam has a plan, at a very early stage now, to create a more cost-effective and quality-conscious town milk-supply scheme."

They turn their attention to their host, walking through the land with its gentle slopes and hollows, cows scattered on the grass like pieces on a child's game board. Nielsen asks both the men about their degrees, where they studied and whether they read contemporary journals. "I suppose the Indian government does send its personnel abroad for a stint of training from time to time. Or is it difficult because this place is, um, slightly remote, even though it is so beautiful?" It happens occasionally, Dr. Dam says, perhaps once in a man's lifetime, but these things have to be approved by ministries in Delhi.

"You should have a chance to see other parts of the world." Dr. Dam shrugs. It does not behoove him to think of such things. "What about your family?"

"I beg your pardon?"

"Would they object if you were to go abroad?"

He shakes his head.

"You have a large family?"

"No, a wife and one son. My son is in school."

"And your wife? Does she stay at home? Or work?"

He nods apologetically that she happens to be a housewife. Both Dr. Ahmed and Knudsen are restless, the former thinking about his son's stomach, Knudsen prowling around, camera out like a sniper's rifle. A throbbing sound begins echoing around the hillside as a Chetak helicopter takes off from the nearby air force base.

They visited the dairy plant and the semen bank, observed the careful regulation of temperatures and the spotless equipment, amazingly maintained by a semiliterate staff, every one of whom smiled shyly and receded into the background as the confident, strong fingers of the visitors probed and felt and watched and converted the observations into rapid notes and pictures.

The objective of the visit had been fulfilled and nothing else of significance remained to be done. Nielsen, who had exposed himself fully to the impressions of the past hour, felt compelled to deal with the awkward silence that was weighing down the end of the visit. Ambassadors that they were, bringing different worlds together, there was always this point where the line flung out between two separate cultures seemed stretched too thin. Nielsen felt the tension threatening to snap the taut line dancing between them, between his world and theirs. At such moments Knudsen was of no help, his very earnestness in matters of development a liability when it came to making a gesture of friendship. "Maybe it would be possible to arrange a visit to Denmark, a lecture-study tour for you, Dr.

Dam. Would you mind if I looked into the possibility when I got back to Copenhagen?"

Dr. Dam smiled. "I'm not sure the government would approve the visit, sir, even if you were to send such a proposal."

"But no harm in trying. We'll convince your Ministry of External Affairs, Dr. Dam. I will write to you." He turned to the other official. "And you, Dr. Ahmed. You must be congratulated for running such an efficient operation. You too should have other opportunities, to visit other countries. Surely you would like to visit Denmark?" Dr. Ahmed's dark, round face showed a strained smile as he contemplated the buttons on the white man's shirt. How did one explain to people from another world the limits one had to set to one's imagination to survive here? He looked at his senior for support and saw that Dr. Dam too was gazing at the visitors with a cautious reserve, his gray eyes measuring the vast distance that lay between them and the foreigners.

Dr. Dam and Dr. Ahmed looked at each other in a wave of silent communication, exchanging notes on the difficult trajectories that had taken them out of their village pasts to this place here and now, to their precarious official positions and fragile endeavors, all of which could be blown to dust. It would not take much; a few telephone calls from ministerial chambers could transfer Dr. Ahmed to a distant outpost in the hills, while a terse set of orders was capable of destroying their best plans about dairy farming.

Nielsen felt the small Indians receding from him across the landscape. He tried to reach out to them, wishing for aid from the taciturn Knudsen but valiantly carrying on by himself as no help came. "How would you like it, if the two of you could somehow be made to visit our university in Frederiksberg? I feel so sure you would spend days walking around the campus, just as we have been walking around your beautiful town. The best place we have seen out of all the places we have gone to. We have three research farms about twenty kilometers from our main campus, which I am sure you would love to see, but this,"—he gestured with his hand, "—is more impressive than anything out there. There is a wonderful sense of peace, yes, a sense of peace."

The humming noise that had been stretching itself in the background grew louder. The helicopter was coming closer, the camouflaged shell of the metal beetle devouring the sun's rays, the only reflections coming from the glass in the cockpit. Pilots newly posted here liked to fly low and observe the farm. Some of them tried to buzz the animals, but the cows usually remained placid, uninterested in their antics. Knudsen's camera was whizzing away, the photographer dropping to one knee for the correct angle.

Dr. Ahmed looked at Dr. Dam and moved off hurriedly, having received a confirming nod. Dr. Dam straightened his back and said, "Come, let us have some tea," addressing the strangers with a sudden flash of pride.

"Helicopter," Knudsen said to Dr. Dam, like a child learning a language.

The visit of the Danes was still fresh in Dr. Dam's mind three weeks later. Ordinarily, he would have been concerned only with the report they would give to their government, since that was what affected him directly. The telephone call, however, had forced him to look at the whole thing in another light. He tried to recapture the details of this entire visit, but what came to his mind was their series of technical questions, their obvious professional competence as they had gone over the machines and animals at the farm. He was sure there was something about their visit that he was forgetting, but before he could recall anything, the two Intelligence men arrived.

They had called an hour earlier and when they walked into his office, they did not introduce themselves. They seemed quite at home in his office, sitting directly across from him without greeting him and looking around while he waited for their questions, a little uncomfortable, wondering if he should ask for their identity cards. "So let's go over this again, shall we? You said on the phone that you took them around to see the farm, this Indo-Danish project, and that you and the manager of the farm showed them around. Is that correct?" Dr. Dam nodded in assent to the small, fat man who was doing the talking, his thin partner silent, twitching his mustache from time to time. "You were with them throughout the trip, all the way from the time they left the hotel up to when they were dropped off back at the hotel. The Ashoka Pinewood Hotel."

"Yes."

"Did they have permission from the Ministry of External Affairs to visit?"

"Yes."

"Did you see their papers?"

"Why should I see their papers?" Dr. Dam said with an acerbic note in his voice. "It's not my job. I was told to show them around by the Chief Secretary. That's what I did. I dropped them off in Police Bazaar, not at the hotel but near the market, because they said they wanted to buy something. They had been invited to dinner that night by the minister, but I wasn't present. I dropped them off and that was it. Never saw them again."

"Yet they were back in a week," the thin man spoke up, "when their special permits for the Northeast had expired. They tried to contact you at your office to ask if you could help them get permits to visit Mizoram and Nagaland, both of which are sensitive border areas. But you were in Gauhati. That was lucky for you."

Dr. Dam shrugged. What was this nonsense about, anyway? They had called in the morning, saying that the Intelligence Bureau had some questions about certain foreign nationals he had been escorting around sensitive areas of national importance. Dr. Dam remained silent, but inwardly he was quite certain that this Intelligence stuff was a pretext for grown-up men to act like children and do no real work.

"Did you take them to the air force base?"

"No, why should I? They were here about the farm, not airplanes."

"They took pictures in the farm, yes?"

"Yes, one of them did."

"They could have been using long telephoto lenses to photograph the helicopters?"

"How do I know? Lenses are not my business."

"Did you take them to the weather observatory?"

"No."

"We have to ask these questions. It is our business to find out these things," the thin man spoke up, giving a suggestive twitch to his mustache.

"It is our business," his fat partner repeated. "Matters of national security. Foreigners walking around sensitive areas, border states, taking pictures. Not good, no sir, not good for the country. One must always be cautious. Even the Prime Minister is much concerned about the foreign hand. The CIA is everywhere," he ended mysteriously.

"Those men were from Denmark, not America," Dr. Dam said.

"The CIA has a long reach," the thin man replied. "A very long reach. If they can infiltrate India, they can do the same in Denmark. NATO, you know."

"The security of the country cannot be compromised for the sake of milk and eggs. National pride is more important than food," the fat one chipped in.

Dr. Dam was beginning to resent the insinuation that he had put his own self-interest above that of the country and he was relieved when they got up to leave. "You must be more careful in the future," the fat man said, pausing as if still unsatisfied.

"Vigilant," the thin agent said.

"Yes, vigilant, always," his partner chimed in. "Anyway, they were asked to leave the Northeast immediately. The big bosses didn't want any fuss. By the way, can one buy some eggs and chicken here? This is hard work, combating the foreign hand."

Dr. Dam called his assistant, Murari, and asked him to take the two men to the sales section and to tell the clerk to release two dozen eggs and two birds from the special quota. The men left immediately with Murari, without bothering to thank him.

After they had gone, he remembered that Nielsen and Knudsen had sent him some photographs from Delhi and this was what he had been trying to recall when the Intelligence men came in. The envelope was still in the office, along with a colorful UNICEF card saying "Thank You." He wondered if he should have told the Intelligence officials about it but then decided it was of no great importance. There had not been a word of their being asked to leave the country in the card. Perhaps they had not wanted to embarrass him by bringing up the boorishness of the Indian government. He reached for the drawer with his personal papers and took out the envelope, fingering the card before turning to the accompanying photographs. Color prints in postcard size, they showed the farm, himself and Ahmed, the cows and the machinery.

He marveled at the quality of the pictures. He too had liked taking photographs once, when he was a bachelor, with a Kodak box camera he bought for twenty-five rupees from a Chowringhee camera store in Calcutta. There were two or three albums full of pictures of the different places he had been to, especially the hill region of Uttar Pradesh—Nainital Lake, Naina Devi's temple, China Peak—which he had liked so much. But these were nothing like the color photographs he had occasionally taken on his Kodak, which looked as if the colors had been rubbed on to black-and-white pictures. He shuffled the photographs around once again, surveying his everyday world with fresh eyes, admiring the Jerseys and Holstein Friesians with their calm faces and perfectly shaped bodies. Nielsen, smiling into the camera, looking as though he had been caught in the middle of one of his questions. But how odd. They had only sent him a selection, of course. Still, it was strange. There was not a single picture of Knudsen, unless one considered him to be the shadow on the ground in the photograph that captured the project sign and the smiling group ranged in front of it.

a tale about tigers
1980

The rain had been beating outside for three days now, the water running in ceaseless pools down the series of steps that led to the two rooms where the Dams had moved in. Small, concrete cubicles of ash gray originally used as storerooms for sanitary equipment, there was just one window for the two rooms. The owners lived above in a mansion that appeared to be cut out of white cardboard, its three stories rising flamboyantly above the tin-roofed bungalows of Jail Road. They were not to blame, however, for the situation the Dams found themselves in. They had offered their storerooms to Dr. Dam as an act of friendship, when the security of the location had become far more important than its inconveniences.

Babu, ten years old, tended to be morose during these long spells of rain. Few of his friends lived close by, and he had little to do when he finished reading the books he had taken out of the State Central Library. The hours at the library were shorter, and even Police Bazaar, little more than a stone's throw away from Jail Road, succumbed to darkness early in the evening. Meanwhile, people had been talking about what was normally unthinkable in the hill town: a flood. It seemed that the low-lying lands of Polo Grounds had been flooded, though all Babu saw, when he peered out through the backyard that was curtained in thick sheets of water, was the uneven, serrated backs of the houses below.

Why is the rain always a part of whatever I choose to remember? Merely because it is the most obvious of traits about the town, or is there something else about it? Sometimes it seems as if it is a blank screen waiting for the credits to start rolling before the action begins, or an empty page that needs to be populated with words and scenes. Certainly, the rain made the telling of stories possible that day, though it was only one of many factors. Our stay in Jail Road, the evenings and nights spent in those largely windowless rooms, had an unusual sense of impermanence about them, the suitcases and trunks unpacked and piled in a corner, no pictures on the walls except for a calendar from the Police Bazaar Pharmacy, a blankness further emphasized by the absence of the once-familiar sounds created by our neighbors at Garikhana. I sometimes felt as if we were on a train, and perhaps it was that temporary air about the house in Jail Road, that feeling of suspension, that led to my father telling me stories, as strangers on a train often do.

I was staring at the calendar, waiting for my father to finish with the *Assam Tribune*. He had been turning its thin, yellow sheets for an hour when he finally folded it away and looked at me.

"Come sit here, and I'll tell you a story," he said, patting the bed.

I was skeptical.

"You, tell a story? About what?"

"About, let's see. What do you want to hear?"

"Enid Blyton. The Famous Five."

"I don't know anything about that stuff. Where do you boys get these things from, anyway?"

"Didn't you ever read story books at school?"

"No. Textbooks were hard enough to get. I'll tell you what. I'll tell you about my school in the village."

"Okay," I said. "But you have to tell me everything. You can't leave anything out. It must have a beginning, a middle, and an end, like a good essay."

"All right, all right," my father said confidently. "Listen.

"The school was in the middle of the fields. It was built of mud and thatch. During the break we went to the playground and played football. Sometimes we played catch."

"No cricket?"

"Only a few times. I was one of the fielders. And when you try to catch the ball in the air, you must pull the ball toward you."

"I know, I know. Go on."

"The school was big and there were many boys. We had to study very hard, Arithmetic and English and Botany. But nothing was so hard as Sanskrit."

"This is getting boring. Who wants to know about what you studied? How did you go to school?"

"Why, we walked. We came out from the neighborhood and walked in a group. During the monsoons, we went in a boat."

"You went to school in a boat? Who rowed?"

"We rowed, all of us. We rowed across the fields that had become the river, we rowed past hills that were now islands and we sang as we rowed to keep time."

"What did you sing?"

My father began singing in a very unmusical voice.

"Come, come, come on, let's go,
Rowing this boat of wood,
See the black waters swirl and flow,
Brother, it sure feels good."

I was delighted. My mother, who had come in from the kitchen to fetch something, stood near the door and laughed. My father suddenly became self-conscious and stopped. "Now, did you like that story?" he asked.

"What story?" I was astonished. "Nothing's happened. What happened next?"

"Something has to happen in a story, does it? Well, okay, this one is where something happens. Listen.

"No one in the village wore shoes, except for the rich landowners and their sons. Apart from the germs, this was dangerous in the monsoons, when you could be caught by hookworms or leeches, or worst of all, bitten by a snake. When we played football, we learned to kick the ball with the side of the big toe, so as not to damage a bone. But football wasn't as important as climbing trees for fruit or swimming or rowing, none of which you needed shoes for. Still, I began to feel ashamed as I grew older, especially when the school inspector came on his annual visit and we were lined up outside in the yard. All the masters wore something, at least slippers, and the headmaster and the inspector wore shoes and walked past us very stiffly. In the fourth grade, I won a government scholarship. This meant my tuition was free up to my matriculation and my textbooks were provided for. They also gave me an annual stipend. The stipend was four rupees."

"Four rupees," I laughed. "To buy sweets with?"

"Four rupees was a lot of money. You could buy a whole goat for five."

"Why would anyone want to buy a goat?"

"To eat it, of course. Four rupees was a lot of money. They informed me of the scholarship and gave me my first stipend on Tuesday afternoon, along with a lecture to study hard. There was a *haat* that day on the way home."

"What's a *haat*?"

"Weekly market. They don't have permanent markets in the village, so there were weekly markets where traders brought in all sorts of things you couldn't buy otherwise."

"What kind of things?"

"All sorts of things. Toys, mirrors that were evenly polished, condensed milk, tinned biscuits, cigarettes, and shoes." He paused for breath. "There, I found these shoes exactly my

size. They were not boots, the black boots some of my classmates or the masters wore. They were canvas shoes, with two
colors, in brown and white. They had green rubber soles."

"You bought them? They were sneakers—you'd never seen
sneakers before?"

"Forget me. No one had seen sneakers or any other sort of
tennis shoe for that matter in the village, not even the land-
lords. I bought the shoes, and wore them with my short pants.
I wished I had a pair of long pants to go with them."

"You mean trousers?"

"Yes. So I wore them to the house, feeling very smart. Then
I reached the house and began taking the sneakers off before
climbing onto the veranda. My father had come in from the
fields and was sitting there with his hookah.

" 'What's that?' he said.

" 'Shoes,' I replied. He looked at them and asked me where
I had stolen such strange things from. I told him I had bought
them with my own money."

" 'What money?' he said. I told him. 'How much did you
pay?' he asked me. I told him that I had spent all the money I
had been given, four rupees."

"Was he unhappy? Wasn't he pleased you won a scholarship?"

"I don't know about that. He came down, looked at my
shoes closely. Then he went and got his stick, the one he used
to guide the bull with while plowing. He made me take the
shoes to the cowshed and put them in the dung. Then he beat
me for the next ten minutes."

I was stunned. "How strange. He beat you up for that? But it wasn't even his own money."

My father smiled serenely.

"Did you go back for the shoes later?"

"My sister did, at night. She washed them secretly and dried them. They could be washed because they were of canvas. But they didn't look the same. And they always smelled a little of dung after that. Not that dung smells bad."

"What an awful story. Don't you have any happy stories to tell?"

"Sure. Listen to this one." I think he developed a story-teller's block at this stage because I remember he tried to gain time. First, he asked me to go and see whether the rain had stopped, although all he had to do was open the door and look out. Then he sent me to the kitchen to find out when dinner would be ready. "Maybe you should study a little," he finally suggested, perhaps as a way of saving face, when I came back.

"That's cheating," I said indignantly, "you're not keeping your word. Besides, homework's all done."

Perhaps he was thinking about the past, about the village life that had come up so suddenly in his stories, and maybe he was overwhelmed by the memories, each bit that surfaced revealing only a small part of the whole, fragmentary and uncertain. Or am I transferring my own uncertainties to him? He may have thought about telling the story about the first time he had come to this town. That was when he was still in school, when it had been part of the same country and the country itself ruled by the British. Along with his father, he had walked from their village in the plains of Sylhet up the hills to this town. They had come to visit someone. A relative on his mother's side, her brother, who had been a civil servant.

If he was thinking about such things, he did not bring them up. He sat there for a while twirling a shirt button, looking away embarrassedly when he raised his head and saw me waiting. Then he suddenly cheered up. "I'm sure you would like a story about tigers."

"Yes! Were there tigers where you grew up? Royal Bengal Tigers?"

"Well, not exactly where we lived. But I ran into a tiger when I was posted near Aizawl, in Mizoram."

"Okay," I said, somewhat doubtful.

"Listen," Dr. Dam began. "When I was posted to Mizoram, when it wasn't Mizoram yet but still a part of Assam, I worked in a very isolated place. People came to the veterinary clinic in the daytime, from faraway villages. I lived in a small bungalow, but there were very few houses near it. There was a man who came and cooked for me during the day. But at night I was alone."

"Weren't you scared?"

"Nothing to be scared of. Just no people there."

"Robbers?"

"No robbers. Very honest people."

"What about ghosts? Maybe the bungalow was haunted."

"There are no such things as ghosts," my father said.

"That's superstition. Didn't they teach you that at school?" He was probably annoyed with the school and the amount of money it cost him to send me there.

"Sure. But the class teacher also reads us ghost stories during story hour. Second World War ghost stories. Like the man who they thought had been killed at Dunkirk but who turned up in London to fight the Battle of Britain."

"Nonsense. Do you want to listen or not? Tigers are real, not ghosts."

"Okay, okay. Go on."

"So I was there one night by myself. There had been a difficult case in the morning, this calf and its mother, both of which were sick. Village people are very poor, sometimes all they have is one cow. If they lose that, they are finished."

"I thought this story was about tigers," I said.

"I'm coming to that. One more interruption and I stop."

Receiving utter silence from me, he went on.

"I tried my best, along with my field assistant, but both mother and calf were suffering from severe infections and were very weak. I suggested they shouldn't be made to walk back to the village, but there was no place to keep them, the owner said. So I told him the animals could be kept in my quarters. There was this little shed that was meant to be a garage or something, I think. They wouldn't be cold there and it had proper walls and a door, so they would be safe from wild animals as well. Anyway, I was writing my diary after my dinner by the light of a kerosene lamp—there was no electricity in these parts then, remember—when I heard this sound outside my house. Someone was walking around the house, someone heavy."

"Then?"

"I turned down the lamp, and went to look through the window. Luckily, I had shut them all. There was no moon and where the sound had come from, behind the house, there were a lot of trees so I couldn't see anything. I came back to my chair. Then I heard the sound of coughing."

"Coughing?"

"Coughing. Like this." Here my father provided a modest imitation of a tiger's cough. "Tigers cough, when they are stalking prey. It had smelled the cows."

"Maybe it had smelled *you*. Perhaps it was a man-eater."

"Maybe. I went to the window and there was just a tiny bit of moonlight now. I saw it as it circled the house in front. It was big, muscled, with black stripes on its back."

"Didn't you wish you had a gun?"

"I turned up the lamp to its brightest, and made sure every single door and window was shut properly. Then I began singing very loudly, so that it would know that I wasn't scared."

"What did you sing?"

"I know only two songs. The rowing one and the national anthem. So I sang them one after another."

"Then?"

"It was very late. I didn't dare go to the bathroom that night since I had to cross an open stretch to reach it. But I kept my electric torch in my hand and went to sleep. But I didn't sleep at all. All night long I heard the tiger circling the bungalow, and later on it began to roar from time to time. The villagers heard it too and thought I was dead. In the morning, I waited until the sun had come up properly before I went out. The tiger had left its footprints all around the house. The animals were terrified, but they were alive. They recovered later."

"That's it?"

"What do you mean, that's it?"

"But there's no adventure, nothing really happens. Not unless you went after it the next day when you got hold of a gun."

"Why would I do such a thing? You wanted a happy story. You boys are difficult to please these days," he said. "Everybody's fine at the end. Me, the cows. The tiger too," he added.

"Any more stories?"

"No, not today."

I quickly got up and put on my slippers, my hunger having overtaken my greed for stories. He sat there, silent once more, and I wondered if he had really been in a bungalow with a tiger circling outside or if he had made it up. He said something as I opened the door. "Boots." I turned to look at him, but he shook his head and asked me to run on to the kitchen.

It was not a story he could tell me that day. Not then. And not now.

blackout

1979

Ever since they stopped the bus coming in, picking out seven passengers in the swiftly falling evening, something changed. He was out of town when it happened, a small bureaucrat making a small official trip, or it is possible that he would have seen the policemen—maybe even some blood?—on the road a few meters beyond the edge of the staff quarters. When he came back there was only the winter.

He is a man graying faster than his years, sitting with the lights out in his room and the curtains drawn, filling in these evenings by himself. He has sent his wife and child away to a distant mining town in the plains and even the neighbors do not venture out after dark any longer. It seems uncertain how he spends these long evenings, for the files he brings back home cannot be that big, with the mass of papers always yielding swiftly before the steady beat of his hand. The rooms in the government bungalow are many and large, and no doubt at nine he walks softly to the kitchen, pours milk into the big aluminum bowl, breaking up the bread and waiting for the milk to soak up the pieces, eating swiftly as the darkness of the curtains changes shade with the entry of the moonlight.

The man and his background, his thoughts and his experiences, are not important or even interesting in themselves. It is just that there is something in the situation that seems significant, in the darkened room and the calm pierced every hour or so by the sentry's call, in the sense of waiting permeating the scene and in the fact that the solitary figure, oblivious to all this, seems to have found something important in the papers he has taken out of a creased, heavily marked buff file.

December, and against the backdrop of the streamers and little stars studded with silver dust in the shops near the bus station there is the slow boarding of the ASTC (Assam State Transport Corporation) bus, then the pause inside the second-class railroad car in Gauhati at the end of his journey. There he has a hurried lunch that his wife has ordered for him from the railway base kitchen, working his way through the food tray divided into various compartments, the small boy looking on. The bangles on his wife's thin wrists clink as she hastens to take his empty plate. Then the swift departure with a quick reassurance and the four-hour journey back to the hill town that has been home since the early seventies.

He is accustomed to this leave-taking, sending his wife and son away every winter to his in-laws. This time is only a slight variation. He will do much the same things as usual: go for a morning walk, but a little later when there are more people around, inhaling deeply at the wind blowing through the conifers in a cascading waterfall of sound, his blunt, boxerlike nose always taken a little by surprise by the warm smell of the coal fires that arrives as an aftershock. At these moments he is as much at home as he has ever been anywhere, belonging, in his patched-up overcoat and the cheap shoes bought off a wizened Chinese shoemaker at Burra Bazaar with its slush-filled alleys, belonging to this hill town with its golf course and elegant missionary schools and the red cheeks of the tribal children bundled up in tartan checks behind their mothers. And perhaps it is when he sits at his desk at the Additional Secretariat a little later that he is most at home, among the papers, checking the figures and statements and notations, cocooned safely in his work, oblivious to the corridor outside where the workers clatter, erupting in a frenzy when the tea lady comes in at eleven with her steaming kettle and dry, flaking pastries.

The enforced darkness in the evening, yes, that makes things difficult. But it is not as though he has no knowledge of loneliness. There are years of solitary evenings accumulated from bungalows in far-flung places where the twilight narrows to a slit through the windows and the sky slowly subsides into the dense earth, leaving only the massed sentinels of the trees to stand guard. There are all the long journeys he has made, from village to veterinary college, to solitary postings throughout the Northeast, making unsuccessful surveys of cheap plots of land even as larger political boundaries are drawn and redrawn, demarcating new countries and fledgling states.

And being forced to sit in darkness? That, too, he has done before.

That was eight years ago, 1971, one year after the birth of the boy, when the town was still part of Assam and had not become the capital of a new hill state, when this same house in the veterinary compound awaited his return, the evening rapidly papering over the windowpanes of the bungalow. Then, as now, his wife had gone to Dhanbad with the child. He had sat with a kerosene lamp, with the giant Philips transistor turned low, sat by himself as the sexless voice of the announcer spluttered and died down. He had turned the red battery onto its side to coax a little more life from it. Carefully closing his files, separating them into two halves, he had given himself a break. Unfolding *The Statesman*, now beginning to look like parchment paper, he had read laboriously through the editorial page, turning back once in a while from analysis and comment to the news scattered in the other pages, delving into the story that had unfolded with a single, sharp headline emblazoned across the front page: IT'S WAR.

The only sound would have been the occasional drone of aircraft engines, Dakotas chopping their way through the skies toward the delta plains of East Pakistan, rising and fading through the house, their piston beats reverberating through the tin roof. Maybe he had become emotional at the thought of a war machine moving toward a land that for all the liberation to come would never again be home. Did he feel something, reading those place names that had been left behind the border of '47, or was that space with its tempestuous rivers and fishes and snakes, its groves overflowing with mangoes, guavas, and jackfruit, lost to his mind? Irrevocably gone, like the matriculation certificate he never claimed because he did not have the required fee?

Tonight should not be difficult after such knowledge, but how far does the current darkness stretch? Beyond the house with its blacked-out windows, and surely far beyond the solitary sentry posted there after the incident with the bus. The darkness races across the highway to Gauhati like a military aircraft, like a monsoon cloud, moving on to the small settlements where the knives of the long night are being sharpened, and yet never seems to reach far enough to affect the big cities in the plains. Why does no one in Delhi know what is happening here? Why do the killings and the lootings not appear in the Calcutta paper that now gets here three days late?

As if in response to the indifference elsewhere in the country, he turns the flame higher, holding up the papers he has been scrutinizing that evening. There is silence everywhere, from the cicadas, the highway, even from the sentry, all of them watching and waiting. And feeling that what had been intended as a signal to the larger world has instead drawn enemies closer, Dr. Dam turns the kerosene flame low. And listens. Only the sound of the air rushing through his ears, the silence of the room roaring in to balance the pressure created by an emptiness inside his head. He understands perfectly now the persistent invitations from his colleague to come for dinner and stay over—he would be quite safe with him—the pleas to take care of his health and to go easy on the paperwork. The figures lie before him, limp and ragged, their code now breached to reveal the transactions, the fake purchase vouchers, the supplies that could never have reached the government depots. As he goes over in his head the report to be made the next day, calculating the sum total of the loss to the state, he feels a sudden pity for the man whose glances have frantically wooed him the last few afternoons, sees the small, friendly face emerging from the neat, well-cut suit that could not have been paid for with a government salary. Then, as he hears the crunch of feet on the gravel, he feels fear, frozen in his glance toward the telltale lamp. The feet, more than one pair, are coming closer, the marching of confident leather so unlike his own. Boots, he thinks automatically. Boots, not like the shoes people wear to work wherever people can afford to wear shoes, but boots coming up to the ankles, maybe with spurs. He waits in the darkness, wishing the moon away from its dispassionate role as an observer of events. But there are shadows across the drawn curtains, figures on the grass waiting for him to make a move. He wipes the sweat beads from his forehead, looks around at the files and grips the heavy glass paperweight. There are murmurs from outside, then the figures separate and one of them approaches and knocks lightly on the window.

As if reciting a charm or a sacred mantra to ward off evil, he thinks of the town, of home in the faces of the tribal women at the fish market with their sudden laughter, the stubborn resistance and slow yielding of the boat at Wards Lake, of the gardens and markets and cottages and stone-chipped paths and thinks that maybe it will remain for him, if not in quite the same way. Because there is no doubt that an uncertainty will linger, a raw nerve, a tic to be brought back by the sound of marching feet that is for now passing him by, fading, as the men outside decide to leave for some reason he cannot fathom.

Many years later, in a sudden burst of confidence, he will tell his son, "Boots, marching up and down, that night," handing over his memory of that fear and uncertainty. And his son, though he will never know it, will acknowledge the gesture, deal with it in his own way, his high lace-up boots crunching down the concrete of the places he has lived in, places like Calcutta and Delhi, all those lonely places that have never been home, the tread of his feet just a little unsteady when he recalls his father and that night of fear.

2.
Departure

new year's eve
1987

The days between Christmas and New Year's Eve had passed in such a strange manner that as I walked to Police Bazaar that evening for the medicine, it seemed that I was on the same mission I had begun on Christmas Day, the bus tickets still in my wallet, yet to be disposed of. It was easier to believe this than the images I had in my mind, of my father being taken to the hospital in Dr. Chatterji's car, the bed in the general ward, the nurses with their clipboards, the hushed whispers of neighbors discussing whether he would live, scenes that appeared to be culled from a vivid, tormenting dream.

I was walking rapidly, hunched up against the wind, while a part of me remained on the alert, looking out for any groups clustered in the shadows along the road to Police Bazaar. I had taken the shortcut to save time, to get to the big pharmacy next to Kelvin movie theater before it closed, but that wouldn't make any difference if they didn't have the new medicines. It was the last day of the year, the temperature hovering around zero on the Celsius scale. The town was buried deep within itself, the road forlorn and slightly eerie as I drifted past the empty grounds of Lady Keane College, all of it adding to the timeless feeling of my journey. The shops in Police Bazaar were hovering glowpools in the distance as I walked on, the market open later than it would be for the rest of the winter. Who knew what would come after that, beyond the winter, in the new year?

It was a relief to reach the rows of shops, to forget the strangeness of the week in the immediate worries that presented themselves at the pharmacy. They had the Threptin medicinal biscuits and the pills, but the injections would take a couple of days, maybe three. I waited impatiently in the brightly lit shop, among the reflections from the glass-covered shelves and plastic panels advertising tonics and pills, waiting for the man behind the counter to check with the manager about the injections. I could hear the sounds of revelers in the streets, little bursts of music and the impatient rap of car horns floating into the shop to die among its array of medicines. They would try to order the injections from Gauhati, but if the distributors there had no supplies, the injections would have to come from Calcutta. I was troubled by the prospective delay, my mind returning of its own accord to the image of my father lying on a hospital bed, the strange words tumbling out from the lips of the doctors as they discussed his condition. I had no time to linger, though, not with people waiting for the medicines back at the hospital, with the winter night marching all over the landscape except for the marketplace, the last spot of light and life in the town.

Casting a last, backward glance at the stores with greeting cards in their windows, some of them still festooned with Christmas wreaths and paper spikes of mistletoe and holly, I began walking back to the Civil Hospital. It was almost eight now so I took the main road, past Peak Studio and the high court, on through police headquarters and the State Central Library, turning past the obelisks in front of the library toward the white building with its ambulances and stray scraps of gauze and cotton wads in the front yard, stepping finally into its hospital smell of disinfectant and disease and despair. The turbaned attendant was settling in for the night shift, patting the cushion on the little stool in front of his electric heater. He greeted me immediately. "*Arre*, Babu, why is your face so cloudy? Cheer up, everything will be fine. Come down later for a cigarette. I'm right here."

The sweeper didn't really know my name. He used it as a term of endearment, which was how I had been stuck with the ugly nickname in the first place. It didn't matter here, where I was just someone accompanying a patient, and the nurses addressed me by room number rather than name as they spoke about the various rules of the hospital, tapping impatiently at the charts on their clipboards. That was what the hospital seemed to be about, a grid of rules that descended upon those who entered here, lifting only at the very end when the patients left the hospital.

❀   ❀   ❀

The first night at the hospital, on Christmas Day, Dr. Dam had been put in the general ward, on one of a row of beds with identical red blankets and cold white sheets. Babu squatted near the bed, his mind divided between his father's illness and the aborted trip. Whenever he looked at his father lying unconscious, a saline drip stuck into his arm, he felt ashamed that he grudged the change in plans. But he could not stop thinking about it. They were to have taken the bus together to Gauhati. His mother and he would have set off for Dhanbad, while his father went in a different direction, to Silchar—almost like those times when Babu had been very small and Dr. Dam would accompany them to the railway station in Gauhati, scrambling off the Kamrup Express as it began pulling out of the platform. As Babu sat in the general ward on a hard metal chair, he recalled the train journeys of his childhood as if across some distant, immeasurable stretch of time, the crescendo of the coal-black steam engines as they thrust themselves forward with a sudden jerk, the arbitrary stops and cries of tea at lonely stations, the glimpse of an old, deserted house from the train window. From Calcutta, Babu and his mother would have boarded the Coalfield Express to Dhanbad, where her brother Anil lived, and he would have met his uncle and aunt, his grandmother and cousin, all of whom he had not seen in years.

Instead of that, he was sitting in a cold chair in the long room on the ground floor of the hospital, close to the emergency ward. He could hear the gurneys being wheeled around occasionally, stifled moans of pain punctuating the creak of their wheels. When the lights were dimmed at eight, the figures prone on their beds made the place look as if it were underground, a cemetery of some sort. Was that what catacombs were, underground cemeteries? The relatives and friends who had chosen to spend the night in the general ward with the patients, mostly poor people, had nodded off on the floor, exhausted and cold. Cries and whispers came through the night as the inmates—patients, relatives, it didn't matter—stirred and felt their hopelessness or pain, but he was awake.

Dr. Dam's bed was toward the front, in a straight line with the door, and Babu could see the turbaned attendant in front of the heater stretching himself periodically. Dr. Chatterji had asked him to see that his father did not pull off the drip in his arm. He had pointed out the bell for the nurse and put Babu in charge of an enamel bedpan before leaving him alone with his thoughts, the almost imperceptible flow of the saline and the uneven breathing of the man on the bed providing the background to his loneliness.

Babu had bought a full packet of cigarettes for the journey, but in the mad rush from home in Dr. Chatterji's car there had been no time for him to get matches. They had bundled Dr. Dam into the little Standard Herald and headed for the hospital, the money from the canceled bus tickets still in Babu's wallet. He felt very sorry for himself as he reflected on his situation: he had no matches, it was six days to the end of the year, he was seventeen years old and watching a bottle hanging from its plastic vine and metal branch, the dull juice trickling slowly into his father's blue veins.

Around midnight, when Dr. Dam seemed to be breathing evenly, completely unaware of the drip or the surroundings, Babu walked carefully toward the door, looking out for a limb that might lie in his path. The corridor was sterile and empty, and through the metal gate pulled across its end he could see the thickening winter fog and the distant blinking of the taillight of a car. Sikhs don't smoke, he muttered to himself, seeing the turbaned man sitting on his haunches and looking at him with inquiring eyes.

"Come and sit in front of the fire," the man said, indicating the heater. "Young bones, I know, but come and talk to me. Can't be liking the scene in there." He spoke quietly but in a normal voice, making it seem almost as if this was not a hospital. Maybe a bus station, or even a sleeper compartment on a train. "Tell me who it is you're with." Babu told him. The sweeper nodded. "What's the number of the bed? I'll take special care." Babu sat by the heater, lit a cigarette from its orange coils of light after asking the man for permission. They talked as the boy smoked, dragging the fumes into his lungs, talked about school and hospitals, about the town and the winter. Then he fell asleep and the attendant woke him in the morning, saying that he had been checking on Dr. Dam through the night and that he was fine.

Dr. Chatterji was waiting for me in the little hospital room on the third floor, holding a lively conversation with the neighbors who were gathered there. They were talking politics, debating the state assembly elections in February, most of the men deferring to Dr. Chatterji, his bulky, suited figure dominating the scene as he talked about what the Bengalis should do in the current situation.

It was Dr. Chatterji who had made it possible, the admitting of my father on Christmas Day, calling up senior doctors and administrators once they got back from their holidays so that he could have a private room. "One more night for you, Babu. Take good care of your father and use the time to study," Dr. Chatterji said as he collected his bags and the men began to file out. I resented the advice, the assumption that one could turn one's mind on and off like a tap, anytime, anywhere.

I was lonelier up here on the third floor than I had been the first night at the hospital. I had to go down the stairs to talk to the turbaned man but I didn't like leaving my father alone. The attendant came up to the room periodically to take the bedpan and put a fresh one in, but he hardly had time to talk while doing his rounds. He had been true to his word, I thought, he did take special care of my father, coming in and doing his work lightheartedly, asking Doctorsaab to piss as frequently as he felt like, assuring him that there would be an empty pan for him even if all the other patients had to soil their clothes.

The nurses on the night shift were strange, not like the

attendant at all. They had hard, glittering eyes behind identical steel-rimmed glasses and they turned the door handle noisily and shone their flashlights around the room like policemen carrying out a search. They were usually noisy and bad-tempered and if I had shut the door against the wind, they rapped loudly on the window with their flashlights. I tried to spend as much time as possible outside the room, smoking, thinking, looking out through the windows along the corridor.

The private rooms were toward the back of the hospital, the windows looking onto Lady Hydari Park. Not much was visible at night and in any case the shrubbery and fence behind the hospital concealed the park with its birdhouses and lawns and canals. But invisible as it was for the most part, I found myself staring into the blackness, painting in the shapes and colors of the park from memory, a book dangling from my hand, my finger on the same page for hours. I had been to the park so many times, but I had never looked up at the hospital windows where I now crouched at night, bunched up against the wind streaking through. The night we moved up to this floor I had been startled by strange noises, a metallic sound like creaking shop shutters but also resembling the hoarse wheezes of a man whose lungs are gone.

They were cranes, I later said to myself, those cranes I have seen so many times walking in their funny, fastidious way through the shallow water, looking really serious although they were only thinking about fish. Just cranes. How quickly it had fallen into a pattern for me: the night stays at the hospital, going home early in the morning when a neighbor—usually one of the Goswami brothers—took over, grateful for the relief as I drank tea at the stall near the entrance before walking home. I came back in the evening, carrying a few textbooks with me although there wasn't much light in the passageway. Not that I felt like reading anything. There was so much to do during the day. Blood samples to be dropped off and reports picked up from a private lab in Laitumukrah; the hospital's pathology section took three days to come out with the results of any tests. Medicines had to be procured from different pharmacies, the food for my father delivered from home by someone or other. The room was freezing cold at night, and I had had to tell Dr. Chatterji, who asked me to pick up a heater and a thermos from his house.

A few days ago I had accompanied Dr. Chatterji in search of Dr. Borgohain. Dr. Chatterji had been dissatisfied with the hospital doctors and wanted to bring in a specialist he had heard of, an M.D. Dr. Borgohain was supposed to be very young, extremely brilliant, and on the staff of the best hospital in town, the missionary hospital in Laitumukrah. He lived in a modern block of apartments close to the hospital, but the clerk at Nazareth Hospital was unable to give us the number of his apartment.

Dr. Chatterji was not put off by this at all. He had been very confident that not only would he find Dr. Borgohain but that he would also be able to convince the specialist to take up the case. His large body tucked into the tiny Standard Herald, he told me genially, "Now let's see who finds the apartment first, you or me." When we got out from the car near the block, I wondered how we would ever find the doctor from among the rows of identical balconies sprouting from the concrete we were standing on, with not a single human being in sight. Dr. Chatterji smoked and pondered, then he pointed and said, "Third floor. On the left. You go and tell him I'm waiting downstairs."

I later asked Dr. Chatterji how he knew that was where the M.D. lived. Dr. Chatterji enjoyed explaining his detecting skills very much. "Ah, we looked at the balconies. All those clotheslines hanging in the balconies with washing. There was a *gamucha*, white with red borders, on Borgohain's balcony. You'll never find an Assamese without one of those towels." It was that easy for some men. Everything came together for them—money, strength, confidence, social skills. And then there were people like my father, reduced to this, lying helplessly on a hospital bed, retired, a house half-built somewhere in Silchar.

I was trying to read, sitting at the foot of the bed by the heater, when I heard my father stir restlessly. I didn't feel as tired as usual, since I had stayed at home last night. My mother had come in the morning and replaced the red hospital blankets with some from home, so that my father looked a little better in spite of the bristly white stubble engulfing his face. He now seemed to understand where he was and what had happened to him. There were even moments of lucidity when the doctors were here and he asked them questions about the drugs being administered. But as he sat up now, leaning against the pillow, his eyes were squinted in concentration, looking past me. "His vision's gone," I had heard Dr. Borgohain whisper as he put him through some tests, right finger to the tip of the

nose, now the left one, bring them together now, that's ter-
rific, and my father smiling at the end of it like a child. He
looked at me and said something.

"What?" I said, trying to catch the words.

"Who's in the next room?" he asked.

"I don't know. Why? How does it matter?" I realized that
my tone was peevish even though I hadn't meant it to be.

"They make a lot of noise," he said, his words clearer now.
"Partying into the night. Drinking, gambling. Leapingstone
and his cronies."

He's delirious, I thought, talking about people he knew so
long ago. He can't let go of anything.

The little room on the third floor of the Civil Hospital was
what the lives of Babu and Dr. Dam had been reduced to. Every
single detail in the room—the musty odor of disinfectant and
urine, the metallic smell of the filaments on the heater, the tea
stains dribbling down the side of the thermos on the bedside
table, all this made up a self-contained world absolute in its
hold over the two. What lay outside—the town with its expanse
of memories and experiences—seemed to have disappeared,
pared down to the frailty and uncertainty of the human mind
and body. In his fitful dreams, Dr. Dam sometimes saw scenes
from his past life, but he could no longer quite place them or
understand what they referred to. As for the boy, he was still
raw with the pain of the disrupted journey and his father's
illness, suffering from the premonition of an entire life gone

to waste, caught in the afterburn of a youth that had disappeared before he had had the chance to taste it in full.

Babu saw his father attempting to rise, a hand precariously close to the borrowed thermos. "What do you think you're doing?" he said as he hurried over. His father's face carried some emotion he could not fathom.

"You'll see, they're in the next room, having a party. I know Leapingstone's voice. It's him." Dr. Dam allowed himself to be tucked in without protest, looking at his son. His voice sank into a whisper. "He carries a gun." He nodded his head vigorously, eyes glazed over with what Babu feared was madness.

As the last night of the year spread itself like the winter fog around Civil Hospital, preparing to draw the covers of the past around itself, Babu forgot his earlier wish to find out who had been moved into the next room. Leaning on the window, legs folded around the chair he had dragged out into the corridor, he wistfully thought of the magical intersection of past and future that was taking place. The park shrouded in the fog he thought of as his past, as childhood and the absence of responsibility, a place that had always belonged to him but was now slipping away like the shores of a country seen from the guardrails of a ship. Barely visible, the receding country that lay behind was still fathomable, if only through memory. But what was to come, the future holding itself coiled and ready in the room with his father, remained utterly unknown. Resolutions, he thought, I've forgotten to write down any resolutions for the new year.

He had his diary out, full of fantastic scribblings: song

lyrics, poems, quotations, and lists—of things to do, places he
wanted to visit, addresses of colleges and universities in Australia, England, and America. There were some photographs
of him with his friends, with Moni, Michael, Partha: standing
near a food cart at a fair in Garrison Ground, holding bats and
stumps in their hands, leaning against the curved bridge over
Wards Lake. Partha had come to see him in the morning,
slightly embarrassed and apologetic about the fact that he
wanted to borrow Babu's Russian Army jacket. Partha had
wanted to be serious and solicitous about his friend's father but
then his excitement broke through and he began talking about
a girl he had met at a party. He was going to meet her again at
a New Year's Eve party. She was older than him and worked in
the administrative division of the Northeastern Hill University. "Study for the board exams," Babu wrote, "especially
chemistry. I mustn't be a burden to the family. It looks like I
have to try and get admission to an engineering college." He
knew he would rather do anything else.

He heard the people in the next room when he came up,
having gone down to talk to the attendant. There was the sound
of music from behind the thin wooden door. He was familiar
with the song because he had the same Smokey album at home
and he would normally have appreciated the sad, sweet lyrics
of "Living Next Door to Alice." The door opened in a flash
of light and loud music that was abruptly filtered down as it
swung shut again, a man stumbling to the end of the corridor
toward the public bathrooms and being violently sick, retching into one of the washbasins. There was laughter, squeaks of

excitement from the room, cards being called out, the clink of glasses. Babu realized with some amount of surprise that his father might not have been delusional. But how could he have been so certain who it was in the next room, unless somebody had told him?

The man who had come out so unceremoniously did not return and when Babu looked around later, he was no longer to be seen. In a little while, the bells from the churches would sound, pealing beginnings and endings into the sleepy night spread over the town. People dancing and drinking would embrace, while those in front of television sets watching the programs produced in Delhi and Bombay would turn toward each other with their greetings before going to bed. He heard the cranes setting up their wild, shrieking ritual again, harsh cries accompanied by the flapping of wings, their urgency voicing an animal murmur that was relayed to the other creatures, traveling through the chattering monkey cages and the solitary wildcats before vanishing into the trees and walls that surrounded the park.

If he could somehow go to a college in Calcutta, what would the next New Year's Eve be like? What would he see at the end of a long night in the city? He imagined narrow pavements where the street dwellers were setting up morning fires, sending up smoke signals that rose to meet the first, tremulous rays of the sun spreading over the jagged rooftops of a great city, the early risers beginning their day by putting out washing on lines strung across the rooftops, solitary walkers and runners already in their energetic morning rhythm, the winding-up of squeaky shop shutters.

The door to the next room had opened to the sounds of another Smokey song, "I'll Meet You at Midnight," and people spilled out into the passageway. Somebody turned the music down at a sharp command and he saw the man who had spoken so tersely in the half-light, dressed in crisp white pajamas, coming toward the windows. The bells had begun pealing, not loudly but almost a little sad and uncertain, and a few solitary fireworks set off in Laban lit up the sky over the park. There was a rumble of greetings from the men behind, the sound of drunken slaps on thickly padded backs. The man in the pajamas was standing next to him, aloof from the noise. He turned a little toward Babu and looked at the boy standing in the corridor. "Happy New Year," he said softly, "May the Lord give you peace and happiness."

"Happy New Year," Babu replied shyly. The group began walking down the corridor, a little quieter after the man who had greeted him told them to shut up. The corridor emptied out, leaving him a little blank inside, the images of the big city and of another life that he had conjured up suddenly gone. He looked at his father's room and moved toward the door.

learning to walk
1988

If Babu and his mother had held on to the hope that things would someday go back to normal, that feeling ended with Dr. Dam's return home. In some ways, it had been easier to go on during the month at the hospital, living with the shock of the event and the faint hope that was its shadow, taut and trembling. Now that there was no crisis to be warded off and that death—or the awareness of death that had hovered around the hospital room and in the murmurs of the doctors—had receded, there was no longer an expectation of sudden miracles. A change for the better would come only gradually; what was real was this routine revolving around sickness, the worries about money, and the move to Silchar, the realization that the former shape of their lives would not be found ever again.

At night, crouched in front of his science books, Babu was aware of a different kind of tension in the house, sensitive to everything that was new: the weight of one or the other uncle in the next room, the uneven texture of the floorboards across which he guided his father on his way to the bedroom window or to the bathroom, the slow accretion of medicinal things around his father's bed and the early tread of the visiting nurse who came twice a week to test his father's blood sugar level. These changes were hard enough; what made it even more difficult was the specter of another transformation, the impending move to Silchar. Babu appeared calm and mature to visitors but, inside, he was deeply unsettled by the state of suspension. He felt himself stretched out, spread out thinly over the surface of sickness, trying desperately to reconcile his different roles—from studying for his high school exams to forging his father's signature on bearer checks.

Dr. Dam had planned well before his stroke that they would leave for the house in Silchar once Babu had taken his exams. Neither Babu nor his mother had any idea, however, about what those plans had consisted of. It fell upon them to work out the move, beginning with the painstaking business of becoming familiar with the landscape of Dr. Dam's financial affairs. In those months, Babu probably learned more about the real world than he had in eleven years of schooling, as he found out the difference between a fixed-deposit account and a five-year savings bond, between a recurring deposit and an *Indira Vikas Patra*, and discovered the absolute power that a single clerk at a government institution is capable of wielding over hundreds.

Dr. Dam was not unwilling to help. He felt deeply the responsibility he had burdened his wife and son with, both of them utter novices with respect to the larger world, but there was little he could do. He had trouble remembering the details of his accounts and he couldn't even sign the bearer checks that had to be cashed at the bank. When Babu decided to try an old skill picked up from friends at school, Dr. Dam watched carefully and admiringly as his son's dark hand produced the squiggles and curlicues that had been his own trademark. After Babu and his mother presented these forged signatures successfully at the State Bank of India and their immediate worries about meeting daily expenses were over, Dr. Dam asked his son for a few specimen signatures. Armed with blank sheets of paper, he tried meticulously every day to reproduce his son's efforts, devoting the rest of his time to carrying out the exercises the doctors had recommended for him, right finger to the tip of his nose, then the left, then both of them together.

To the external observer, the separate efforts of father and son complemented each other, creating a design and a symmetry around the change of guard taking place, even though the actors themselves were unaware of this. Against the backdrop of the freezing month of January, they tested themselves against these new skills demanded of them, even as Mrs. Dam kept the house running, ensuring supplies of hot water and food and medicines and tea. She wrote to Biren, asking him for his help in moving to Silchar, and talked to the visitors appearing on their short visits of sympathy. Dr. Dam listened silently to those who came to see him, to the stream of advice that poured from their lips about the miraculous possibilities of homeopathy, ayurvedic remedies, charms, or the specialists at Christian Medical College in Vellore, while Babu stayed away from everyone other than his parents. Biren wrote back tersely that he was conscious of his family duties and that he would fulfill them in due time. Dr. Dam's two other brothers visited for a few days each, meeting their obligations by buying some fruit for their elder brother during their stay.

There wasn't much that was not hard in those months before my high school exams and the move to Silchar, as it became clearer that my father would take a long time to recover, if he ever did. The little relief that came our way, the slight lightening of mood, was produced by Anil, my mother's brother. It had taken him a while to have his leave approved— he was a clerk for the railroad in Dhanbad—but when he did arrive, it didn't take him long to revert to character. He was a nervous, funny little man, somewhat awestruck by my father and the town we lived in. Humor was his defense, I realized later, the defense of a powerless, harried individual whose character had been shaped by the reservation counter he manned, where he was often caught between angry passengers and remote, imperious officers.

Anil liked mimicking people, sometimes with unfortunate results, as in the stammer that had begun as an imitation of a particular official and then became a permanent feature of his speech. He was clearly downcast on his arrival, the invalid state of my father more of a shock to him than to us who had seen the transition, but after a few days he recovered. He declared that he was heartbroken by the fact that we would be leaving this town on the edge of the country, as he liked to characterize it. It was not that Silchar was any less remote, but Silchar was hot and flat and had neither pine trees nor bungalows with sooty fireplaces. Anil also decided that my father's recovery was only a matter of time and that the use of a cane would enhance the necessary dignity of a retired officer. To this end, he bought an expensive cane for my father from Superbazaar, not a heavy wooden stick but a light, fashionable aluminum tube with a rubber grip at the bottom. He presented this to my father with a flourish, advising him to grow a goatee to complete the air of distinguished retirement, stroking his own thin beard hopefully.

Anil had visited our family only twice in about a decade and although this trip was not a happy one, he seemed to be extracting some pleasure out of his stay until the tail-end of his visit, which overlapped with Biren's arrival. For Anil our town was "very English," with its smooth little roads and parks, and even our house with holes in its canvas ceiling and its oddly shaped rooms was a bungalow. Everything was different here, he informed my mother and me, from the fact that my father was a retired "officer"—he laid particular stress on this designation—to my small collection of Hemingway and Steinbeck. Anil had not been to Silchar, and what he had heard of it had aroused no desire in him to see the place for himself. "You people are not going to enjoy living in India," he repeated to all of us until we got sick of the joke.

In fact, he made such a fuss about our move to Silchar that my mother had to comfort him instead of the other way around. Still, it was fun to have him staying with us because he talked so much and was full of questions about the most commonplace of things, from the plants in the backyard to my clothes and books. "No, you have no idea what you are getting into," he said one night at dinner. My father had already been fed and it was just the three of us sitting around the table, tired and cold. "If you knew what India is really like, you would not take this business of moving to Silchar so calmly. I know," he said, thumping himself on his chest, "I have spent all my life in the backwaters. How would you two know what it feels like to live in Jhumritalayia?" The latter was a fictional town, and it was meant to indicate the most boring and rustic of small places in the plains. "Unimaginable disorder. I feel that I'll go crazy one of these days. You can't even imagine the kind of things that happen, like . . . like elephants at a train station."

"Elephants at a train station?" I knew a tall tale was coming.

"Happened just the other day. I almost had a heart attack," Anil replied. Then he said, "Let's wait till dinner and I'll tell you about this in your father's room, so that he can hear the story too. He'll be interested in it, since there are animals involved. Well, I suppose, everybody's an animal out there, even me," he said, cheering up at the thought of an audience. After dinner, we moved to the bedroom and sat around the heater still on loan from Dr. Chatterji. My father looked bewildered at first, but he sat up happily enough when he realized that there was going to be some deviation from his usual routine.

"Well," Anil said, clearing his throat a few times, "as I was saying, we had a little trouble with an elephant at the station the other day. We're quite used to animals. We had a monkey for a while, and that guy was terrible. All the stray dogs living on the platform were terrified of the creature and it was also quite lecherous, so that women passengers had to be especially careful. So we had a resident monkey for a good six months, and in December two Frenchmen came into our office and began asking us questions in French, creating total panic, and in January we had a politician passing through, one of whose bodyguards went berserk with an automatic rifle. See what I mean about India?" He shrugged his shoulders for dramatic effect and looked quickly at all of our faces to see if we were listening.

"But that was nothing compared to the day this elephant broke loose. We were told later that it was with a circus in town, and it broke free. It must have panicked when it found itself in the streets with all those rickshaws and trucks. Why, *I* panic in the streets of Dhanbad even though I've lived there all my life, especially when I see those small trekkers packed with at least forty people. We had a woman Superintendent of Police who was very strict and she stopped one of those trekkers. When she had finished counting all the passengers who piled out of the vehicle, she told the driver that she would let him go without a fine if he could do it again. You see, she didn't believe that so many people could be squeezed in. Of course, the driver managed to get them all inside and she stood there with her mouth open while he drove off.

"But anyway, we were at the reservation office a couple of

weeks ago when Kanhaiya, the boy who serves tea at the office, came running and said there was a *haathi* on the loose outside the station. Rabbani, Pal, and I decided to see what was happening. We were standing near the gate to platform one. I don't know if any of you remember it, but it's kind of low, with these iron beams across the top. We thought it would be safe enough if we stood inside because the gate was too low for an elephant and there was no way it would be able to break the iron beams. In fact, for all I know the British put them up in the first place to stop elephants from getting in." He paused as this new explanation struck him.

"The British were damned organized, you see, not like us at all. So we were standing inside, and then there were all these screams, and the rickshaw-*wallahs* at the rickshaw stand began running away very quickly, scampering with their *lungis* raised to their knees. A bus that was coming from one of the coal mines swerved and we could see the driver getting off and running back as fast as he could, leaving the passengers packed inside like potatoes in a sack, shouting and trying to get off. Then we saw the beast, massive and slow, looking all confused at the road. It still had a cloth on its back with the name of the circus on it—the Great Indian Circus—and it was standing in the middle of the busiest road in Dhanbad, apparently thinking. I believe elephants are remarkable for their thinking abilities, is that true, Jamaibabu?"

My father nodded his head vigorously when he saw Anil was looking at him expectantly. Having confirmed this bit of information from the great authority on elephants, Anil continued with his story. "It was standing there and we were looking at it when it suddenly turned down the driveway to the station and began coming toward the building. We all stepped back a little.

" 'Yaar, the *haathi*'s heading our way,' Pal said. 'What if it tries to get inside?'

" 'Absolutely not,' Rabbani said confidently, 'the gate's too low. It can't get in from here.' Pal and I looked at each other, because the elephant seemed to have seen the three of us and seemed to be coming straight at us, as if it wanted to ask us for directions or for a special reservation. It had really beady eyes, but it didn't look confused any longer, just really determined as if it had made up its mind to take a train out of Dhanbad as quickly as possible. Not that I blamed it for feeling that way.

" 'Yaar, Rabbani, let's get back inside the office. It's kind of scary-looking. See those big tusks, they're like unsheathed swords. What if it's mad?' Pal said, with me supporting him.

"Rabbani frowned. 'It can't be mad. Shouldn't it be drooling if it's mad?'

" 'That's only in the case of dogs,' I said. 'Maybe elephants do something else. Look, look, it's swishing its trunk.' All of us had stepped back a little more when we suddenly saw the elephant begin to trot, coming straight for us. It came to the gate and stopped when it saw that the gate was low. So what do you think it did? The *jaanwar*, it bent its knees and lowered its head like it was going to offer prayers or something, and then it began to come in. Pal and I ran for our lives down platform one, past the goods section, and when we got inside the reservation office we slammed the door shut. All the other guys looked petrified.

" 'Rabbani?' someone asked.

" 'He's had it,' Pal said soberly. 'Wouldn't listen to us. Was much too close to the gate.'

"Suddenly we heard this sound of running on the platform, and then there were these loud thumps on the door, which was shaking. 'It's Rabbani,' someone said. 'Let him in, quickly.'

" 'No, no,' Pandey said immediately, 'it's the elephant.'

"We could hear a strange squealing outside, along with the hammering on the door. I thought I heard my name. 'I think I'll open it slightly, it sounds like Rabbani's calling out my name.'

" 'Are you mad?' Pandey said, pushing me out of the way and putting some heavy accounting files against the door. 'Those beasts are really clever. They can imitate human voices. It'll destroy the lot of us if we let it in.'

" 'I see the elephant,' Kanhaiya said excitedly, looking through the window at tracks three and four. We all rushed there and saw the elephant get down to the tracks, moving easily in spite of its bulk, getting onto the platform on the other side and then heading down toward the market. Pal and I went out a little later in search of Rabbani, hoping to recover some of his remains for his family. We found a slipper near the gate. 'Looks like his,' I said, picking it up and wondering if this was all we would find of him. We walked up and down platform one but could see no sign of him. Halfway to the reservation office,

we found another slipper. Pal took this one and cradled it to
his chest.

" 'Get me down,' we heard as we passed some sacks.

" 'I think I hear his voice,' Pal said. 'You think he's become
a ghost already?' We were struck by the terrible thought that if
Rabbani had died an accidental death here, he would haunt the
station forever and, because we had been close friends of his,
he might want to hang around with us even after death.

" 'Let me down, you traitors,' we heard again. We looked
up and saw that Rabbani was sitting in the little ledge outside
one of the ventilators, right above the sacks. He had climbed
onto the sacks and managed to get up to the ledge. We helped
him down and instead of thanking us, he said, 'Why didn't you
let me in when I pounded on the door?'

" 'We thought it was the elephant,' Pal said, looking
ashamed.

"Rabbani glared at us and said, 'Fine friends you guys are.'
Then he snatched his slippers, slapped them on one of the
sacks to get the dust off, put them on, and walked off. It took
three days of offering filtered cigarettes and special cups of tea
before he would talk to any of us in the reservation room."

"What happened to the elephant?" I asked.

"Oh, they sent the police after it, and the Superintendent
of Police—a different one, not the woman Superintendent of
Police—tried to shoot it, but he missed and the elephant chased
him halfway across the market into a garbage dump. Finally,
they found the *mahout*, who managed to pacify it. I think the
circus had to pay the Superintendent of Police a lot of money."

It was funny, the way his stutter had almost disappeared as he told us the story of the elephant, but he was so pleased at his success in making us forget about serious things that it returned with full force immediately. Three days later Biren appeared, a little like the elephant pushing its way in unwanted, and the mood of the house became more strained than ever.

If the contrast Anil had drawn between the hills and the plains was between a free way of living and the claustrophobia that comes from relatives with whom one has nothing in common, the arrival of the denizen from Silchar seemed to prove his point. When Biren finally came, he brought with him a bundle of hierarchical notions that Dr. Dam for all his obstinacy had never insisted upon, distinctions of sex and age that were instantly impressed upon mother and son. Emphasizing that a woman's family should have little to do with her after marriage, Biren dismissed Anil from the discussion he was going to have with Mrs. Dam and Babu.

A dour, stringy man, he held forth for a while about how odd he felt they were and the changes that would be necessary now that they were about to enter a properly functioning social system. The house that Dr. Dam had built in Silchar was ready to be moved into, he informed them, though there were no steps leading to the house. It had not been possible to complete them because of the problem with the cement, but those same hardened sacks of cement could be used as steps. They were a little uneven and tended to wobble, but they would get used to it. Nor had the house been painted, but such luxuries were not for people like them, Biren added. He suggested that they should sell most of the things they had acquired here, especially the gas stove and the tanks, which could fetch a decent amount of money.

"If we are to live together," he said, looking his sister-in-law and nephew in the eye, "things have to be different. There must be more discipline, more respect for elders. The common kitchen we will have will be a symbol of our joint household." He looked at his nephew, who displayed no visible response. "This laxness about food, these strange tastes you people have picked up from living among people of other communities, Christians, all this has to change. You, Bordi," he addressed Mrs. Dam, "will do the cooking, since neither my mother nor my wife are in good health.

"What this means is that I will take charge of the family finances. Since I am going to get whatever anybody requires, none of you need interact much with the outside world and that will save you a lot of trouble. You, of course," he said, looking at Babu, "will have to pick up some skills. College education is not for someone in your position. If you must, attend night college and get a degree. That might be useful if you want a clerical job later. But you'd better find some skills, maybe get apprenticed to an electrician or something. You could make decent money that way. Until you are capable of taking care of your family, of course, you will treat me as the head of the house."

Babu's mother sat silently for a moment or two, as the new

joint household Biren had pictured took shape in her mind, a household in which she was the unpaid cook and domestic help, her son the odd-job boy, and her crippled husband a mere reminder of her independent past. The reply, when it came from her mouth, was the expression of all her fear and pride, unfettered by the social norms that dictated how she should address a male relative. "That will never happen. Never, do you hear? Do you think we're refugees looking for shelter and food? I wanted your help, not your patronage."

She paused for a moment, ignoring Babu's unease. "You want me to cook for all of you? I will. But in my own kitchen, in my own house, with food that I have bought. Whatever I can afford on my husband's pension." She spoke calmly, but inside she was seething, much of her anger reserved for Dr. Dam, who, after all these years of stringent authority, was incapable of speaking clearly. "We're still a family, you should know that. And as for my son's education, that's not something you have to worry about. His life isn't over by any means because of this mishap. His father was an officer, and he's not going to be any less."

Biren stared at them both without saying anything. Then he rose slowly and said, "Let me know what needs to be sorted out and if you have worked out how you are going to move things to Silchar." He left the room after this and went out of the house.

The clouds of the dispute were still hovering around the house the next day as Anil and Biren sat in the drawing room, nursing their cups of tea. Anil was embarrassed about the situation, although anyone else would have been offended by Biren's behavior. He had sneaked up to his sister after the talk with Biren, his stutter worse than ever. "Didi, do you think you should have spoken so harshly to him? After all, you're going to be dependent on him in Silchar. None of you know anybody there and I'm so far away."

Mrs. Dam was amused as much as annoyed by his concern. "Forget it," she said. "I'm not dependent on anyone. I've lived through too many things to be intimidated by that unhappy creature. If I were you, I wouldn't talk to him. A woman's family has no part in her life after marriage. Indeed."

It was not in Anil's nature, however, to grant himself such importance and he wanted to make conversation with the gaunt figure sitting on the other chair in the drawing room. As they sipped at their tea, bundled up in shawls and blankets, Babu crouched on the floor, sawing off the top of a plastic bottle with great concentration. Dr. Dam had needed something to urinate in, but both Babu and his mother had resisted buying a bedpan. That would have been too much like accepting his condition as permanent. Babu had been trying out different things for his father to use, from juice bottles made of glass to plastic cooking-oil containers. Glass was too heavy and might break, while the mouths of most plastic bottles were too narrow for Dr. Dam to piss comfortably into, especially as his body shook uncontrollably most of the time. This, however, should do it. Babu finished his handiwork and looked at it triumphantly. With the neck sawed off, the plastic bottle was wide enough for the task.

"The boy's brilliant," Anil said admiringly. "Now, none of us would have thought of that." He addressed Biren. "Don't you agree? He's prime material for the civil services. Thinks on his feet." Biren grunted, not quite convinced that the ability to make something to piss in qualified anybody as capable of solving the country's problems. "I can just see him as an officer, maybe even an officer in the Indian Railway Service, walking into the reservation room." Mentioning the reservation room brought the elephant episode to his mind and he wondered whether he should tell Biren the story. He looked at Biren's face, scowling at the newspaper as if he would like to tear it to shreds, and thought better of it.

Biren was vindicated less than an hour later. Anil shook his head sorrowfully, pointing out the jagged edges of plastic to Babu. "He nearly cut himself. Too dangerous. Doesn't quite work. I'm really sorry." He apologized profusely. Babu didn't take his failure as a prospective civil servant too much to heart and returned to his books. Anil went to Police Bazaar and bought a plastic jug for Dr. Dam, one with a lid, and in the days to come everyone got used to the routine of fetching the jug from the toilet when Dr. Dam got up hurriedly and began to undo his pajama strings.

Anil left a few days later, returning to his work and his family and his ailing mother. Mrs. Dam felt a pang of loneliness as she waved her younger brother off from the front steps and was immediately ashamed that she should feel this way, as if it were an act of disloyalty to her husband. Biren was still there, however, and his heavy, brooding presence unsettled both her and

Babu, especially because he had detached himself from them completely, sleeping and taking his meals in the house but absent for the greater part of the day. When he was at home in the evening, he tended to Dr. Dam's needs occasionally but that was the extent of his involvement. Still, they somehow managed to get the necessary work done. With the paperwork being taken care of by Dr. Chatterji and some of Dr. Dam's old colleagues, they arranged for his pension to be transferred to Silchar and for the payments to be made without Dr. Dam having to appear in person. It was, Babu and his mother told each other repeatedly, just a precaution. He would be able to walk again. Once they moved to Silchar, he would be under a roof of his own. The weather was not so harsh in the winter and even if he used a cane, he would be able to see the garden and his house, maybe even walk to the pension office if accompanied by someone else.

Anil had left, and so had Biren, and our house was down to its usual number of people. February came in a windy flurry, blowing away hats and scarves, taking some of the edge off the cold, but I broke out in a sweat as I looked at the syllabus for the different subjects and realized how little I knew. We would be moving in April, most of the paperwork having been taken care of, and all that remained were the board exams. My father's condition had lost some of its novelty and although we still had visitors every day, their attention had shifted to me and my exams. I had to stand there and listen to these elderly men bundled in old coats, sipping tea loudly, each one of them presenting me with a success story about engineering before telling me to return to my books.

Dr. Chatterji, expansive and full of goodwill, was one of those unwanted advisers, informing me that I still had a chance of making good, of raising the fortunes of my family through academic effort. He regretted that I had dropped biology as an optional subject in favor of additional mathematics. It would have been best for me to study medicine—after my father's illness I surely understood how important doctors were—but now it would have to be engineering. Four years to an engineering degree and then an assured, well-paid job. If my stars had more in store for me, I could add a two-year management degree and find myself jobs in the private sector with even higher salaries. Examples of such perseverance and brilliance were held up to me regularly, along with descriptions of apartments in Bombay, Maruti cars, foreign trips to Dubai and Singapore, those wonderful things that lay at the end of the tunnel lined with arcane formulae, theorems, and experiments.

At that time, the only effect on me of their descriptions was a feeling of boredom at the sameness of their stories. Now, when I look back, I realize that this discussion of careers was the most exciting thing in the lives of these men, and that they were gripped by an almost sexual excitement as they talked of engineering colleges and private-sector careers. It was possible only through their utter ignorance of the lives they sketched out in such an ideal fashion, a measure of their distance from the world they were sending their children into.

The contours of that world were clear to us, who were a part of it, from the desolate descriptions of engineering colleges painted by the seniors, their experience of primitive metal workshops and dull lab work, the sexual frustrations some of them underwent in these remote institutions where ninety percent of the population was male. I thought of Abhijit and Joy at Rourkela, who went to the train station on weekends and waited for the Gitanjali Express, hoping to see some pretty girls on their way to Bombay.

None of this figured in the version of engineering put forward by the adults. But even at a more pragmatic level, engineering was not necessarily the best of careers. This was not the sixties, when engineering graduates were rare and there were plenty of jobs in both the private sector and in the government departments that were being exhorted to build Nehru's temples of modern India. The adults expressed little awareness of the number of unemployed engineers, especially from branches like civil engineering, primarily because those sixties graduates were still ensconced in their jobs, taking bribes and building their own houses instead of putting up roads and bridges. Not that anything came of saying these things to anyone. People like Dr. Chatterji refused to be depressed about civil engineers. Instead, they would talk about the salaries and prospects of those studying computer technology, their voices rising in excitement as they went over the "perks"—car, house with garage, trips to America, servants. Even Biren, with his advice to become an electrician, was an improvement on them.

I knew better than any of them that my chances of studying

engineering were very slim, even if I wholeheartedly wanted to get in. Sometimes I did, when I thought of my parents, but then I remembered what that would really mean and my heart sank. So much effort for so little, all of it in the name of security, as if engineers didn't get sacked or grow old or die. Bent over the heater in the drawing room where I studied morning, afternoon, and night, I tried to inspire myself by thinking of the map of Indian technical institutions in the atlas, the subcontinent sprinkled with hammer-and-anvil signs representing the regional engineering colleges of the country, colleges in deserts, industrial townships, and ports, between settlements on long highways and scattered in sad, suburban outgrowths of the big cities. But try as I might, my mind insisted on diving below those signs and dredging up scenes from the albums of my friends, of desolate engineering colleges, flat concrete buildings against a flat rural landscape of crops and cows, and little double rooms with posters of seminude women and empty beer bottles lined below the windows.

If Babu was fighting a losing battle with his duties and desires, attempting to cram two years of coursework into one month of sustained effort, Dr. Dam had embarked on his own, final project of self-education. He had decided to teach himself to walk again.

The months of convalescence at home had led to some small improvements, but Dr. Borgohain had asserted to Babu and Mrs. Dam that it would take time. The young Assamese doctor knew that he would not be seeing the family again and, in spite of himself, he had become a little emotional. The house had told him all he needed to know, that these people would never be able to afford a long, expensive treatment in Delhi or Madras, but he had scribbled out the names of a couple of former classmates and given this to Babu.

The doctor's instructions had been explicit. Dr. Dam could practice walking only under close supervision, using the cane to balance himself. There were other exercises for the patient, which he could do while sitting down, such as flexing his fists and squeezing a rubber ball.

It is not that Dr. Dam ignored these tasks. He carried them out with the same devotion that he had given to his schoolwork fifty years ago, attacking the repetitive exercises with the single-mindedness he had demonstrated all his life. He swallowed his arsenal of pills and ate the bland food without complaint. He squeezed the rubber balls and flexed his wrists dutifully, practiced his signature over and over again. But he also attempted to walk when no one was around, getting himself off the bed, leaning for a while on the cane before he tried to take his faltering steps. Sometimes he fell and Babu came running in, having heard the noise. So far the threadbare carpet had always broken his fall and no visible damage had been done. There were also occasions when he was quite successful in his efforts and Babu heard nothing. When he came in on a routine check, he sometimes found his father standing by the window, looking at the road winding away in the distance, the thin hand on the cane trembling a little as it took the weight of the body.

Babu was at home alone with his father much of the time, since Mrs. Dam had to go out frequently to deal with the banks and government offices. He worked in the room next to Dr. Dam's, the door slightly ajar, trying to memorize pages of equations, repeating to himself the outdated industrial processes for the extraction of iron or preparation of steel. Then he turned in frustration to the working of DC and AC motors, impossible machines that had to be conceptualized and constructed on the basis of two-dimensional diagrams in textbooks, until he was interrupted by the sound of a table overturning or the crash of a falling glass.

Babu tried to be patient, but each fall made him more anxious than ever. It broke his concentration because he began to spend as much time listening for the telltale noises as on his work. His tone grew harsher and more peremptory, as if he had recognized that in administering to his father, in carrying him to the toilet and holding him while he defecated, in taking on the tasks that his father had carried out for him when he was a child, the roles had been reversed. Mrs. Dam pleaded with her husband a little more softly and Dr. Dam always nodded like an obedient boy. Perhaps it was compulsion of some kind that made him do it again in spite of the requests and commands, perhaps it was plain obstinacy, or maybe somewhere in his mind things had gotten so confused that the contents of these verbal patterns did not register.

Spring began to tease out soft buds in the plants as March came around. The violent winds of February had gone and the trees looked more stable, putting out tentative leaves to the warmth oozing out of sky and earth. With days to go for the exams, Babu stuck to his task valiantly, though he knew it was too little, too late. He could remember nothing, he knew nothing as numbers and names and formulae swam past him, out of reach like the future career that others had within their grasp. He tried again, forgetting about the afternoon sky outside that had spread like a soft, transparent gauze over the town, the sounds of children playing cricket, the sweet, full impact of bat on ball.

The Friday before the exams began, he was working on his chemistry when he heard what sounded like his father's stealthy tread and, close on its heels, a loud crash. He dropped his books and ran in, his heart beating with fear. Dr. Dam was trying, one thin arm grasped around the handle of his cane, to get back to the bed before his disciplinarian came in. He was frightened, but Babu did not see this. Using one hand to yank up the body that had become incredibly light, he ignored his father's cry of pain as he bundled him back into bed, mechanically spreading the sheets out. Then he spotted the accomplice in the crime, the cane lying on the floor. Stooping and lifting it in the same smooth motion, he gripped the cane at both ends and put it across his knee. The hollow tube yielded easily, but he kept twisting it until it was bent in half, narrow and cracked at the point where it had folded.

He went back to his room and tried to continue studying. But he could hear his father's sobs, soft and muffled, emerging from the sheets, floating through the closed door and the vast distance between them.

night journey
1988

Lying awake in the dark, I would hear the trucks changing gears all night as they grunted their way up the slopes. It was better than closing my eyes and trying to count sheep. The trucks went on and on, a live soundtrack throbbing and shaking the wooden floors, the sudden beams of light glaring through deep, dark curtains until the monsters faded into the highways of my sleep.

The trucks occupied my mind on the rain-washed weekdays, as I waited for the bus that sucked me into the comfortable routine of school. But I never spoke with anyone at school about trucks or night journeys, about the visions of distant lands and strange adventures the sound of the trucks brought to my mind, of the hunger they awakened in me. Sometimes, after my biweekly drill for the National Cadet Corps, if it got late while I waited for my father outside his office, I would see the vanguard of the convoys, already on the loose by the time we drove back home. In the shadowy, halogen-swathed streets, the trucks would bear down on us and then race past, disappearing around the frayed edges of the town, on to the national highways.

"Where do they go?" I had asked my father when I was small.

"Aizawl, Kohima, Imphal," my father would reply, naming the state capitals of the Northeast without looking up from his files. At school, in the geography classes, they told us nothing about these places. In the dots and crosses I marked on the map of India during my term exams, I only had to place the big industrial cities and political centers and trading ports of the dusty plains to get full marks for that section of the exam. I would sit in the car and mouth the geography names as they appeared on the windscreens of the trucks going by—"All-India permit for Punjab, Haryana, Uttar Pradesh, West Bengal . . ."—and wonder why the names my father mentioned never appeared on the trucks, as if there was something about these destinations that could not be revealed to the world at large.

But it wasn't as if I had never taken the same road as those caravans with their black water containers made of strips of tire rubber, their sides decorated with tridents, birds, flowers, and eyes that looked at you. There had been a journey once when we traveled past the lumbering vehicles with their long trails of dust clouds. I had seen some of the trucks parked next to a tiny spring, with lines of dripping washing and *coir charpais* set out in the sun, strangely domesticated creatures shorn of their fierce power when seen like that. On the same trip, just after Sonarpur on National Highway 44, I saw a truck lying upside-down like a little toy on the parched riverbed below the road—a glimpse of another kind of fate—before the bus passed the loaders and bulldozers clearing the rubble from the landslide.

That was the extent of my travels. NH 44 was all I knew, for I had never seen what dramatic change took place when 44 became 45. My father had traveled along these routes in the past, and he knew the highways and smaller roads crisscrossing the region so well that when I asked him for help in finding some border outpost like Tawang or Moreh, it took him less than a minute to find the place on the map. But he rarely went anywhere by road by the time I had grown up. He flew to the state capitals instead, going to Gauhati to catch an Indian Airlines flight that would set him down in Kohima or Imphal. When I asked him why he didn't travel on the highways as much as before, all he said was "Too risky," not deviating from his usual monosyllables. It was enough, though, filling my mind with the untold, exotic dangers of carrying supplies to those far-flung places.

Aizawl, Kohima, Dimapur . . . Once, when my father had felt more inclined to talk, he began to tell me of what he saw when he visited these towns. From his account, I could imagine the state capitals ringed by blue hills, the brilliantly white-washed government buildings flying the Indian flag, the state central libraries—each one of them with a captured battle tank set on a podium near the entrance—and the checkpoints bristling with machine guns that came down with the dusk over

Kohima or Imphal, herding people off the streets. And the masked men who walked into his friend's office in Kohima and shot that friend dead, sometime in the early eighties. He had fallen silent for a while after that. When he spoke again, he said something about how one didn't have to go far to look for death. It was here, he had said, pointing to the streets and the houses around us.

Those streets and houses had been blotted out by the suddenness with which our last night in the town was upon us. Awakened by these old images, I sat up on the bed and edged up to the window. The curtains had been taken down and through the naked glass I could see the night sky that had come down to visit the earth, its stars merging with the little lamp left on in the cottage directly across from us. In the bed on the other side of the room, my father was in sedated sleep. I felt disoriented by the vividness and clarity of the dreams, although I was uncertain what disturbed me more, my schoolboy yearning for the trucks and highways or the images of my father talking to me as if I were a child. As I sat there with the night shrouded around me, spending my last hours in the town we were leaving for good, I felt as if there had been no transition from the schooldays of my dream to this moment of departure.

I turned from the window, wanting to impress the room I would never see again into my brain, but apart from the beds I could find nothing that would give me a taste of the years that had flown by so swiftly. It has already become the past, I thought, this place, our lives here, as I looked at the bare walls and the boxes piled on the floor. I turned back to the window and looked at the night lamp in the cottage across the way, above and facing the bungalow occupied by the Intelligence Bureau. Life here had already become memories and I could almost feel them, small and vulnerable, their noses pressed against the window, pleading to be let in.

I felt that I would need to remember this town, our life here, that I had not been conscious of this need in all the years spent here. I had spent the years dreaming of lives other than the one I had had here, thirsting for alternative possibilities. Now I had no time left, no clear feelings that would allow me to take leave of the town properly. I suddenly remembered this passage in *Kim*, which I had liked so much because it had tales of Ludhiana and Lahore and Benares, because it had scenes of crowded trains journeying down the Gangetic plains, alive with the hustle and bustle of *sadhus* and *fakirs* and farmers and soldiers. But now, tonight, what I remembered most was a section set in the hills, toward the end, where the Lama was up on the mountain peak. The Lama, seeing his monastery in Suchzen and the plains of India where he had walked in search of the river, begins blessing everything: the sky, the mountains, the rocks and trees and birds. To take leave properly would involve doing something like that, going early in the morning to Laitkor Peak and seeing the town spread out below like a map and speaking to every inch of it.

But I had ignored everything, the place and the people who lived here, turning my back on them. You will never again walk the road you took to school for seven years, I told myself, and there will be a time when you will sit somewhere far from here and need to remember many things. I tried to begin, to remember, tried to think of the town as if I was up on the peak.

Somebody else lived in the first house in Garikhana, the one with the earliest memories, the garden at the back falling in a steep slope before running into a wall lined with sharp glass triangles. The kindergarten was closed down, converted into a warehouse, the first teacher there long since gone, a widow who had left for Bombay with her only daughter who had been dying of cancer. My father's office had fallen off the horizon long ago, as had the workers and drivers who had been such an important part of my childhood. My father had talked about how one didn't need to go far to look for death, but the same was true for life as well, surely? It seemed everything had been here, in this town—life, journeys, adventure, death—and I had not recognized it.

I heard my father stir and turned toward him. He was fumbling with the knot of his pajamas unsteadily, squinting in concentration. I stepped off the bed and helped him untie the strings, handing him the jug and waiting so that I could empty it in the toilet after he had finished.

All the middle-class odds and ends my mother had acquired over the years, the pots and buckets and torn mattresses and papers that had collected under the beds, they had been taken out and packed. Everything that could possibly be of use was being taken to Silchar, while the rest had been distributed between neighbors and acquaintances, some things given to old servants who had turned up in the days before our move, others sold to a *kabadiwallah* who had weighed each metal object carefully, with the demeanor of a goldsmith determining the value of a bangle. My mother and I spent a long time thinking about my father's papers, tied together in massive bundles with fraying red tape and packed inside two old, rusted trunks. An entire life was in those two trunks: academic certificates, a couple of medals, strange color photographs that looked as if someone had painted over black-and-white pictures with watercolors, piles of correspondence about the land in Gauhati, a series of diaries beginning in 1947, accounts written in a minute, spidery hand. When we asked him whether it was necessary to carry these things, he waved his left hand in a gesture of resignation, asking us only to hold on to the financial documents. We thought of burning the papers and selling the trunks to the *kabadiwallah,* but at the last moment my mother and I could not go through with it and decided to take the trunks and their contents to Silchar. There was enough leave-taking happening as it was.

The house with the triangular rooms had been stripped bare by early afternoon. Even the bedsteads had been broken down and loaded onto the truck carrying our belongings. After the truck had departed, around four, there was nothing left in the house except the three of us sitting in chairs provided by the Goswamis next door, a couple of small bags with my father's food and medicines on the floor.

❀ ❀ ❀

Just before seven, when night has come down on a crystal-studded sky, we move. Everything is seemingly in order: the weepy faces of the women, the friends patting me on the back and asking me to write, my father wrapped and cushioned, my mother's last gesture of supplication, hands raised to her unseen, silent gods. We set off in the taxi, its headlights picking out the empty roads of a deserted town. Most of the shops are shut, and under the halogen lamps on the main road I see the glint of the leather and steel of a police patrol. We are leaving the town behind—the courthouse, the schools, the jam factory—looking at the hazy outlines of meadows and trees we have always taken for granted.

We passed a small convoy of trucks an hour later, each of them laboriously moving in toward the cliff face to let the car pass. Then, for a while, only the sound of the engine, the swaying of two arcs of light, a black world framed in tar and stone. We went through Jowai, a small highway town asleep amid the vacant stare of solitary lamps looking over the shops and garages, and I thought of my father traveling with the policeman in the truck with bags of cement. I felt the world asleep around me, collectively dreaming away the night that was separating my parents and me from the past, and felt the night behind us rising like a fortress wall. So strong was this image that I felt compelled to look back from my front seat. In the darkness all I could make out was the swaying heads of my parents, bobbing shapes stripped of all expression.

The car slowed and the driver nudged me, pointing out an obstacle ahead. I looked, seeing a fox frozen in the headlights before the driver turned them off. Released from the grip of the car, the fox scampered off the road and disappeared into the bushes. I felt something of its animal joy as I tried to keep my eyes fixed ahead, the images caught in a flashing instant—the locked gates outside a timber camp, heaps of coal on the road, the embers below a drum of tar—growing inside me like a fever as the road steadily grew worse and the car bounced over large rocks.

I sat back for the last leg as we began descending and a whiff of lime trees came into the car. I remembered them from that trip long ago, coming back from the wedding of my youngest uncle, Naren, when they had rescued me as I was overcome by nausea. I remembered, and dreamed—of border countries with olive-green trucks, machine guns mounted on them, of road gangs piled on the backs of trucks releasing the smoke of a hundred *bidis* into the air. I heard screams of terror and saw, in a close-up view, the contorted face of a driver jolted awake by the earth coming apart at the seams. Like pictures from issues of *National Geographic* looked at in the school library, the road began coming alive in the technicolor of my dreams as somewhere in the background my father's voice told me the complete story, connecting together scraps garnered from the years past and future.

Night had not quite let go of its hold when the driver woke me on a long, dimly lit bridge, its arched back lined with alien-looking soft-drink billboards. The driver was tired and irritable after the night-long drive. "Wake up. Come on, come on, wake up," he was saying, shaking me. "Which way?" he asked. I was confused. "Which way to your house from the junction ahead?"

"Link Road," I said, trying to remember.

"Don't know where that is, you'll have to guide me."

I looked back helplessly.

"It's, it's near the State Bank, the main branch," my mother stuttered.

The driver shrugged his shoulders in irritation. "No idea where that is. Don't you people know where you're going to live?"

"Take the left and keep going. I will tell you when to turn." My mother and I stared at the speaker in astonishment, at the clear voice and tone of command. My father was sitting upright, fully awake, his finger pointing authoritatively at the road the driver should take.

We turned off into a narrow lane and stopped in front of a house, its unpainted walls pale and frigid in the slow dawn. My father spoke again. "That road," he said, looking at me, gesturing back, "leads on to Aizawl. And then you can go beyond, to other places."

3.
Terminal

hometown

People think that those who have gone away have relin-quished their rights to the place left behind, are gone forever. Because most often, those who depart do so under the shadow of the curtain that will fall in between. Memory, visits, photographs with fading colors, a dried leaf pressed between the pages of a book, the snatches of a song that always carries with it the coordinates of the place and time where it was first heard—these are just scraps of meaning blown about by the flurry of a windy day, having nothing to do with life after the departure. Still, as I said, this severance is not as final as it is made out to be. Having lived there once, that piece of earth is never released by our clutching hands, unless it be when we die. Even nomads move before and behind their marks—the black-ened ring of fire, the reservoir hollowed across from the stream—and just when the grass and the dust begin to draw their rags over these cracks in space, time runs a full circle and the nomads return.

Me? I return every day, sometimes under the cover of sleep, at other times stepping in full daylight across the chicken's-neck strip that divides where I am from where I was, when a certain smell or song or face emerges from the city's contested grounds. And almost always when it rains, lulling me into a reverie where I think I am back to the sound of horses' hooves drumming on the slanted, corrugated tin roof, gathering myself in the cold until the moment of awakening drenched in sweat, and the realization of having been torn elsewhere from home long ago.

And I return in words traced on a page, playing resident and guide as well as curious tourist, pointing and gazing at the upturned stone tablet set up to commemorate the poet, the geometric pattern of park and lake, the black texture of berries ripening in the vendor's basket, until between these modes of being and seeing, I truly become the place. I am my own hometown.

maps

You cannot be an exile in your own country. The trick is in the map, in the black line drawn around the edges, from the Arabian Sea to the Bay of Bengal, the political boundary that curves around the open mouth of Gujarat and peaks at Kashmir, the thin neck that broadens out to the seven sisters surrounded by China, Burma, and Bangladesh. This is the frame in which you must operate, the map hanging from the walls of dusty administrative offices, in schools and newsrooms, in atlases and encyclopedias, containing a reality where nothing changes, not since the minor adjustments for Goa and Sikkim, that holds on to its essence even when a rubber stamp proclaims in India ink over Jammu and Kashmir, or somewhere over the blue vastness of the Arabian Sea: "The political boundaries of India as depicted in this map are neither accurate nor correct."

The inaccuracies, you feel, can always be adjusted. There

are problems even in the maps approved by the government of India, but that is merely the result of a need for immediate representation, of utilitarian convenience. If the map where you follow the national highways and rail lines is not to scale, that is simply because it is a simulacrum, a copy of an original where these issues are perfectly clear. You will understand these elisions, or what appear to be evasions, when you have become the complete citizen, when as taxpayer and consumer, as husband and father, you have been mapped demographically onto the system. No one will tell you what you yourself do not seem to know at times, that your forefathers came from elsewhere. From where? It cannot be found on the map of India, which, with its confident peaks and curves and wholeness, eliminates any speculation that in this representation of the subcontinent there are places that do not belong, people who do not belong.

Filling up the line in the application form for a passport that asks for "place of birth of father," you ask a friend, "Undivided India?" "Prepartition India, I think," he replies. And there the matter rests for a while.

history

History, dragged so far from the metropolitan centers, from the rustic mainlands, will tell you nothing. In the Northeast, the way I remember it, history lies defeated, muttering solipsistically from desultory plaques put up to commemorate visiting politicians, the memorial stones fading against the brilliance of the colors in the streets. History is mired in one dirty-green tank captured from the Pakistanis in the '71 war and set on a pedestal in front of the State Central Library, pathetic in its smallness even in childhood, its rusting gun aimed far away, beyond the hills, at some distant and ideal enemy settlement.

When I do turn to history, it offers me little in return, sometimes only a meaningless account that does not seem to further my own story. History tells me that on the night of October 19, 1828, Henry Walters, Esq., began traveling from Dacca, crossing the Pandua Hills near Sylhet in Bengal. With baggage, tent, and coolies, Walters made a journey to the hills in less than a month, mapping the route that strings out three generations in my mind, a connecting line from the emptiness of an ancestral village in Sylhet to that place in the hills I nominate hometown.

Walters, when not scared of being trapped in a tribal village, was happy. He wrote in his journal that "it is proposed to establish a Sanitarium at this place, for English soldiers and sick people, from Calcutta, & c. The elevation is about five thousand feet above the level of the sea. The air is cool, light, and refreshing; and although the sun is hot, it is innoxious. The hill is free from jungle, covered with fine pasture and flowers, but rocky—and the ravines filled with trees and shrubs—I can almost fancy myself on the top of the *Bannerdown!*" Moreover, in the inhabitants of the hills, Walters found a happy contrast to the dark, querulous population he presided over in the plains of Bengal as a judge. "Theft is unknown among them," he wrote, "and they are true to their word. In their moral character, they tower, like their mountains, over the natives of the plains."

Why did they move, these natives of the plains, bringing their noxious, dark, sunburned faces to blight these mountains? Did they not foresee what would happen when such opposites met, the cool and the hot, the light and the dark, the honest and the thieving? Why did they not know their history?

ships

The first foreigners brought the town with them. Before them there was nothing, not even the countryside, because there was no place from where one could demarcate it, nowhere to measure it against; just the valley rising and falling, nestling against the mountains. The first outsiders, with their surveyors, planners, and administrators, their foremen and coolies, constables and postal runners, wishing a sanctuary among the hills and afraid, still, of its uncontrollable and unknown nature, raised this town from the turf. Casting about in their minds for the likeness of this place, searching their precarious memories for what it should resemble and remind them of, they visualized the stone-chipped paths and raised cottages, the honeysuckle and the common and the church spire swelling its sound through the mist on Sunday, so that they finally created this town in the composite image of what they had left behind across the black waters.

In some way, long after they had left, the otherness recalled from so far away remained—thin, spectral, and yet the essence of the place, making its way into the tourist brochures speaking of a Scotland of the East. Given this, one could not blame those curious plainsmen I encountered in my childhood on a hot, crowded train burrowing its way out from a mining town in Bihar, moving toward Calcutta. Having asked me where I lived, they performed a different mental operation on this remote place, saying, half incredulously, half patronizingly, "Ah, so you'll be going home by ship, then?"

memories

What recourse, then, but to the map? The heads of friends, teachers, editors, a girlfriend, all bend over the representation, my finger pointing out the unfamiliar territory beyond West Bengal. There, you see that narrow strip of land between Bhutan and Bangladesh, the chicken's-neck corridor bearing the weight of India's seven northeastern states. And there, you see Assam, where the sun slants on the crops and erupts around the red, white, and gold of the dresses worn for *Bihu*. Depending on person and situation, I assemble maps, photographs, and words, call on memory to furnish further details that will impart some sense of where I lived, something beyond a dim comprehension of remote beauty and even more remote violence.

Over the years, memory has taken on the greater share of this burden, each step up in the world resulting in the disappearance of one more artifact from those days. But memory must deal with so much more that is flung in its path by life; it must adjust itself constantly to the headlong rush of the present into the past.

Each churning in the storehouse of memory that is me displaces something, changing the contours of my hometown, merging that place with people and incidents that came much, much later. After the end of a traumatic relationship, I dream of the old walks by Wards Lake, Police Bazaar, reveling in a sense of freedom, the adult coming home to the haunts of the child. Then I am brought short by the figure of a woman I loved. She stands there, shadowy but distinct, at the turning from the lake toward the market. When this happens, I do not wait to wake up. I remonstrate with her in the dream itself. "You? What are you doing here?" It is then that I am aware of the depth of her violation, of the tyranny of the present over the past, of its ability to intrude on the past, the place I had thought was a sanctuary against all failures since the departure.

travelers

Sometimes we floated paper boats on the gutters overflowing with rain, in those early childhood years that were, now I think, left behind too fast. After that nothing could move swiftly enough for us, the trickle of familiar faces every day unsatisfying, too slow to quench the hunger we had for the world. As a result, a large part of our lives revolved around the imaginary figures of outsiders, strangers, foreigners, and all the stories in my head were spun around a lone, mythical figure perched on the edge of the town, ready to enter our world and change it forever.

It is not that I realized this then, because somehow it took me many other boundaries of experience to give meaning and weight to the past. The first sight of Howrah Bridge with the weekday morning strung out on its tarnished metal girders, the thresholds of those South Calcutta houses and apartments with their genteel mockery, the taste of love or what I took to be love in lips tasting faintly, deliciously, of Johnson's skin lotion. All this had to be encountered before I knew of the separate countries that exist in our hearts and then learned of the many that I had collected, like a crusty, seasoned traveler, in my own inner space.

It is as if those images I had gathered in that first place, the picture that I composed of a lonely traveler on the threshold of a new destination, poised uncertainly between past and future, had begun a process that ended only when observer and image had merged into one.

dreams

The town appears different in dreams as the years pass, its features dispersed across a shifting landscape of time. This in itself would not be unnatural. What is there to draw the memories from, anyway, when the images have to feed themselves on a town that is as imaginary now as once it was real? But that cannot quite explain the sheer whimsicality of some of the things I see. The dreams themselves are uncomfortable with the fantastic, dreamlike quality of the town.

In some of them, a river runs through the town, slicing through it in a neat, straight line between the library and the courthouse. As a result, the bus station and the taxi stand, the courthouse and the photo studio where people went to copy their legal documents, these appear on opposite banks of the river, divided, sundered, lost to each other. The people who would have circulated around Police Bazaar, the groups running across each other, now find themselves on two separate

promenades, gravely contemplating the waters that flow in between.

This is such a falsehood that one does not need to be awake
to be aware of the shape of the lie. There never was a river anywhere inside the town. There are other dreaming sessions,
however, that are even more arbitrary. They consist of a landscape full of errors, with glass and concrete skyscrapers—thin,
wedge-shaped towers that dwarf Bawri Mansion, the fifteen-
storied building that had been the tallest structure in the town.
It is possible, of course, that the years gone by have seen Bawri
Mansion shadowed by upstart rivals, but skyscrapers in a hill
town on the fringe of India? One can do nothing when confronted by these fantasia, except wander on, waiting for some
feature or object that will betray this space as unreal. The
school building glows in the distance, ultra-modern, its
smooth glass elevator banks rising into the night. I wander in
awkwardly and find a sheet of flimsy paper pasted onto a wall,
one corner flapping loosely, revealing the congealed gum behind. What can one make out of the words scrawled in blood
red? They constitute an announcement, a warning, and I know
my life depends on my ability to decipher the words properly.
As I bend over the words the walls melt, the glass fades, and I
see the town for a moment as it really is, before the dream dies
into another morning in the city.

airport

I live in Delhi now. After the interregnums of Silchar, Calcutta, I find myself taking stock in a place that, in spite of its
dull anonymity, evokes the small town I left behind. At the end
of winter, an unseasonal rain comes accompanied by cold air,
the parks blossom in an uncertain, fragile spring. When I first
moved here, and would call my mother on weekends, I would
say, "You'd love it. It's just like home." Meanwhile, the city
growls along its axial and radial roads, the offices swell with a
familiar, frustrated ambition, and the crowds on the streets
flow through the body of this traveler.

Perhaps this is the true return, the completion of a cycle set
in motion long ago, and if it seems lonely, maybe it is because
migration is a reductive evolutionary principle where the
sprawling, oppressive family gives way to its streamlined nuclear
descendant, to be replaced finally by the individual straining at
the limits of memory.

In Delhi, I dream of my father. We are at an airport, and he does not look the way he was when I last saw him. He hasn't had a haircut for quite some time and seems caught up in what he is doing. It is dark at the airport, there are numerous staircases, corridors with sharp turns. We could do with a map of the place, but then we would not be able to read it. Then I notice that we are both shuffling like old men, hesitant in the dim light. Walking behind me, my father holds a flashlight in his hands, and though I think he needs the light more than me, I say nothing. He keeps moving the beam, shining it alternately at my feet and his as we move slowly through the dark.

4.

Travelogue

learning to run

I had moved far away from fear.

Just how far I realized only this afternoon. At the end of the interview the minister held my eyes in his and whispered, almost imperceptibly—*Dkhar!* Foreigner. Now it all comes back to me, sitting in the hotel room with the windows looking onto Wards Lake, the bridge arched over it like some prehensile serpent poised for a drink, turning that whispered word over and over again in my mind, that lifetime of fear. And the first time I walked into enemy country.

I couldn't have been more than ten years old, accompanying my father to the little alley below Police Bazaar where the Bihari cobbler sat. It was not one of our annual walks, back from the Garrison Ground after the Independence Day parade, with the promise of *puri-sabzi* and orange juice hanging in the air. This was an important weekly ritual that began on Saturday evening with my father's careful examination of the brown shoes he had bought from a Chinese shop in Burra Bazaar, always ending with a visit to the cobbler the next morning. The cobbler was there every Sunday, usually bereft of customers, waiting, it seemed, for the sole purpose of adding a few more strips of rubber to my father's brown shoes. Hammering together bits and pieces of rubber for the soles to hold out until the next Sunday, exhibiting threads of different tensile strength to my father for his careful appraisal and approval, trying out different shapes of castaway leather, they talked meanderingly of farming, the Bihari with many nods and assertions and grunts, my father replying in his bad Hindi. It was an embarrassing routine, with my father's feet inserted into torn rubber slippers provided by the cobbler, one heel shining through a hole in his sock, while the upturned shoe went through its weekly routine of maintenance, spread out on the anvil.

We walked slowly that day, me because of my short reedy legs, my father to conserve his breath, climbing past the army movie theater and the officers' apartments, the washing on the balconies fluttering in the afternoon breeze like kites broken on telephone wires. Then it got easy as the road sloped down past Lady Keane College, rising a little at the end when we reached the greasy automobile carcasses in front of shuttered garages, opposite which the cobbler maintained his post, hunched between a cigarette shop and a photo studio.

That Sunday, when we saw an empty spot where the cobbler should have been, a bare space unoccupied by his narrow frame or the bony anvil that so resembled him, we paused. My father did not accept this absence and looked around hopefully, perhaps thinking that the cobbler had changed his place. I followed his gaze, and the sudden appearance of the men from the direction of Police Bazaar did not register with either of us. They must have been spots on the horizon, half a dozen blobs that magically doubled into a dozen hands enclosing us, jabbing at my father, the air turning solid with their curses and blows, a series of curiously flat sounds produced by their open hands as they struck him in the face, chest, and stomach. I remember falling, scrabbling around looking for my glasses until I found them a few feet from me, thankfully not broken.

We stood there on the road, brushing the dirt off our clothes. My father looked more embarrassed than scared or angry and the arrival of three policemen did not help. They wanted to know what we were doing there, and why we had not seen the posters in the marketplace.

"We did not come from that direction," my father said, breathing heavily, "and I heard no announcements on the radio last night."

"They put up the posters early in the morning," the biggest policeman said, eyeing us warily.

"Who did?" my father asked him.

"The student union," the policeman said, laughing. "When the student leaders announce a public curfew, everyone stays off the streets, even the local people. And you choose to go for a walk in a deserted street with a small boy. Don't you know that the curfew is a protest against the presence of foreigners?"

My father said nothing. The implication was clear.

"You want to file a report, you have to come to the police station."

"I'll do that at the local *thana*," he replied.

The policemen, to their credit, found us a cab from the bus station, bullying the driver into taking us home. There were more questions from the neighbors as we got out of the taxi, questions directed at my father, blood on his shirt, dentures in his pocket. Everyone but us knew of the latest public curfew, it seemed, and as we walked into the house a crowd of nontribal neighbors followed, talking excitedly of writing to the governor and to the newspapers in Calcutta and Delhi regarding this latest assault on another nontribal.

The event brought a sudden sociability to our house, with so many of my father's colleagues and our neighbors crowded into the drawing room through the next day. The nontribals were excited, even a little exultant, about this fresh piece of evidence. An honest man, a quiet man, they said approvingly of my father, although I think they were really characterizing themselves as a group. The tribal officers who came to see my father felt the unsaid accusations around them as they sat silent for the most part, apologetic and a little uncomfortable. The conversations drifted around the situation and someone told my father to be less strict about regulations. The other visitors had left, and I caught snatches of the dialogue between the two of them. "Times are changing," this last nontribal visitor said, shaking his feet vigorously, "and the government is not going to do anything for your family if something happens. Don't be a fool, Dam, you're not in the army." It was after this that I started running.

Every day, at 4:30, when the alarm suddenly sounds like a foghorn in the cold and the dark, I'm up, tying the laces of my running shoes, flapping my arms around, and fixing a handkerchief over my mouth so that I'll breathe only through the nose. Then I let myself out silently, bolting the door from the outside, reluctant because the first steps have no promise but only the possibility of defeat. My feet begin to tap out an unsteady rhythm on the road, breathe steadily, but how can you when your nose is running and your lungs are on fire and the sun chooses to make its first sharp sortie straight into your eyes. I feel my legs going heavy, I don't see anything, I even forget the busy clatter of Colonel MacPherson's ghost putting his latest steed through its paces, all I know is that I can't stop now. Then, when I'm least expecting it, the air clears around me as if I have run past rows of seats in an empty auditorium, right through the screen onto the beach in *Chariots of Fire*, the cold around me and the burning in my lungs falling away simultaneously to the sound of music and I am no longer running but swinging through the air. I've found the pace and I'll stop only when I want to.

Now that I can sit and remember with such clarity, having come home to fear after ten years, its salty taste arrives with pulsating quickness to the tongue, the premonition of a cut lip flooding my mouth. Now if I were to get up and move out of this room, past the receptionist at the front desk incessantly patting her hair into order, out from this false paradise of lake and garden to the road that sways and curves between the two poles of the town, I would know how to walk. Avoid eye contact, look out for little groups bunched together on the pavement. If a shout or insult starts trailing you, don't hear it. Get off the curb and give way if someone approaches from the opposite direction, swinging his shoulders exaggeratedly. The sound of footsteps behind and again the words: "*Dkhar!* Foreigner." But I walk on—the first rule of fear is that you don't show it—listening for a change in rhythm. If that happens, I will take a quick look behind and, putting into use what I have learned with such dedication, run for my life.

This, then, is a retracing of that runner's route, from the first awareness of what it meant to be an outsider to a final settlement of accounts. Past and present brought face to face at last, strung out on two ends of the long run; father and son, characters and narrator, the town and the self, all come together—here, now, at this whirling, dizzy point of vertigo that is the return. The lake shimmers in the distance, as if shaken by ripples from a thousand children trying simultaneously to send their stones leapfrogging over the water. Lies, half-truths conjured by the mind, irrelevant details—is that not what memory amounts to? But we are close to the end. There are a few hours left to the bus that will take me away from here, one last walk from hotel to bus station. This final act of remembrance must attempt, through the taste of fear, to freeze the images for a moment.

Hometown.

It is possible to think of that day in Police Bazaar as the first experience of fear only because that is the way it seems now, in this collapsed and condensed version of the past. That could not have been the case then, even if I did begin running immediately after the assault on my father. The truth is that the running was not for my father but for myself, and what I was reacting to was not so much the attack that had taken place but the violence that was yet to come. It doesn't make sense, I know, to think of reacting to something that was still to happen, but it is the only kind of sense I am capable of. It is the return journey that has done this: space bends, time folds, and the past I attempt to talk about is impregnated by what comes after, laden heavy with all the failures that were not apparent then.

The first time I saw the future leader was on a day when my friend Moni and I were walking home after the Saturday laboratory session in school, past the handball court across the field where a game of cricket was in progress. It was a practice session with not too many players, none of them from the school. Moni nudged me. "Look at the keeper, first time I've seen that."

The wicketkeeper, fully padded up, was an easy six feet, a long, rangy figure in a cowboy hat, smoking a cigarette as he crouched uncomfortably behind the stumps. The ball was wide, both batsman and keeper missing as it skidded past and ricocheted off the wall enclosing the handball court. The keeper remained sprawled on the ground, the cigarette in his mouth sending up little smoke signals as the fielder from the slips came toward us to retrieve the ball. Moni didn't make a move toward the ball. Normally he would have grabbed it for a throw. He waited until the fielder had returned to position.

"Know who the cowboy is?"

"No. Looks an outsider. I mean, not from the school."

"As far as he's concerned, we're the outsiders. You more than me." Moni was Assamese.

"Who's he?"

"Adolf," Moni said thoughtfully.

"Adolf?"

"Adolf. Hitler. The short guy running in as if he's really fast? That's Goering. At square leg, let's see, that's Himmler. Dönitz at gully, Goebbels's batting."

"Do they call him the Führer?" I laughed.

We started walking, hidden from the players by the embankment looming above the road. Moni started to goose-step. "You should see them in the evening around Don Bosco Square, doing this and throwing Nazi salutes. They're regular student-union guys. Got it in real hard for nontribals."

It was nothing, one could argue, just a set of foreign names that had come down to the field of burned yellow, almost as unbelievable and comical as a UFO invasion. Everything else was the same: the school building in blue and white in the background, its unchanging coat of arms casting a Latin spell of stability and perseverance—"Facta non Verba"—across the fields, the pine trees standing as silent sentinels all around, the path dipping between the hostels of St. Edmund's College before jumping up to the stretch of paved road in front of that Golden Store, where, it was rumored, one could buy heroin if one had the money.

Nothing had changed, not just then, and yet everything changed. In essence, the cricket game being played that day was the same as thousands of other acts of play: innocuous, predictable, and replicable. What meaning my memory gives to it comes from my perception of events that came later, through the growing knowledge of those names Moni introduced me to that day, of the agenda and vision of the world that naming had sought to capture.

Put too much weight on any particular moment, force it into an epiphany, and experience cracks in half. Before that sighting, the trouble and fear had been no more than little blips on the radar of my existence. The killings of '79, the move away from the house in Garikhana, even the assault on my father, these were anomalous events that would not be repeated. They were part of the adult world that one could always run from. My world was different, it was whole, it was the taste of a beef sandwich offered hesitatingly by Rishan Bhor—"Man, you're Hindu, you know. You sure you want this?"—the weight of the reference books sneaked out of State Central Library with the help of Sokhlet, the satisfying click of a cassette borrowed from Michael.

Adolf changed everything. It seems impossible now that there could ever have been a time not contaminated by all that happened afterward. My past, after all, holds meaning purely through memories of his presence, their presence, and I can only measure my youth against his rise from the captain of a local cricket club that called itself the Aryan Club to the point when he became the dominant leader of the tribal students' union and the German names he and his followers had taken on became official, used even by the local newspaper as it mentioned Adolf Hitler's latest opinions on what should be done with outsiders.

The acts that came with the rise of Adolf sealed us in, forcing us to read the landscape of our everyday lives in terms of a new lexicon of outrage and fear sweeping through the town—strikes, demonstrations, public curfews, rallies, extortion, assault—dividing people into insiders and outsiders, laying down the rules of existence. Meetings held by the student union ended with demands and exhortations, with outcries of rage against the foreigners who had settled in the state, an exhilarating flow of political action that hurled itself in successive waves on anything perceived as alien outgrowths on native soil. On the night wind the smell of the burned flesh of the slaughtered cows of Nepali milkmen and herders, the rumble of jeeps with loudspeakers blaring out another act of assertion and demanding that the outsiders stay home the next day, the steady tapping of policemen's sticks on the dark, deserted streets. On the way back home from an early-morning run, while taking a detour through a colony emptied of most of its nontribal residents, the graffiti on the wall of a lonely and shabby cottage: WE SHALL COME TO THIS HOUSE AS WELL.

Where did they get the faith in their righteousness from, and which absurd world gave them the symbolism of the Third Reich as a way toward self-assertion? During the deliberations of the student union, the town held its breath, waiting for the declarations that would come after, ranging from punitive measures against an offending nontribal family to an increase in taxes for nontribal businessmen. The larger decisions were placed in front of the tribal political leaders, from a ban on construction of the railway line because it would only bring in more Bangladeshis, to the demand that Bengalis carry identity cards at all times to prove that they were Indian citizens.

Adolf was the most visible, terse symbol of the fault line running through the town, slicing up quadrants of time and space into zones of fear. He was to be seen often in Laitumukrah, around the school and the college, driving around in a Willys jeep that mapped out a route of dust, stray guitar chords, and violence. When my friends and I walked out of the school grounds, we stayed in groups through some unsaid agreement, avoiding looking up toward the figures lounging around the shops leading up to Don Bosco Square. If we went to a film at Anjali or Kelvin and saw his cropped head waving above the melee around the ticket counter, we left and ate in a restaurant instead, careful to head out of Police Bazaar before sunset. And what this meant was that by some undefined process, the "we" became composed exclusively of nontribals, and the tribal friends who had been a part of my life since the age of six faded away, joining groups of their own.

I have no doubt that I created as many shadows out of that collective unease as those that actually fell across my path, shirking and flinching at the end from the very roads and houses and trees as if they were all ranged against me, whispering conspiratorially to each other. After the incidents of 1979, people had moved away from places like Mawprem and Malki where the majority was tribal, coming to rest around the few Bengali and Assamese neighborhoods. That was why we left Garikhana—where the killings began when some people stopped a bus coming from Gauhati and hacked seven non-tribal passengers to death—and moved to Jail Road. The government had started arresting large numbers of people in response to the riots, and because there weren't enough cells in the small jail, most of the rioters had been left to wander around the big courtyard. As we walked home from school and passed the jail, we could hear shouts and jeers, sometimes followed by showers of stones across the wall.

Then we came to the house with the triangular rooms in Rilbong, moving over to the other side of the central spine of the town, with library and hospital and government offices and marketplace flung out in a straight line. It was a small nontribal neighborhood squeezed between the hills and the army quarters, and as I explored the winding streets and the houses stacked one behind the other, it seemed as if Rilbong had been positioned with a siege in mind. From the window in the room

I shared with my father, it was possible to look at the curving road, in the far left corner across the shallow gorge, the stone tablet speaking of Tagore and the books he had written here. Within a year of our arrival there, it had fallen down, the smudged letters speaking of the Nobel Prize worn away with every passing month.

It remained like that right up to the time we left for Silchar. Why, in any case, should the tribals care about honoring a foreign poet when their anger directed itself at every stranger, and every Bengali was seen as an outsider from Bangladesh, as an illegal immigrant regardless of when and under what circumstances they had settled here? I can't deny that there was a certain justice in their indifference to this announcement of Tagore's distant literary achievements. When I read one of the works he had composed here, a tiresome drama of Calcutta relationships being played out in this hill town, I looked in vain for any reference to the people who had always lived here, to the landscape as something more than a backdrop for Tagore's literary abilities or the amorous impulses of his characters. I could have taken the side of the people here, agreed with them that they had for too long been treated as exotic props in their own land, had I not been denied that possibility by being who I was. So Tagore remained, face-up to the monsoon skies, ignored by Bengalis and tribals alike, while the Intelligence officials who occupied the bungalow behind the memorial filled the evening air with their radio signals, sending reports of growing discontent and the possibility of a secessionist movement to faraway Delhi.

Still, it was safe in the neighborhood. Once you stepped out of Rilbong and touched the main road near Garrison Ground and the army movie theater and moved a little away from the other memorial, the one to the unknown soldier, it was a world of clots of people hurling stray words of abuse at you, of black, streaky posters saying, "Nontribal boys are warned against talking to tribal girls. Or else steps will be taken against outsiders." At other times the language of the posters took up the larger issue: "Go back, foreign dogs. Go back, Bangladeshis."

Where could one go back to? What had been left behind could not even be given a name. My grandparents had spoken of East Pakistan, my parents referred to Bangladesh. To me the notion of an ancestral village was quaint and distant, far from the school building and lakes and parks and houses that I had thought was home because I was born here and because the land was in my blood. I wish I could say that I learned to love it anew, to see things afresh. But I had no understanding that accommodated these opposed points of view. Instead, I went through periods of completely different emotions, oscillating between a desire to blend with the town and the insiders and a virulent hatred for the place and a desire to leave it forever so that I would never hear that word, *Foreigner*, again.

My father and I never spoke of the way things were, keeping our separate worlds to ourselves. He had taught me very early on about the trees and the flowers, pointing out the vague shapes or smudges of color and assigning names to them. "That's a willow, and that's a weeping willow."

"Which one? The wavy one?"

"Yes."

"Why is it called a weeping willow?"

"Because it looks like a person weeping."

I suppose that was my first lesson in abstract representation. It was easy to accept it as fact then, just as easy as the notion that ancestral villages are something people leave behind for good, something they can never return to. Unlike others who had migrated from East Bengal through the years following the Partition, my father spun no myths of great tracts of land and feudal ownership. The grimy, much-folded piece of paper that charted out our genealogy stopped at my grandfather's father, a small peasant like his sons and grandsons. Before that there was only a blank, while in front of me, where there had once been the solidity of this place, there was a town slowly being stripped of its characteristics. The trees were no longer pines or firs or weeping willows. They had been assembled into a landscape of words, foreign words whispering "*Dkhar, Dkhar,*" German names marching like storm troopers toward us, the nonpeople, the outsiders.

At some point Adolf stopped playing cricket, having moved on to higher things as a student leader, but by then it didn't matter. The rules had been established. No matter at what stage of the game we were in, the sight of tribal boys walking deliberately across the field meant the pitch had to be vacated. If they were particularly kind, we would be allowed to play a curtailed version of our game at the edge of the field. It depended on the individuals involved and their mood. Often enough we were told brusquely to clear out from the playing area. Then we took out the stumps and collected the gear, careful not to display a good bat that might be confiscated. We watched their game for a little while from the sidelines before leaving. It didn't do to leave straight away, without having applauded politely at a few preliminary deliveries or strokes or fielding stops. That could be construed as a deliberate insult and had been known to result in immediate reprisals.

The plastic Ping-Pong ball loops and falls in a different way, spinning and bouncing in accordance with its own separate laws on the little wooden tabletop. Partha and I slap it around in the school common room, bored and fidgety after half an hour, ready to pack up and walk home toward Rilbong. Partha lives in Bishnupur, fifteen or twenty minutes from my house, in an Assamese neighborhood where it is still safe after dark and we can hang around for a while.

The ball bounced off the edge of the board from a mishit and rolled into the corner, hiding among some dismantled benches. The windows looking out to the back of the school were open. There was a loud noise, the opening bars of a song leaping through the windows. A lead guitar cut in, picked up the tune, molding it into a recognizable shape. "Rock concert, at Sinanthony's," Partha said. "Want to go for half an hour?" I agreed, because it should be safe enough as long as we left before dark. We set off for St. Anthony's, passing the statue smeared with pigeon shit, Don Bosco's finger open to a book, probably preaching the gospel to the fawning, kneeling children cut out of gray stone. Or maybe they were angels telling him he was in heaven. I could never be quite sure about the scene being enacted and, insular outsider that I was, had never bothered to find out.

The square was rippling with a festival atmosphere, of spring and romance and sex and youth, high-school and college students hanging around in their best clothes, some of the lucky ones in couples, the girls giggly and cloying, the boys wide-shouldered and macho. They had assembled here as if this was the center of the world, which it was, this square with festoons and signs announcing college festivals and spring fever, shiny bikes and cars parked in a heterogeneous mass along the pavements.

Inside the grounds of St. Anthony's, the space in front of the stage was packed, the alcohol breath and cigarette smoke and loud guitar chords being blasted around the arena by the sound system, people swaying with their hands held up in "Long live rock 'n' roll" signs. We made our way in just as the group finished its cover version of an Iron Maiden song, guitars and drums dying into the screams and shouts of fans, the women raising plaintive white arms toward the lead guitarist. The bass player slammed a closed fist on the strings, then turned away from the crowd in displeasure.

They were beautiful on stage, with the unfettered movement of long hair and their stylized guitar duels, far from the Bengali teenage world of exams and schools and careers. Here was freedom and joy, life itself in all its force. Their fingers flickered over the strings, riding the fretboards with an intense pain and sweetness, spreading their magic from the stage toward the crowd and the square and the town to engulf the world in a sea of sound, blurring every single face into the same rapture. There were loud screams when they finished, the bouncing, bobbing lights over the stage steadying their focus on the singer, who remained frozen, drenched in sweat, shirt ripped off long ago in the course of his demented progress through the song.

The sound of murmured endearments, loud conversations, whoops and shouts of recognition throbbed back over the space of the break, as the crowd shifted itself. Leave now, a voice inside my head whispered, even as I drank in the sensations greedily, devouring the images and texture and odors. It was a moment of lightness in which it was possible to make stupid mistakes. With the lights on the stage reduced to steady concentration, the crowd around us swelled and bubbled in the darkness, expanding in its own sensual glow. Laughter and yells everywhere, the occasional high-pitched sounds, the tinkling of a bottle on the concrete floor, the rise of voices to sharp, angry shouts, then oaths, insults, protests overlapping with each other. This was happening in a group in a distant corner; we were still away from the disagreement and the voice in my head flashed out its warning with the steady flicker of a red light. Leave now leave now leave now.

There was a ripple that ran through the crowd, bodies moving differently, someone running into me and forcing me back. "Sorry," I said automatically, turning around, seeing the hand in a blur as it met my face, bringing a sensation of pain and fear, knocking my glasses off. My hands went up to my face in reflex as I felt myself drowning in the waves of fear. The figure in front raised his hand as I heard Partha go down somewhere and I was struck again, the bones of a hard knuckle riveting into my lips. I was hoping the police would come soon.

Looking back on that scene it seems amazing how total the control of other lives can be, how much the world is capable of being swallowed into the small but absolute dimension of fear. There was nothing other than the host of faces rising like a wall around me and that one man asserting his right to my life and consciousness. Everything else was far away, on another planet, the announcements on the microphone for calm and peace, even the retching sounds of Partha somewhere near me. All that was real was the laced-up leather boot in front of me and the hand with the metal-studded wrist band that made for the left side of my face methodically.

The cordon of fear lifted and reshaped itself as suddenly as it had come down upon us, the arrival of Adolf and the union members bringing a sense of purpose to the crowd. The bodies that had been ranged around us moved back, heeding the call for discipline that came from the union members. Partha and I waited numbly, and then we hurriedly began to make our way out in response to the voices hissing at us to leave, but in a knot of people somewhere behind me there rose a sudden wail before it was silenced swiftly. We would read about the two corpses found near St. Anthony's the next day.

I had found my glasses and Partha and I were carefully

making our way out, trying to avoid all contact with the bodies packed around us, when we were brought to a standstill by the sight before us. The scene had clicked back into vision like a slide show. With the crack in one of my lenses running across the crowd, I saw the faces around filled with a strange fervor as Adolf's cronies went into a ritual of Nazi salutes, goose-stepping behind their leader as he headed for the stage, slicing through the mob.

The world had not stopped while this was happening. Instead, the crowd around Don Bosco Square had swelled and there was more music, dozens of different songs from the speakers of cars parked near the sidewalk, a collage of sound pasted on the blackboard of the evening sky. But the population had become more homogeneous now, mostly male, many of them drunk. The temperature had dropped. My face hurt and the crack across my left lens gave the scene the quality of a delirium. "It's dark," I whispered to Partha. "It's a good thing it's dark," he replied. "You look like shit."

We wanted to go in the direction of Loreto's, toward Dhanketi, but the street was so crowded with cars and people that we couldn't move. From a distance, I caught the eye of Bantei, a tribal fellow student, his long curls bouncing on his shiny leather jacket. He began making his way through the crowd and caught up with us easily. We exchanged meaningless greetings in that crowded square, his eyes staring at us and then flickering around restlessly, ill at ease.

"You guys live around Laban, don't you?" There was a burst of firecrackers nearby but we could see nothing over the heads of the crowd that had swelled ahead of us. "You should have left before, guys." Lowering his voice, he whispered, "Don't you notice you two are the only nontribal faces here?" We looked around furtively. There was a sea of alien faces everywhere and Bantei's stopped short of that description only by virtue of his concern. He began pushing us. "Come on, you have to get off the street. You can't go now. They're setting up an effigy there right now. Come on, we have to find a place where you can wait." There was a rush of flames behind, reaching up to the night sky like a hand raised in admonishment.

Partha and I began to hurry along behind Bantei, our faces low. The shutters were coming down on the stationery shop on one side of the entrance to St. Mary's and we hurried up its steps. The owner, busy turning off the lights, began to protest, but changed his mind as Bantei stared him down. "I'll return when it's okay for you guys to go, but don't come out until the cops have cleared the streets." He turned and ran back down the steps, hair bouncing on that shiny jacket, until we could no longer tell him apart from the mass he had dived into.

All lights inside the shop turned off except for a little lamp at the back, the owner tested his shutters and nervously fingered the handset of the phone. There was no sound; the phone lines had been cut off. Then he sighed softly and bent down, peering through a chink in the metal shutters. We watched the owner's curved back, a bulky shape in the darkness, the sounds coming through the shutters now distant and now near, first muffled and then sharp. It sounded like a February wind whistling through trees, howling and raging against the landscape, but it was composed of human voices, cries opening up to the screech of tires and then swallowing up the lesser sound, waves of tinkling glass racing along the beach of the background noise and finally the crash of gunshots on each others' heels.

When we came out, the street was empty of people except for the paramilitary troops in their riot gear. Partha and I hurried our way through broken glass, past three or four car shells and what looked like patches of blood, past stones and cans with burned rags, past all the debris left behind by the receding tide of fear and hatred. At regular intervals, slightly away from the street lamps—where there were still street lamps—the soldiers stood like warning signs, their bulbous helmets bobbing in the dark. We slowed down when we came to these spots. They hefted their sticks thoughtfully and the flashlights seared our faces. Looking at us with hard, alien eyes, they waved us on.

the local archive

So I went away more than ten years ago, giving in to that impulse to leave, hoping to find other things, other places. Now I'm back for one final visit. Why come back, you ask? What happened in between?

Nothing, really—a room here, a room there.

Old age, sickness, a man lying on his bed for over five years, death on a hot summer night that brings in the flies to settle on his lips within an hour of the ceasing of the heart. A room here, a room there. My mother, she who always accepted things with far more generosity than my father or I ever mustered, she departed without fuss. As in life, so in death, the spirit slipping away through the billowing curtains with the faintest of signs, leaving at the most convenient of times so that no one had to sit up through the night, no extra charges to be paid at the crematorium, no worries about the indignities the body might suffer from the heat.

As for me, the teller of tales, the inept archaeologist of memories, there were mostly failures. Failures in love and work, moving from town to city, from city to capital, restless and uncertain. A room here, a room there.

I make no bones about my failure. Things could have turned out differently, but they didn't. If I foreclosed my engineering career, choosing what I saw as freedom over following an unexciting if well-honed groove, the illusion of that freedom disappeared soon enough in the face of everyday routine, during the evenings hunched over a computer at the newsroom, assembling stories of injustice and banality from various corners of the world. An unappealing job editing news reports in the evening, an empty apartment to go back to ever since my mother died, the weight of books on dusty shelves, memories in some distant corner, the strangeness of one's own face when seen in a cheap mirror over a small sink, the sudden awareness of my alcohol-tinged breath as I bend over the lock at the front door.

If there had been a future, or even a present worth paying attention to, had there been something other than an infinite, monotonous, endlessly repeating assembly line of days, perhaps my thoughts would not have turned so obsessively to the past. It was not a question of roots or origin, you understand. That was not possible, not now, not fifty years after the notional ancestral village had ceded its place to the modern nation state. If we were all to do so, we whose lives are flung around in Pakistan, India, Bangladesh, if we were to let loose our songlines, our routes of memory, our pilgrimage paths, we would find them faltering against the documents and borders and guns. Perhaps rightfully so; maybe this is the way it should be. One can cling too much to such things, like the followers of Godse, the man who killed Gandhi, who swear upon his ashes every year that the Indus and its tributaries must flow once again within the boundaries of India, that the crack of 1947 will be layered over again some day, but on their terms.

Where was I? Talking about past and origins. No, I let go any idea of an ancestral homeland long ago and it would never have surfaced at all in my life had those days of fear not brought it up so sharply: "Go back, foreign dogs. Go back, Bangladeshis." But this was home, surely, this space of childhood, the place where I had last seen my father on his feet, this confluence of childhood hopes and a faith in the future. All concentrated in the word *hometown,* a definite point in the curve of the earth, where the monsoon marshals its forces and bursts through rooms and windows and staircases with a wet, cold smell, where the winter months swivel from light to darkness and the halogen lamps that come on in the evening create little pools on the met-aled roads, broken up momentarily by the rumbling wheels of supply trucks.

Therefore, the return, as a taciturn figure bunched up on the swaying seat of the Northeast Express to Gauhati and then boarding the bus nosing its way up cautiously to the land of clouds, to see it again one last time.

The traveler's eyes are always subjective and biased, but to return in this strange way, caught between alienation and familiarity, was to peer through some inverted telescope which distorted the scale without any gain in clarity. The changes had been visible even on Thursday, the day I took the Assam State Transport Corporation bus from Gauhati. Standing at the bus terminus next to the railway station, it seemed that I could not have chosen a worse time for this trip. There was a 100-hour "*chakka* jam"—locked wheels, a transport strike—throughout the Northeast, and none of the private services were running their buses. The state transportation companies with their inadequate fleets had put up handwritten notices everywhere, stating that their buses were full up to the next day. One could not travel to Dimapur or Aizawl or Kohima or Itanagar. What was left, then?

Men in striped underpants scurried around near the toilets, holding mugs, while in the corridors and in the open spaces of the yard I could only see clusters of despair and futility, sullen bus porters eyeing their railway counterparts, who carried in the luggage of the passengers arriving by rail, adding to the human mass curdling around the bus terminus. The afternoon fading rapidly around the ticket counters and the empty buses parked in the yard evoked a feeling of desperation, but then I felt the initial stirring of excitement as the collective began to delineate itself before my eyes. What a range was to be found here, in this gateway to the furthest corner of India. There were well-dressed, middle-class tribals perched on shopping bags filled with consumer goods they had bought in Calcutta or Bombay or Delhi, surly army *jawans* strolling around in pairs, shabby Bengalis and North Indians who snapped at their tired, resentful families. I picked up scraps of conversation, shouts, comments, words uttered in languages I had not heard for over a decade. For a while, it seemed possible that the journey might give me something in return.

I did not spend much time at the bus terminus, just long enough to drink in the sights and sounds. My first impression that it would not be possible to travel further proved false when I checked the counters. There were tickets available, on an Assam State Transport Corporation bus, to one state capital. As if the fates had planned it, my destination could be reached. Even though the people looked hungry and dirty and hopeless, no one was going to my old hometown, it seemed.

Riding up Highway 36, crossing the state border almost as soon as we left the suburbs of Gauhati, the bus with its scattered passengers settled into a steady climbing rhythm, circling back laboriously as it made its way up the hills. I saw frequent bald patches on the hillside, clearings in the forests that had the effect of little explosions, trucks carrying rocks and earth and tree trunks not yet shorn of branches and leaves, the humming of mechanical saws. There were sweat beads on the inside of my elbows, even though the air blowing in through the window was cool and fresh. I looked out for the first houses on the outskirts of the town as we made our way in, eyes peeled for the high walls of the veterinary compound and the small gate behind which the childhood years lay buried. They had put up a steel gate where the old one used to be, between the dairy plant and the veterinary hospital. There were new buildings on the vacant lots where the empty trailers had rested in permanent retirement, along with skeletons of old jeeps brown with rust, and patches of tall grass one could spring an ambush from. In that compound, my father had bought me my first soccer ball, trying to teach me to kick it properly as I resisted his advice, convinced even at that age that he had little to show me.

I could not stay long in the Ashoka Pinewood with its colonial air, among its Burma teak doors and cane chairs, in spite of the fact that I had deliberately chosen this ostentatious hotel, wanting at least an air of worldly success around myself. It was, after all, a meeting between two beings long sundered. I was drawn irresistibly to the streets outside, lying just beyond the shaded grounds of the lake. It was all partly familiar, but there was so much that was new. As the sights flowed in and my mind tried to make sense of architecture and landscape, people and place, the ghosts that I had nurtured over the years broke through, scattering like loose change. This was no longer remembrance. It was the place itself, imposing and resonant, hurling its roads and Maruti taxis, its shopping plazas and air-conditioned hotels at me.

Some of the old jaggedness still existed, in the series of steps sprinting up from G.S. Road and cutting through Police Bazaar as I followed it up to the road with the pharmacy and Delhi Mistanna Bhandar. The alley still crouched over the Punjab Hotel, dark and musty—which we had always taken to be a brothel—but most of the small jewelry shops once populating this row were gone. Here the Bengali women would come to sell their jewelry, a gold chain or a pair of bracelets bundled up in cloth and tucked deep inside their handbags as they scanned the shop for a familiar face before declaring their poverty. Sometimes they would enter laughing, accompanied by friends to place an order, assessing the heft and shape of the shiny new objects that would be theirs. I came here once with my mother—she had something to sell—though she must have made many visits on her own. She would have walked up the steps and entered the shop alone on these occasions, casting off each little gold piece that her father had given her, a pair of bangles in return for my admission to the best school in town, a necklace so that she could purchase some medicines my father needed, perhaps some money for the electrical wiring still to be done in the shell put up at Silchar.

Beyond the shadow of this alley, the roads were wider than I remembered, although I had expected to find everything scaled down from the landscape of my memories. Where the Mordanis had a department store, there was now a shopping plaza sunk deep, five levels below ground. There was no elevator, or if there was, I did not find it, and I climbed down the stairs, passing shops crowded with leather jackets and jeans and sneakers. At a cosmetic shop there, a smart-looking young woman told her customer, "Yeah, I can give you the Indian Revlon, the stuff they make here. But we have the original thing. You sure that's not what you want? Most people prefer that. You sure? You can't depend upon the quality of the local thing, even if it's licensed by the company."

It didn't happen in a minute; it took the day after and the next, all the way up to today, the day of the departure, for the impressions to sink in. But from the moment of my entry into the town I could feel myself disoriented by the sights and sounds, in the diminishing, uncertain nature of the past I sought out even as I was assailed by the newness the town was trying to assert, like fresh skin growing around old sores and burns. I wanted to find a place for the new next to what I had carried with me for so many years, but the present had no patience with my spectral, half-fashioned memories. The town that I had invented and refashioned in words and images was caving in under the weight of this, the real, the present, the now.

How often had I compared settlements in the plains to my hometown, weighed them with the hillman's eyes and always found them wanting? Here there was none of that awkward eruption of concrete boxes packed together, roofs colliding with each other, dusty roads stuck between vacant patches of land not quite pasture or forest or field. Instead of that two-dimensional, flat nature so characteristic of the plains, there were sharp angles here, the opening-up of space into a sudden gorge or ravine, scissored-out peaks and cliffs reworked into the sloping roofs and wavy lines of tin sheets drenched in flowers and ivy vines. But that was a simple, ideal contrast that allowed for neither the change that had overcome the old neighborhoods, nor the fear that was an integral part of our former lives here.

How did I achieve this unlikely feat of forgetting in the very act of remembrance, if the fear had been as overwhelming as I

say it was? I don't know, but the answer must be that I chose to
forget. Memory is also about what you decide to remember, so
that you can make sense of what has been irrevocably lost. That
was the only way the past could be recovered, in the writing of
stories in different voices, sometimes across the distance of the
third person, sometimes through the eyes of the boy who lived
here. Change a name there, add a street, put in the rain, as if
by doing this there was something that could be reached, a way
for the waste to be negated. If the fear found its way into the
stories, it was through a screen, somewhere in the background
of my father's affairs and failures, little details tucked around
that most unremarkable life as I attempted to give it a shape. It
is not that the stories are lies, any more so than this final section. Each group has its own truth, but there is no way of putting them together to form a complete picture. There is no way
the feeling of loss can acknowledge the sense of fear.

I came back to find an end to the story other than Dr.
Dam's death, and to find something that would recover the
voice of the boy who had left with dreams of night journeys, of
another future where he would be free and successful and un-
afraid of his alienness. But I also came back with the distance
of more than ten years, with the experience of adult failures
and a perspective gained from the death of my parents, in the
knowledge that there was nothing with me that was alive. In the
streets that had once been so familiar, there would be two
ghosts, one that of my father, the other of the child that was
me. I thought it would be a way of seeing the two of them closer
together than they had ever been in actual life, without the wall

of fear rising between them, without each trapped in self-doubt.

In the eighteenth century, nostalgia was diagnosed as a medical condition, arising from a lesion in the brain that in turn was caused by homesickness. Who would you say had the disease? Me with my constant rewriting and recharting of the landscape of a childhood hometown? Or my father, who never allowed himself to acknowledge the loss of this place, to whom it was the most unspeakable of loves? The last doctor we took him to said that he had a tumor in his brain, that it would not be long before it was over.

The stories about my father's life, of life here up to the day we left, were attempts to find a site for the fleeting emotions and images that came up again and again, in places as far apart as Silchar, Calcutta, and Delhi. Yet how does one find a justification or a story around such intangibles? There is so much I have left out, so much of pleasure and happiness. Listening to a Walkman on a night bus to Tura, playing an ELO song called "Rain Is Falling" over and over again, hearing the guitars and violins rising against the hillsides, the hopes and desires and friendships of that time weaving a thick mist around me, casting a spell over the waters of Barapani Lake, the condensation of so many presences, the fingerprints of Michael, who had lent me the slow-rock cassette I was listening to and who I thought would always be my friend, the feeling that I would like to come back to this town some day, maybe when I was married or when I had children. To be able to do what my father had always been unable to say or do, to point out, "This is where it all began."

In the spring, the gardens flowered from house to house, and in the backyards, along with shrubs and weeds, there were vines of squash, their prickly golden-green skin rough with fiber and indentations and little hollows like a piece of the earth itself. There were butterflies, berries, and rare orchids in the forested walks up toward Laitkor Peak, crabs that scuttled along the slippery, stony beds of streams. Years later, in Calcutta, I edited a story for the city pages about butterflies from this region being smuggled out through the Park Street post office, hundreds of them, butterflies that had been captured in the hills before being sealed and shipped out to foreign lands to lie in some cold, sterile collection. I felt as if I had been robbed a little more of the past.

My father had had little to say, about the town or anything else, in those final years of his life in Silchar, his skin worn and creased like an old sheet, the arms bent and fragile, reaching shakily for a cup of tea or a newspaper. When I went through his diaries, there wasn't much about his life here, or anywhere. He had taken most of his memories with him.

I left the hotel early on Friday morning, the day after I arrived, planning to walk to the old neighborhood of Rilbong. The weather was pleasant enough, mildly warm with an occasional breeze that came up from the lake, although I recognized the telltale sign of the monsoons in the fleeting darkness cast by clouds overtaking the sun. There was a turbaned military policeman directing traffic in front of the Governor's House and a scattered flow of office workers entering the massive gates of the Additional Secretariat, the pedestrians outnumbered by the cars and jeeps honking their way to the office buildings. I paused outside the State Central Library, my eyes drawn to the tank, rusted and discolored in spots, the lid of the turret lying twisted on one side. The tank looked as if it had fought at least another war since I had last seen it, while a strong stench of urine suggested that some new uses had been found for it.

The corridors of the library were empty as I made my way to the information desk, but the echo of my footsteps on the polished concrete made me expect an approaching patron or librarian around the corner. Nothing, save the high ceilings, the inaugural stone tablet, vacant sofas, and a few magazines—*Span, National Geographic, India Today*—on a coffee table in the reception area. I continued along the passageway that skirted the building and found myself near the main hall, its doors wide open. There were rows of metal folding chairs stacked neatly inside, and two men were spreading a large white tablecloth over three trestle tables set up at right angles to the stage. Somewhere in the background there was the faint smell of food.

I turned back toward the information desk of the library section, to the little plastic box on the desk with a bunch of tourist guides, the words *Scotland of the East* printed in black, bold type on the leaflets. Behind the information desk was the glass door that had led to the main stacks. I looked in, but although the fluorescent lights in the room were on, it seemed empty of human beings. The olive-green metal shelves were the same, their recesses packed with books whose titles I could not read from this distance, and I felt myself drawn back to the past, to the smell of paper and binding glue, the room suffused with soft light and the hushed tread of browsers. I had not been allowed to go in here until the age of twelve, although I had tried often enough to sneak in. Why twelve? Was there something about the age that made it a definable boundary and allowed one to cross over to the world of adult books? The first such venture was *Lady Chatterley's Lover*, I remember, which I read only after having covered it first with brown paper.

In those years before the adult stacks were opened to me, my greatest ally had been a tribal clerk called Sokhlet, who was in charge of the reference section. He remained much the same through all the years I knew him, seemingly unchanged from my first glimpse of him at the reference desk, a sober young man with wisps of facial fair, leafing through a thin mathematics primer, unheeding of the heavy encyclopedias and dictionaries stacked around him. He must have been in his early twenties, although to me he seemed very adult, and if our relationship found a point of equilibrium, it was when he told me that he was trying to pass his high-school exams for the fourth time.

When his boss was not around, Sokhlet let me treat the reference section as my personal domain, allowing me to smuggle out as many books as I wanted as long as I returned them. They were an odd assortment that I carried home with me, books about the solar system and Jane's *Encyclopaedia of Military Aircraft* squeezing E. Nesbit's *The Railway Children*. Sokhlet displayed only perfunctory interest in the reference books I wanted to borrow, his entire universe revolving around his examination syllabus. Sometimes he wanted my help with English, taking out a dog-eared grammar book from his bag. This could hardly have been the motivation for his friendship, since I got so much more out of it than he did and because his main worries were not about English but about Mathematics.

"Are you sure you don't know how to do these sums? Eh?" he would ask, when we went out of the reference room and sat near the battle tank. In his hand would be an arithmetic textbook, equally battered, which he leafed through with a wary expression, shivering ever so slightly when his eyes fell on a particularly difficult section. Our conversation was usually one-sided, a slow, halting monologue from Sokhlet that sketched in his village background, his modest ambition to get a job as a schoolteacher back in the village. He was grave and decorous and about the only time he was visibly excited was when he tried to get me to repeat the name of his village, going into peals of laughter as my tongue twisted the name and disgorged it in his bemused face.

There had been another permanent figure, a little Bengali man with the air of a minor Dickensian character, shuffling around the corridors under the burden of a great suspicion. Unshaven, small, and shoddy, he carried the appearance of a hunchback without actually being one, always ready to ward me off from my forays toward the adult stacks. One day he demanded to see my bag as I came out of the library and I had the feeling he had been watching Sokhlet and me for some time. Fortunately, I did not have one of those volumes with the incriminating "For Reference Only" stamp on them, but he marched me up to the deputy librarian's office anyway, accusing me of theft. He had always given the impression of great erudition, but I realized that day that he was illiterate, unable to read the date of return stamped on the books I had checked out. The librarian let me go, meanwhile remonstrating with the hunchback. This story, when related to Sokhlet later, added to his small store of mirth. It strengthened the bond between us and we shared many laughs at the expense of the hunchback as he walked past us, glaring and muttering, a stooped and suspicious malevolent spirit lingering around that dusty place.

None of them would be around, I thought. Sokhlet had perhaps realized his ambition, and the hunchback was certainly dead. He had seemed very old even then. I was picking out a tourist brochure from the box on the desk, ready to leave the empty library, when I heard shouts behind me, followed by a patter of bare feet coming down the corridor from the hall before a man burst into my view. A man, I said, but it was more like a beast, a small, bent creature with a wild beard that ran out toward the garden, leaving a faint stench of urine in the air. One of the men who had been setting up the table came running with a stick in his hand, pulling up short when he came upon me.

"Which way did he go? Did you see him?" he asked,

holding the stick a little away from his body, as if he was embarrassed to be seen with it. I pointed outside, and he hit the ground with his stick. "The second time today. They'll blame me."

"Who's he?" I asked the man, a stocky tribal in his forties, neatly dressed in jeans and a thick plaid shirt. He tapped his forefinger on his head. "Lives in that tank, quite mad. Sneaks out to steal food sometimes."

"But how long has he been doing this?"

He shrugged. "I've been working here for a year and he's been around all that time. Someone told me he had a job in the library a long time ago." Was it the hunchback, I wondered. But I had no reason for assuming that; I was only making an arbitrary connection between my memories and the present. "The library's closed," he added. "There's a function later in the evening in the main hall. You a tourist?" He indicated the brochure in my hand.

"Yes."

"Take it," he said.

I took the brochure and left, noticing, on my way out, that there were old, stained rags spread out on the tank's gun, weighed down with what looked like stones, adding to the air of defeat around the emblem of victory.

The Civil Hospital came up on my left, then Garrison Ground, from where I turned left. They had done something to the Memorial to the Unknown Soldier across from the army movie theater. The gun and the helmet were the same, but the surroundings were more deliberately imposing: gold chain, regimental flags, an announcement of military power in a land that had emotionally seceded into its own space long ago. The bridge was no longer a ramshackle affair, the roads were freshly paved, and there were metal signboards with names for those little connecting streets that crisscrossed the neighborhood. The road that ran up from the bridge toward Kench's Trace and Bishnupur, past the timber factory, was called Oxford Hill Road now. So I stood on Oxford Hill Road, facing the new houses that had sprung up, caught by the pathos of the grandiose name given to this little strip of pavement. Why Oxford, of all things? Why not a local name, if every little thing had to be named and entered on some municipal map? No answers came from the cars and motorbikes changing gears as they took the slope, and the stare of a motorbike passenger only planted a growing unease in my mind, opening me up to a strange feeling of vulnerability.

A man with a pair of crutches limped up the road, about a dozen yards ahead of me, cursing at a yellow jeep that forced him to one side as it came up the narrow road, the back of the jeep spattered with mud as if it had come from the outer fringes of the town, its license plate illegible. There was no one else on foot apart from me and the man on the crutches, only souped-up motorbikes, the latest automobiles, and dozens of Maruti taxis, one taxi every six minutes or so, I calculated. Not a single one of those horse-drawn carts that had been so common, little carts pulled by shaggy hill ponies that would nod and jangle their way up the slopes, often leaving a trail of steaming dung behind. I left Oxford Hill Road and went back to the bridge, taking Zigzag Road to the old neighborhood. As I walked, the paint seemed to run ahead of me, changing shades as it touched each house like a mad artist trying out different possibilities from his color palette, light blue to pastel green to faint yellow to white, all of its stages retained by my eye through some strange working of REM vision.

The houses had been much like each other in the past, green or earth-red roofs perched on white walls that consisted of cement and plaster set over a skeleton of cane reeds. Now the old Assam bungalows sat uneasily next to new structures of concrete and glass, a piece of American suburbia implanted into the remote Northeast and crowding out the houses that themselves had been put up by the first white men to come here. Most of the open spaces were gone, the uneven fields and wild scrub trimmed into narrow lawns and driveways where they had not been built upon. Before things got really bad, before the public curfews and assaults, some of us would walk back late at night, sleeping over at either Moni's or Partha's house. We told exaggerated ghost stories to each other, and Colonel MacPherson always came up, trying out his latest steed early in the morning, bent on winning the next big race. Or the one about the girl this boy had danced with on Christmas Eve, and when he went back to see her the next day he found her name carved on a tombstone.

I don't know if those friends of mine remain in touch with each other and if I am the only one who has broken the circuit.

Although I have little news of them, one feels that they too are dissolved in the vast spaces that opened up once we left the town. The sporadic correspondence we maintained for a while ultimately ceased, each step one took in the adult world—career, marriage, children—serving to increase the distance from the past. Some of them decided to live in places where they were sure they would belong; the Assamese boys in Gauhati, the Bengalis in Calcutta or thereabouts, some of them in Delhi or Bombay, where the anonymity of the metropolis was compensated for by a sense of safety. There were others who were unable to give up their memories of long, frost-encrusted winters, obdurate souls who had been unwilling to exchange the neat cottages and lawns of their childhood for hot, vertical apartments crammed together in the housing colonies of big cities or suburban sprawls. These were the ones who left altogether, touching down in places as far apart as Massachusetts, New South Wales, Rotorua. Small-town boys settled in the United States or Australia or New Zealand, where they will become old men and sit on their front porches or lawns at the end of their lives, trying to remember whether the decades have taken them across many continents or if they are still in the first, original place where their old friends live around the corner.

There were two new houses in the sloping land between the bungalow owned by the Duttas and the house we had lived in. The rooftop of our house had been an independent little world, with hordes of rats in the space between the sloping tin roof and the canvas cloth that functioned as a ceiling. I remember how their scurrying feet would leave a faint little trail of indentations on the cloth, moving so rapidly that I became dizzy as I followed their trace, as if looking at an upside-down sea. Sometimes the rats fell through a rent in the cloth and landed in the middle of the room, scrambling away when they realized they were among people. After dark they became much bolder, making calculated expeditions to the kitchen, sometimes overturning the lid of the metal bucket in which the rice was kept.

They were not the only enemies who came in from above. In the rainy season, my mother stood on a strange column of chairs and stools as she sewed patches of cloth into the canvas with swift, flowing strokes. It was only a temporary shield. The patches stopped the leaks for a while but the rainwater would collect there, forming little bulging sacks until the pressure became too great and the water cascaded down everywhere, indiscriminately drenching different household objects, so that my mother had to fall back upon the time-tested solution of placing pots and pans under the holes.

The house now had new doors and a fresh coat of paint. There was a new railing on the front porch as well. I looked at it from the road, walking slowly so as not to appear to be staring at it. There was an air of permanence to the doors, bolted fast, reluctant to allow any ingress to my senses and thoughts. What could I expect? That they would fly open to reveal everything the way it had been and that I could walk in and make straight for the kitchen to ask my mother for a cup of tea?

The bungalow where the Intelligence people had had their office had been taken over by the state government. The plaque about Tagore had been carefully moved aside, placed near some bushes sprawling in the dirt, even more meaningless in its assertion of lasting fame than before. A long, narrow driveway wound past the trees scattered through the grounds of the bungalow, the grass and dried pine needles checked by the fresh, spaded earth where new flower beds were in the process of being laid. A signboard at the beginning of the driveway declared that the bungalow was now a state archive, committed to preserving material relevant to local history and culture. I walked up the driveway, as much to escape the sight of our old house as to see something new, something I could enjoy as a first-time visitor, like a tourist. An archive was impersonal in its version of the past, I thought, as I approached a gardener tending to patches of flowers. The clerk in the front room said he would let the director know there was a visitor and disappeared into one of the inner rooms.

I looked around while he was gone. It was not a particularly large bungalow, two big rooms and a smaller one to the right where the clerk had gone to talk to the director. I thought about the IB men crammed here with their files and wireless equipment, perhaps sleeping and eating in the smaller one, cooking their rudimentary meals on a kerosene stove as they counted off the days before they could return to their families. There was nothing left of them, though, as if they had vanished with their ghostly radio signals into the airwaves, and the solitary desk was as bare as the room. To my right, there was a calendar from the state tourism corporation with a picture of the golf course that was modeled on St. Andrew's in Scotland, according to the caption. I checked it with the photograph on my brochure; they were identical, with the very same caption. I peered into the room behind it. It was a mirror image of the one I was standing in, down to the empty desk and the calendar on the wall, but a little dustier, the floorboards bare and scratched, the canvas ceiling sagging in a couple of places that were stained yellow.

In Delhi, I once had occasion to visit the National Archives on Janpath. Visit is the wrong word. One does not visit national institutions: one awaits permission to enter them, sometimes endlessly, as in Kafka's parable. It was like a fortress, the sandstone walls stiff and hard against the trim of the lawns, even the trees carefully lined up, much like the soldiers and weaponry paraded down this road twice a year. After I was admitted into the visitor's room, a square of sofas, tables, and shelves with arcane periodicals, I waited for an hour for the requested material to come down. It was a little bit like waiting for a god to appear. I needed a collection of prints, watercolors done by a French artist, some eighteenth-century claptrap about "Costumes of Hindoostan." My job was to match a list I had been given with some of the plates and then request photographs of these prints. Some professor was writing a piece for a special issue in the features section.

As I faced the counter then with its two clerks, a little like guardians to some mythic netherworld, there was an awareness of hidden depths behind the heavy doors, of corridors and stacks and cubicles and offices crammed with whatever archives are supposed to keep: gazetteers, documents, correspondence, files, proclamations, maps, census data, land records. But even if the past was codified and accounted for, it had lost none of its mystery, ranging over some vast shore inaccessible to those merely mortal.

That was an archive, certainly, but what was this? Here there was nothing save the rooms swept bare, only the dust-balls in corners left unswept, one bundle of files on the director's desk in the little room to which I was led, pictures of her family and friends encircling the file, and at least three calendars on the walls. "Yes?" she said primly, adjusting her glasses. I said I was a journalist passing by and wanted to know a little about the archive.

Her defensive aggressiveness was not unusual; I had encountered it in countless petty officials throughout the country. "The place isn't open to the public as yet," she said, "and permission is required from the state secretariat before someone can visit." The two statements seemed a little at odds with the bare rooms, but I let it pass.

"So you are going to be moving things here at some point?"

She nodded sullenly.

"What kind of material will the archive have when you are ready for the public?"

"I cannot tell you, not without written permission," she said, standing up from the chair and rearranging a picture frame. I took this opportunity to pass my ID card to her.

"You're from Delhi?" she asked, looking at my card. "We don't get many press people from Delhi."

There was almost a pleading tone to her comment and I felt some sympathy for her. In her place perhaps I too would have interpreted the visit as an act of invasion. I could hear her saying that she was not used to people from the capital dropping in so casually and that her inertness was only because she was afraid of doing something wrong. The face was made-up carefully, but there were wrinkles around the eyes. Who was I to think I knew what her troubles or worries were?

"Oh, I was here for other things," I replied, "and I thought I would just stop in and see what kind of things you have here."

She said nothing but returned the card, dropping it on the table an inch from the edge.

"I used to live here, you see," I told her, weakening somewhere inside myself.

"Where?" she asked.

"Right across from here, out there, that house with the triangular rooms at the two ends."

She hesitated, then pushed her chair back a little.

"There weren't so many houses then. Things have changed a lot since I lived here."

She became almost perky.

"Of course things have changed. Things should change. Change is good." She sat back down in the chair now with a brisk, businesslike air. "Get permission from the secretariat. No unofficial visitors."

I said good-bye and turned around. She seemed not to have heard me. "Change is good," she repeated to herself, as if that gave her some conviction about the empty archive. She raised her voice as I left, a little harsh, slightly triumphant in her recognition of an enemy of her people. "Tell them when you get back home to Bangladesh that change is good. People who cannot adjust to change are no good."

a lesson in history

The church was in the same grounds as the All Saints School, a quiet space in the heart of the administrative section, directly across from the state library. Behind the church, half hidden by trees, was a small cemetery, the Old Military Cemetery. The English historian A. L. Basham, whose wife had been from this town, was buried here. One more foreigner embracing the earth of India in a bid to atone for the imperial past, disappearing behind gravestones with fates not too different from those of their colonial predecessors, forgotten and left alone.

The congregation that had gathered here was not a neighborhood crowd. The wealthy and powerful sat in front, shining and clean, while old ladies with lined faces were scattered like petals throughout the hall. The service had already started, the words echoing oddly in the dim interior, released without the aid of sound system or natural acoustics. Impelled across the rows of listeners, they seemed to transform themselves at each stage of their progress, disembodied from any larger unit of meaning, word floating away from sentence and paragraph, from idea and story, an unbridgeable gulf separating them from the book on the lectern, the fragments finally dropping around me as if borne on the shock waves of a distant explosion.

Still, some of those words were insistent, forming a ragged structure of meaning. "In my father's house are many mansions; if it were not so, I would have told you." The voice of the priest droned on, flailing against the sunlight creeping in under the door and the humming of the bees on the lawns.

"In my father's house are many mansions; if it were not so, I would have told you. And we are told that it was Simon's son, Judas Iscariot, that betrayed him, taking the sop that the Lord offered unto him, knowing that the betrayal had already entered his heart." The diary had been lying with other odds and ends in the trunk. A medal from the Bengal Veterinary College, a receipt from Cherra Cement Factory for sixty bags of cement. The diary was old, and the binding had split like a husk to reveal the bent cardboard frame underneath, the pages curled with age. The entry was a page long, the scribbled script running halfway across each line. The sentence was short. My father had chosen a fresh line each time he rewrote the sentence, as if he had been practicing his handwriting. Over and over again it said, "Leapingstone has a gun."

I woke up with a start, to the rustling of feet and the blaze of light from the doors flung open. The old lady across the aisle had fallen asleep as well and was helped to her feet by a grandchild who had accompanied her. She leaned on her cane and moved her jaws slowly, as if tasting the residue of the pastor's words, the cross on a thin chain around her neck trembling as she flexed her chin.

I set out for Malki, passing the Civil Hospital once again. The slopes of Malki were full with people dressed in their Sunday best, released from the dark interiors onto the streets. I walked slowly—there was still an hour to go before lunch at Dr. Chatterji's. There were the occasional glances from passers-by, neither hostile nor friendly, merely reserved and distant. There were few nontribals to be seen on the streets. Even on weekdays, those I had seen on the main streets walked quickly and unobtrusively, heads down, eyes averted, nonbeings moving from point to point along the shortest route.

It did not take me an hour to walk to Dr. Chatterji's place, no matter how slowly I moved. Nor could I stop even if I wanted to, there was too much of the shadow of the stranger hanging around me. There was a sign at the turning into Dr. Chatterji's neighborhood, a quiet group of expensive bungalows looking down to the main road. Freshly painted, nailed high to the trunk of a pine tree, the sign demanded that no outsiders "loiter" in the streets of the neighborhood after ten, by order of the local residents and their committee. I was to find out later that the sign did not refer to ethnic outsiders of any kind and that all the people in this mixed neighborhood— tribals, Assamese, Bengalis—were happy about the sign. Most of the prosperous localities had begun to find the presence of drunken young men an annoyance and a danger, and even the well-off tribals were concerned with protecting their new houses from the stray stone that might be hurled in a fit of anger.

The house Dr. Chatterji lived in was an old bungalow that had retained its weathered charm, warm and comfortable with the feel of aged wood. The owner, too, was much the way I remembered him, a large man whose muscles had run to flab, comfortable and bourgeois in his bungalow in spite of his references to "DPs," displaced persons. His grandfather had been among the first Bengalis to settle here, and with three generations of medical practice behind him, Dr. Chatterji was confident in his knowledge of human affairs and motives. His eyes still bright and enthusiastic, his manner graciously feudal, Dr. Chatterji was willing to talk about everything from political issues to my father's career. Somewhere in between, I felt, was his own life, inviolate and untroubled, a still center in the turning world.

Although I was early, Dr. Chatterji's wife greeted me without surprise and with affection, quite willing to begin lunch at once and leading me into the dining room. We should eat first, then talk, she insisted, plying me with questions as she laid out the different dishes. Dr. Chatterji sat down at his place with what I took to be a sigh of satisfaction, his sides spilling over the chair. He was dressed in a sleeveless undershirt and checked *lungi*, and I chided myself for thinking that he would appear in a suit with his little car, just because that was the way I remembered him. His hair had grayed at the sides, but it was his wife who showed signs of age, her entire head a shock of white hair, wrinkles around her eyes.

There was nothing much I could tell them about myself as we worked our way through the meal. They, on the other hand, had a lot of news. The eldest son was married and lived in Gauhati. The youngest was going out with a girl whose father had been killed in '79. Before long, the conversation turned to how bad things were here.

"But what about you?" Mrs. Chatterji asked. I tried to answer as best as I could, picking out the slivers of fish bone carefully. I was noncommittal and reserved, since I had no desire to go over my failures with them, they who had been so far above us socially in spite of their kindness, perhaps especially in their kindness. We moved back to the drawing room after lunch, watching the sun's rays fading rapidly in the chilly afternoon. Dr. Chatterji lit a cigarette, telling me that his wife had increased his smoking quota as a concession to my visit. She sat a little aside as we talked, knitting a pullover, joining the conversation with sharp comments of her own. They wanted to know about my father's death and listened closely as I told them the bare facts.

His wife spoke up. "Your mother would agree with me, Babu, I know, so don't mind what I'm telling you. I hope you will be different from your father. As a boy, you were not like him at all. You took after your mother." She looked at her husband and he nodded his large head in peaceful agreement. "Your father made too much of regulations. One doesn't have to be corrupt to take care of oneself, you know. He had no understanding of everyday affairs, of matters concerning his own family. Look at Hari's father. You remember Hari?" I didn't, but I pretended to. "Hari's father was, what, a clerk? Now he's got a nice house in Silchar. Got his three daughters married off, both the sons have good jobs. He's bought a car. He drives to the market everyday. Who'd have thought that when they lived here, the seven of them in two rented rooms across from our old place?"

Mrs. Chatterji was a tall, beautiful woman who had grown up in Calcutta. Bengali women of my mother's generation had not been reserved about expressing their opinions and she, we had all known, had a master's degree in chemistry from Calcutta University.

Her husband, who had listened carefully while she summed up my father's life, spoke up. "Of course, your father was troubled, very troubled, but he made things hard for himself. I often told him, 'Dr. Dam, ease up, one must fight to survive, but one can still enjoy life.' "

"It was first the '79 killings, and then Lister's fraud, that unnerved him," his wife said, as if they had worked out his whole life between them and that was when I began to resent them a little.

"Yes, that was the first thing," Dr. Chatterji agreed. "They threatened him after he found out about the fraud and sent some boys to assault him. You were probably too young to remember."

"I remember."

He waved his large palms in a gesture of understanding.

"What is there to say? Things became hard for all of us, especially since '79. It's been downhill all the way since then. That was the beginning of the end for everybody, for your father more than most people. Imagine, close to fifty thousand people living like refugees four decades after independence."

His eyes had lit up at the prospect of telling the story all over again, at the possibility of finding a willing audience for his tale of woe. I suppose he had a right to tell the story, if anybody did. He had championed the cause of Bengalis in this region for decades, but without remaining aloof from the local people. He maintained close connections with tribal political leaders even as—like his father—he sent streams of letters to officials and politicians in Delhi, to the press everywhere. All the letters were signed "In the service of motherland," as if to negate the accusation of treachery that must fall upon those raking up the issue of nontribal rights in a protected tribal state.

"But your father remained aloof when we appealed to him to join us in our efforts to make our position known in the national arena. He would not put his signature on our appeals. The reason he gave for this always was that he was not an independent person but a government official. He didn't say official, of course. The phrase, if I remember it correctly, was 'government servant.' As a result he was quite alone in his troubles."

There was a minute of strained silence after this, as if they felt they had gone too far. "What happened to him after he became director?" I asked. "He was always so tense, but Ma and I never knew why. There used to be this minister who always called at night. He was drunk whenever I happened to answer the phone. After the first week or so, my father took to waiting by the phone all evening, as if he didn't want whatever was happening to reach me."

They were quiet for a while. "I was unfair, ungenerous," Dr. Chatterji said. "I had forgotten how much he was dealing with. He was afraid, very afraid, you see.

"The fear became tremendous when Leapingstone's nephew became minister of the department. He lasted only a few months, because he was an uneducated buffoon from the villages who wasn't cut out for politics here, but those months were enough for Dr. Dam. It was terrible, terrible to see a grown-up man sweating with fear. I went to visit him one day when Leapingstone had been there. Leapingstone said hello to me on the way out, joking about how I was the one Bengali he would not want to get rid of because no one could cook fish like my wife."

Mrs. Chatterji smiled. "Whatever his politics might be, he always had wit, that man."

"Yes," Dr. Chatterji said, "except that he misunderstood your father. I don't think he quite anticipated the effect some of his actions had on your father. I'll tell you about it, since you want to know. But that day, your father was sweating profusely when I went in. That was shortly after the milk-booth thing had happened and Leapingstone had come to see your father about an acquaintance of his who had applied for a job. I told your father to loosen his collar and tie and to drink some water. I was afraid he was going to have a stroke. He just sat there, staring at me as if he didn't understand. It was difficult to believe at that moment that he too was a doctor, even if his patients were animals. Afterward, when he calmed down, he whispered to me, 'Leapingstone carries a gun.' "

Dr. Chatterji paused here to light a cigarette, letting the sounds from the street flood back into the house. I felt I was viewing the scene in the minister's chambers again, the three men inside it trapped in a world not completely of their own making. "You see," Dr. Chatterji went on, "Leapingstone and his nephew the minister were doing something one might consider illegal, but they had more than their own self-interest in mind. They had seen the politics of the state changing under their eyes. When the student union became so popular, they were threatened as much as anybody else. They wanted nontribals to leave too, but they were more circumspect in how they went about it. The whole milk-booth thing was one of a series of populist scams to retain their power base, to keep some kind of hold over the people because they had realized, much too late, that the fires they had stoked would overtake them. They were against mass killings because the one thing they didn't want was a suspension of the assembly and the imposition of central rule. If that happened, they felt, the student union would only grow stronger and they—or those who sympathized with them, the hard-liners—would be the ones to win when elections took place. Or worse, the really radical fringe among the students could take to arms, go underground as in Nagaland or in Mizoram. Then the focus would shift to secession and the army would come in.

"Leapingstone was right about what he thought could happen; he was wrong about how effective his strategy would be. Your father only remembered the end of his beloved milk-supply scheme and the fact that he had been humiliated, that Leapingstone's nephew had pulled a gun on him in his chamber and said that he could get away with anything and that one more foreigner's corpse wouldn't make any difference."

"So it wasn't Leapingstone who had the gun?"

"No, no. Leapingstone's much too suave for stuff like that. Old school, you know. It was his bungling nephew who did that, on his own. Hothead, like most of the youngsters. Believe me, Leapingstone felt bad about it. I don't know if your father knew this, but after he retired, it was Leapingstone who called the veterinary minister and asked him to make sure your father's pension order was passed quickly. I don't know how your father got the idea that Leapingstone was the one who threatened him with a gun. Maybe he got confused or something—he was frightened, after all.

"I can understand his feelings," he said heavily, "how helpless he must have felt after those decades of entirely selfless work, of wearing threadbare clothes and never using the privileges of his office for himself. Did he ever let you use the office car? Did he let you learn to drive? No. And after that, when he felt he had been stripped of all power, he must have felt the weight of his whole life upon him, and seen it as one big failure. He was older than me and saw many more things. The World War, Direct Action Day, Partition, riots here, wars across the border, so many things.

"Only the strong survive, Babu." He put a large, calloused palm on my knee. "This you must understand. This is something your father refused to understand until it was too late. It's not ethics or honesty or professionalism or kindness alone, though these things are important. It is strength that determines the winner. Look at me," he said, leaning back into his couch and looking like some strange, gargantuan idol. "My father taught me one thing and I never forgot it. Strength. At medical school in Gauhati, I lifted weights every day, even when I was sick. I bench-pressed 250 pounds at my best. No one dares touch me even now, though there are reasons other than physical strength for this."

There was the loud throbbing of a motorbike outside. The engine died down, giving way to ear-splitting barks from Dr. Chatterji's dog, who was craving attention from the younger son, who had just come in on his Royal Enfield.

"I taught my son too. He may not be smart, but he has the confidence of his father's wealth and his own health, what do you say? But there are other strengths, which you have. Your IQ. Show them that we are not helpless, that we too can bite when cornered. Babu," he said emphatically, "I've got it: you must interview Leapingstone."

"What?"

"Interview him."

"Leapingstone? He's a minister now?"

"Yes."

I didn't want to do it. This was not what I had come here for. But something, maybe just politeness, maybe curiosity, drove me to ask, "What's Leapingstone's portfolio, his department?" Dr. Chatterji was staring through the door at his son, who entered carrying a helmet fit for a Neanderthal's head, jeans clinging to his legs. He crossed the floor noisily, big and loud, his head half-turning toward me in a curt greeting. Dr. Chatterji, who had followed his son's progress through the house, looked at me with a distant air.

"Youth," he muttered. Then he shook his fat, cracked fist emphatically. "That is what you must do, Babu. Yes, use your contacts. Flash your press card. Publish an article. Let the world know about our sorrows, beaten from place to place across fifty years. Yes, I know you're thinking I'm rich, that I've held on to my property in spite of everything. But I'll tell you something, I'm tired too. Tired and sick of seeing the others being destroyed, those who are not strong. In the village, they would have been peasants, petty officials and servants who would have been taken care of. Now I see them go down, without a fight, without a spark of spirit in them.

"Chowdhury was a clerk with one son and a daughter. They cut him to pieces when he was coming back from the market with two small fish that all of them would have shared at home. The son got into an engineering college, was a good student until this happened. Now he's a drifter, a salesman for some company manufacturing GI pipes or something. Sold all his mother's jewelry to try and go to America for higher studies.

Didn't get a visa. Doesn't ever come and see his family in the rented house where they live on his father's pension. His sister couldn't get married, she's turned to other things, I don't have to tell you what things.

"They see nothing, Babu, in their hate. They kill the odd businessman now and then, but the people who really suffer are nothing. They stabbed Upen in Umpling because he argued with them when they refused to pay his fare. He got the taxi on loans from different banks, so that his younger brother could stay in school. You remember the blind man who used to sing with his harmonium in front of the Shani temple? You remember how during Durga Puja he would have a sari next to him as he played, a sari he had bought for his wife? They set fire to him when he was walking back home with his harmonium one day. I was told they laughed as they broke the harmonium. What difference was there between him and the blind man playing the guitar in Burra Bazaar? One wore a hat and sunglasses, the other wore a *dhoti*. They were both poor and tried to find a way to earn something.

"People in the plains hear the word *tribals* and have rosy visions of innocent people, living off the earth, singing and dancing all the time. That's what they see when we appeal for our rights, as bloodsucking exploiters who want to continue what the British did. But we're not the ones so proud of our white skin, are we? No, because we don't have white skin. We don't go to church, or at least most of us don't, and we don't hear those sermons about the heathens who must be wiped out before they overrun the kingdom of Christ."

His wife, who had gone in, following her son, returned and was listening closely. "Tell him about the schoolboy," she said.

"Which one?"

"The one in Mawkhar, coming back home from his board exams."

"Yes. Well, the school board doesn't assign nontribals examination seats at schools in tribal areas, did you know that? There were too many incidents that happened. Well, they slipped up on this one. A Bengali Muslim boy, he was given a seat at a government school in Mawkhar. They poured kerosene on him when he was coming out of the exam hall, looking through his question papers. Then they set him on fire. Sixteen years old.

"You think these are crocodile tears, Babu? Well, let me tell you. I had to sell the other bungalow, the one up there. Look what they've done to it. All the trees are gone. I could have sold it to someone like your father if I had not been prohibited by the land transfer act to sell it to anyone other than a tribal. I sold it, I got my money all right, but that's not the point. Your father put in more in the service of these people than most tribal officers. Here, look." He gestured toward the front veranda, at the garden where his son could be seen, tall and straight with the strength his father had passed on to him. I understood a moment later what Dr. Chatterji was talking about.

"See? That dilapidated structure, that's what is left of Dr. Dam's milk-supply scheme and his milk booths. Anyway, where do we get milk these days? They went after the Nepalis after that, burned their sheds, butchered their cows, killed those who tried to resist. They thought the Nepalis were stupid Hindu heathens who would die to save their gods. What they could not see was that the desperation was economic, that those cows were the only hope the Nepalis had for making a living in the world."

"Let it be," his wife broke in. "Your blood pressure is going up."

"Let me finish. I have one more thing to say. We were not perfect, we are not perfect now and never will be. We were insular and narrow-minded, with a false sense of superiority when we first came here. We saw the honesty of the tribal people as stupidity, and through that we taught them our own deviousness. That is the irony. Irony," he repeated, evidently liking the sound of the word. "That we should have learned to be more human only when they became less so. But we did not learn most of our lessons well, Babu, because we are ignorant people, stupid people, thinking only about degrees from high school, sending our sons and daughters to study engineering or medicine, unable to comprehend that we live in a world of other people who speak differently, eat differently. We keep our sons and daughters cloistered within the ties of community, refusing to let them bring friends home, not knowing that their world must necessarily be bigger and more flexible than ours.

"It was much the same when Partition happened, and Hindus and Muslims both paid the price for their certainty that the world would not change, that they could go on observing their taboos and rituals and distinctions forever, until they were taken by the scruffs of their necks and deposited into a new world where you had to be very strong to survive. That is why I have this rage, this anger at what is being done to us here. That we should have suffered once from one of the cruelest jokes in history, only to suffer again. You and I were comparatively lucky, for different reasons. But there were so many who rode those trains of death, walked miles to reach the safety of the borders that made their new nation, working their way through those decades after Partition painfully, selling vegetables, teaching singing, mathematics, anything, to the children of rich people from their community. And then, just a few years later, after this place became a hill state, they discovered that they were foreigners once more because of the language they spoke.

"We are a dispersed people, wandering, but unlike the Jews we have no mythical homeland. Nor do we have their achievements that would make the world recognize and fear us one day. My two brothers have not been here for years. They left as soon as they could, but they found Calcutta too narrow, too alien, after their childhoods here. No doubt you face the same problem. One of them lives in England now, the other in Belgium. They send photographs of their houses, their cars, and their fair children with red cheeks who write *Shubho Bijoya* in English every year until the time comes for them to grow up and leave their homes. My brothers chose that way to become safe, to go where it began, to the European countries, so that with each passing generation they will become whiter, safer. Stronger.

"As for the rest, the majority, who will not have enough intelligence or money or strength to take that route, they will dwindle and die here. Some of them will move to the suburbs of Calcutta, crowded together in the East Bengali ghettos. They will never look back to what they left behind, here or in Bangladesh. In Calcutta they will be mocked by those who didn't suffer from Partition or are more educated, they will be disavowed even by those East Bengalis who have become genteel.

"And one day the student union leaders here will rejoice, when the last alien presence among them is dead. Do you know who that will be? Me. Yes, I will stay here to the end. I've made it easy for my sons. They can settle in Calcutta or Silchar or Gauhati if they like, there is land there, houses for them, because I know they will not want to remain here. But I will not move, I won't budge from here, I have a right to die here after three generations have put their work into this soil.

"After that, this story, these appeals I make, their killings, it will be meaningless, Babu. They will have outsiders here, in the form of officials and policemen from the central government, and big businessmen. Oh, the powerful businessmen they'll never get rid of, but they will live in an easy compromise with them. You know what an Indian Administrative Service officer had the nerve to tell me once? He said this place was a model of how the central government should run the states in the Northeast. He talked about how happy the tribals here were, how they realize that they could never have it so good in any other nation in the world. They pay no taxes, sell all the trees in the forests, have the right to exploit the only coal mines in the country that are not nationalized, and they can kill all the outsiders they want as long as the outsiders are not important central government officials or big businessmen and as long as they do it discreetly, in reasonably small numbers. They—this Indian Administrative Service officer told me, someone who has never known what it is like to lose your home over and over again—they will never raise demands for secession from India. This is the way Nagaland and Mizoram and Manipur should be run, he told me. That the government should let them feel like they can do anything they want as long as they don't raise secessionist demands."

He was clearly worn out, but he still went on. "I will be here to the end. My wife says we should move to Calcutta, but I'll tell you the truth. I can't stand the place." He laughed painfully, shaking in his angry mirth, which turned into a coughing fit. His wife looked at me and made a sign that I should leave soon. "Calcutta," he coughed. "Their smugness, as if they are the only Bengalis in the world, with their oh-so-proper language in comparison with our dialect, which is rustic. It's okay for a visit, but when I run into tribals in Calcutta, tribals on their shopping trips, we stick together. We who will come back and be ready to murder each other in this place, we feel united in our common dislike of the city and its people."

He raised his massive body as I got up to take leave. Coming closer, he touched me on the back. "You'll do well. Write many things, but don't forget us. Remember. That's right, remember, I ask that of you. Criticize this old man, say that many of these views are biased and need to be balanced. But somewhere, if people still believe in truth, it must be true that fifty thousand people who fled in the night with bundles on their backs can't all be evil and exploitative. Somewhere, on some map, there must be a place for them too."

Outside, the clouds had retreated and it was bright again. The younger son was standing on the front lawn, an airgun in his hand, his leashed dog yapping excitedly beside him. He smiled when he saw me. "There's a street dog that's sneaked in through the fence. Look." I saw it, an emaciated creature with sores and scald marks on its back—somebody must have thrown hot water at it—which was scurrying between the flower bushes, whimpering, tail down, dropping to the ground in a crouch as it gave up hope, then scurrying a few yards as it found some courage, followed by the steady barrel of the gun and the salivating glance from the big, well-fed German Shepherd on a leash. "Can't make up my mind," he muttered, his finger on the trigger, "whether I should take a shot at it or let Tiger go after him? Tiger will eat him alive, but he's going to be sick afterward if he bites that creature."

"You decide what should be done," I told him, turning once to wave to the strange, elderly couple inside their sitting room. I walked out of the gate and began following the hedge down to the road. There was a cascade of howls punctuated by a terse, sharp command, followed immediately by the pop of an airgun.

leaving home

This is what it comes to in the end, then, the shape of a life in my hands, brief and inconsequential, summed up by the Chatterjis.

My father was forty-four years old when I was born. This fact doesn't come easily to me. I have to calculate it each time I need to remember the number, unable to recall his age except through the relation between events in his life and mine. When he retired, the day he returned home alone, cut adrift from his working life, I was sixteen and he was sixty; we were forty-four years apart from each other. He began working at the age of twenty-one, a veterinary surgeon for the Assam government. The year was 1947, the year of Partition, of independence. The family that crossed over across the new border, especially his parents, knew nothing of the world they had been catapulted into, the nation state they had been fortunate to reach, given those who didn't make it. He looked after them, took care of the three brothers, the youngest a full nineteen years behind him. He took on the responsibility for a nephew almost the same age as his youngest brother, and for the sister who had retreated into her own deranged corner after her husband's death. He put the men through school and college, saw them to their jobs or the threshold of a career before he got married. On the day of his wedding he was thirty-eight.

It is not surprising, then, that he should have had so little to say to me, that he should have been unable and unwilling to acknowledge that he had not only lost youth and home but also everything that should have come after as some kind of compensation. At the age of fifty, it must have been impossible to understand how he remained an alien, an outsider in the new land he had come to love and had hoped to call home in some fashion. There you have it, the strangeness of it, that those who had left their homes forever to try and find themselves within the nation that was supposedly for everyone should have found that the journey was not over. The hills that appeared beyond the horizon were only another mirage, their destination just another place that would reject them as not part of it.

If it is true that our first journeys contain the seed of all the voyages we go on to make in the future, if it is true that each life has only one story that it must ceaselessly repeat, then I suppose my father's first visit to this town prefigured everything that came after. I found out the details of the story long after we had left, when the three of us were in Silchar, alone once again; Mayarani was dead, my uncles had moved away with their families, and we were on our own. My mother was remembering the past, as she often did, while my father lay in his bed, his gaze following us as we lingered over the scraps of our late dinner. Even then it was not the clearest of stories. My mother told me about Mayarani's brother, an Indian Civil Service officer posted in this very town and the way my father and my grandfather came to meet him, to ask him for some help so that my father could take up his chosen career. He had wanted to study medicine.

They walked up through the Pandua Hills in Sylhet, arriving at the edge of the valley that rose and fell, nestling against the mountains. It was a strange, almost fearful place, a sanctuary for British bodies ravaged by the plains, administrators and rulers of the empire recuperating in their home away from home, surrounded by their *chaprasis* and *khansamas*, police constables and postal runners. There were some people from East Bengal even then, mostly petty clerks and shopkeepers. There was also the Indian Civil Service officer they had come to see. My father and my grandfather must have stood there in silence on the edge of the town, uncertain of the changes that would come upon their lives if they entered it. They were turned away, the uncle did not meet the schoolboy, and they went back to the village in Sylhet—until the schoolboy grew up and returned to the very same town in the early seventies as a district veterinary officer.

When he did settle in this town, I think it was with the hope of beginning afresh. He was in his forties then, with a family of his own. Much of the surrounding hill was free from jungle, covered with fine pasture and flowers. There was an old

Chinese shoemaker at Burra Bazaar whom he would visit once every two years to buy a new pair of shoes, picking his way through its slush-filled alleys in the old, patched-up pair. On weekends, he would walk with my mother and me through the golf course, looking at the elegant missionary schools and the red cheeks of the tribal children who were bundled up in tartan checks behind their mothers. He promised her that he would send me to one of those missionary schools, where the children looked so smart and happy. Those early years here had been permeated with the feeling of being at home in the world around. At his office there were the workers clattering and erupting in a frenzy in the corridor when the tea lady came in at eleven with her steaming kettle and dry, flaking pastries. Outside the Additional Secretariat, he knew, were the faces of the women at the fish market coming alive with sudden laughter, the stubborn resistance and slow yielding of the boats at Wards Lake, the gardens and markets and cottages and stone-chipped paths of the town telling him that he was where he wanted to be.

All this until the first killings happened outside the veterinary compound, the seven passengers pulled out of the bus coming in from Gauhati, the seven knifed to death on the road where his walks had begun. Sitting at night alone in the bungalow, caught up in the papers that gave meaning to his solitude— he had sent my mother and me away to Dhanbad, to be with her brother until things settled down—he uncovered those strange numbers and figures that indicated something he could not reconcile with silence. How insignificant that amount must have been, but for him it was a matter of defrauding the state, and duty demanded that he report this to his superiors. That bungalow, the town that drummed its message of death through the long night, must have seemed like a lost spot on the map of the nation, its remote beauty and even more remote violence surfacing in the national newspapers only as little single-column reports of "disturbances." The fear of being the stranger who could be knifed to death, the one whose presence must be exorcised, had returned again.

It is all conjecture on my part, of course. Who can tell how much he understood and what he felt through the years? The face, when I try to recall it, is impassive, caught up in its own trials, asking nothing of me. Did the nights spent alone in the house in the veterinary compound infect him for good, with each little incident adding to his store of miseries, or did he let go of them as they passed away? After he vacated the bungalow and moved to a safer place, to the temporary rooms in Jail Road, the killings must have appeared as an aberration. One cannot be an exile in one's own country, can one?

When my mother and I came back from Dhanbad, with the violence having subsided—or so we thought—he was more human, more fatherlike than he had been before. At the same time, he was more alone than ever, and when the assault at Police Bazaar happened, totally bewildered at the motive behind the aggression. He did not understand that it was not simply a matter of the fraud he had reported but that it was the outcome of an inevitable process, the result of a meeting of opposites. There were other incidents that unfolded themselves around him, but he did not realize their import when they did not affect him directly. The Danish professors he had showed around one of the farms were suspected of being spies. He dismissed the very notion as absurd, not understanding that paranoia was very much a part of the India he served so eagerly, and that the nation he imagined being shored up through the efforts of people like him was ultimately a fortress, that everywhere around him new battle lines were being drawn and fresh groups of people were being defined as outsiders, borders bristling with barbed-wire teeth.

He had not understood that his own brother had turned against him, though it became so clear to my mother and me that Biren had not wanted us in Silchar. Even after the riots of '79, the assault, he had thought of the possibility of a new distribution scheme, had envisioned lines of supply running through the state, bringing the lost hamlets and far-flung places of this impoverished hill state into the fold of the modern world. What he had forgotten was his own place on the map, until the minister pointed a gun at him.

That was the day things changed for him in many ways, when he walked home from the Additional Secretariat building via a long, circuitous route, deciding to go on a walking tour of as many of the milk booths within the town as he could manage, as if he was bidding farewell to a part of himself in visiting each one of them in turn, as if he was blessing them before taking leave, or asking forgiveness of them. Who knows what his motives were? The diary entries around the day in the minister's chamber are what I have, his reiteration of the gun that had been aimed at him and a list of the booths he had visited, seven of them. Apart from that outburst of anguish and fear, nothing of the mind and heart is recorded in his diaries; just the bare facts of the passing days, the years, until the time when he could no longer write his own name. He was not heroic, which is why his story has been so difficult to write.

Perhaps it is the biographer who is at fault. You will notice that I find it impossible to say anything of his life away from the town. Without stories, without photographs, I can only imagine him where I had always seen him, in this town, walking that winding road curling around the hollow, coming up the steps with that curious tread of his, carrying different offerings for my mother and me—a small fish bought with boundless pleasure from the evening market, a set of three oranges, his shoes and mine wrapped in newspaper after he had had them patched up by the cobbler at the bridge below the market.

What went before, in the years other than those spent here, I don't know. There are only images in my mind, a scrap of scenes to be wrested free somehow, to be retained against the excesses of history, of time. As human beings, we move against the flow of the world. What was before, when we were young, is also the point farthest from us so that our childhoods must, by this paradox, be the oldest, most ancient world we know, curled and stained by time like old black-and-white photographs.

I wonder if there was something that could have been

recovered, whether there was no way for him to ease the burden that weighed him down constantly until the day he fell face forward in the passageway. No matter, it is all over now.

The interview was not difficult to arrange. It took a phone call to the Principal Secretariat, identifying myself through my big-city paper, asking for a brief interview with the minister for youth affairs. It was as formal as it is possible to be formal across a constantly interrupted phone line. I called on Monday morning and arranged an interview for the next day at ten o'clock. It left me plenty of time to come back and check out of the hotel. I was going to take the bus to Gauhati at three, spend a little time there before catching the Kanchanjunga Express in the evening.

The minister's office was in the Principal Secretariat building, in keeping with the important status of the youth affairs portfolio. It had been drizzling in the morning when I stood at the window, looking out to the lake, but I had not yet seen one of those full-blown assaults of rain that held back for no one. The moisture was in the air, thick and taut, but reining itself in and letting the chilly wind do the work of keeping people off the streets. The Principal Secretariat was fairly close to the hotel, but I took a somewhat circular route, emerging from the grounds of Wards Lake to the road in front of the governor's residence, passing the building where the pension office had been and walking past the unyielding facade of the Additional Secretariat. I turned right from the State Central Library and there was the Principal Secretariat, its whitewash dulled by the clouds, police jeeps and white Ambassadors with red lights scattered across the driveway. I went through the usual motions of presenting my ID card, waiting for the bored policeman to call upstairs while I signed my name in the book, until I was waved to one of two elevators. It was like a government complex anywhere in the country, I thought, as I squeezed in among the clerks and assistants holding those buff government files, the kind of space that was the same everywhere, flattened into an evenly dull and bureaucratic oppressiveness. How would Leapingstone ever justify any grand vision in this kind of place? Unlike Dr. Chatterji, I thought it possible that the violence in the streets that had been hurled against us had had some grain of idealism in it. But that language of purity, no matter how misplaced, could only be spoken on the streets; here it was only corruption, boredom, rot, no different from the oppressive shades of power to be found elsewhere in the country.

As I moved through the crowded cubicles of the clerks and typists lounging around their typewriters, past the officers rising in rank, the rooms became cleaner and more thickly carpeted, until I reached the reception area in front of the minister's chamber, with its burnished flower vases and the shiny steel frames for pictures and citations. The minister's secretary went through her business with practiced ease, asking me for my ID card and speaking in a low voice on the intercom at the same time. "The minister will see you now," she said, putting down the phone. A worker in a khaki uniform appeared magically at the desk, summoned by some invisible bell.

As he led me down the carpeted stretch of corridor that ended at the door to the minister's chamber, I felt her gaze following me. The worker knocked lightly once, then held the door open.

The minister was signing some papers, dressed in an olive-green safari suit, the double pockets bristling with pens. He looks young, I thought with surprise. I had met Leapingstone once, had seen him that New Year's Eve at the Civil Hospital when he came out of his room. This, surely, was not him. The minister gestured to one of the seats facing him without looking up and even though he was behind a desk, I could see that he was tall and muscular, with close-cropped hair. I advanced on the hush of the carpet, moving one of the chairs to take my seat, fingering the notebook and pen in my pocket. As I sat, he pushed away the paper he was signing and sighed. He looked up at me at the same instant as I saw the gold-edged nameplate on his table. The honorable minister Adolf Hitler was asking me if I had enjoyed my stay in his town.

So it ends. I feel I've seen this scene in many films—the last, long walk, the music fading, dying out against the frame of the town dissolving slowly, the trees and houses blurring into an outline, merging into the horizon running its cracked line against the smooth sky. I walked with my bags, a few shards of memory, with the fear that had been the one familiar face I found in my hometown, the whispered words of the minister, the derisive reminder that I was a foreigner here.

Walked. To the bus station. I looked up at the sky from time to time, where the clouds hung like wet patches in the canvas of the house in Rilbong, like a map drifting along the sky, isthmuses and peninsulas and gulfs running into each other, creating new continents and countries.

There is an image in my mind, though where it comes from I have no idea. Perhaps my father described the scene to me one night in Jail Road, though I am not sure, as I am unsure about everything I have written about him. Still, he must have told me about his early work as a veterinary surgeon in Assam, riding his bicycle to see the elephants used by the logging camps in those days right after independence. The elephants were expensive animals and often enough he would be asked to write a fake cause on the death certificate so that the owners could claim the insurance money. He was not a brave man in the way we understand bravery these days, in close nexus with bravado, but he always rejected the bribes. He had no money to boast of, but he was not conscious of any heroism in refusing to make out the false reports. He had quickly passed on to the point of the story being told, the work involved. He described how difficult it was to operate on an elephant, of the special anesthesia required and the hours it took to cut through the epidermis, narrating the medical details with pleasure. Riding to those logging camps was full of danger for him. He remembered a British planter who ordered him off the track he was cycling along, claiming he was trespassing on private property. This was well after independence and he was surprised, even angered, at this planter who did not accept the change that so many other people had paid so heavily for. There were also the wild elephants one had to look out for, he told me, especially since they were often drawn to the camps by the smell of the domesticated animals.

That is the image of him I love the most, of a shy and earnest young man riding a bicycle along a jungle track. It is a moonlit night and his little lamp wavers in the darkness as the cycle bounces on the rough, stony path. He is afraid of wild elephants, of Englishmen who might point a gun at him and order him off the path and into the forest. But he rides on, smelling the jungle scent, riding to save the life of some beast because that is his duty in the service of the government of India. And as the forest swallows him up completely, he is happy, not because India or the government means anything to him. India is just a name, but this forest rising around him is a country without boundaries, whose borders cannot be mapped, where the most the cartographers can do is mark, in bold letters: HERE THERE BE ELEPHANTS.

The diesel-smeared creatures at the bus station were emitting low growls of smoke, ropes snaking up to their backs where trunks and bags and suitcases and holdalls were being lashed down. What I had I could carry with me, so I found my bus and put my bag on the seat. I waited outside, smoking a last cigarette before the journey, taking one more look. There was a woman dressed in black, a baby on one arm, wailing loudly. She was Nepali and her thick, dark mountain clothes clung to her like a shroud, the face red with exertion as she alternated between consoling the child in her arms and giving vent to her own feelings, tearing her hair and crying. A few bags were strewn around her, little bundles flung carelessly around, the debris of her sorrow. People hesitated, halted, and then looked away. I was one of the wavering crowd, unsure of her pain and of my role, always the powerless observer.

A stocky Nepali man leaned against one of the pillars, smoking a cigarette as he eyed her. It became clear that he was involved and responsible, at least in part, for her misery. He tossed his cigarette butt away and circled her swiftly. Then he approached her and kicked her in the stomach. The woman fell on her face, still holding on to the baby, as her voice was drowned out by the man's shouts and curses. "Whore, *randi*," he screamed, drawing closer for another blow, this time to her face, and then turning around at the crowd and offering his abuses as an explanation.

Behind me there was a cacophony of horns and the rumbles of an exhaust pipe, cries of "Gauhati, Gauhati," I looked behind and saw that it was my bus, preparing to depart. A tribal official appeared from inside the office. "Hey, hey. You. Stop that."

The Nepali paused in his circling. Cringing a little, he said, "She's a whore, sir. Just a whore."

"Get lost. Now. Or I'll turn you over to the police."

The man muttered something to himself but he began to move away. The officer bent to the woman and reached out toward her. There were yells from the bus in response to my raised hand and I ran toward the closed door. The conductor held it open, his expression impatient, while I paused, looking once more.

I look at my birthplace, knowing that I will never see it again. I want it to be home for everyone who lives there, for everyone to have a place in it that cannot be lost or stolen. But how you achieve that future is no longer my concern, I tell my hometown. I have truly let go, I know, as I step past the impatient conductor and the door closes behind me.